Hazards of Time Travel

NOVELS BY JOYCE CAROL OATES

With Shuddering Fall (1964)

A Garden of Earthly Delights (1967)

Expensive People (1968)

them (1969)

Wonderland (1971)

Do with Me What You Will (1973)

The Assassins (1975)

Childwold (1976)

Son of the Morning (1978)

Unholy Loves (1979)

Bellefleur (1980)

Angel of Light (1981)

A Bloodsmoor Romance (1982)

Mysteries of Winterthurn (1984)

Solstice (1985)

Marya: A Life (1986)

Hazards of Time Travel

Joyce Carol Oates

An Imprint of HarperCollins*Publishers*

HAZARDS OF TIME TRAVEL. Copyright © 2018 by The Ontario Review, Inc. All rights reserved. Printed in the United States of America. No part of this book may be used or reproduced in any manner whatsoever without written permission except in the case of brief quotations embodied in critical articles and reviews. For information address HarperCollins Publishers, 195 Broadway, New York, NY 10007.

HarperCollins books may be purchased for educational, business, or sales promotional use. For information please e-mail the Special Markets Department at SPsales@harpercollins.com.

FIRST HARPERLUXE EDITION

ISBN: 978-0-06-286100-9

HarperLuxe™ is a trademark of HarperCollins Publishers.

Library of Congress Cataloging-in-Publication Data is available upon request.

18 19 20 21 22   ID/LSC   10 9 8 7 6 5 4 3 2 1

For Stig Björkman,
and for
Charlie Gross

A self is simply a device for representing a functionally unified system of responses.

B. F. Skinner, *Science and Human Behavior*

They would not have come for me, naïvely I drew their attention to me. Willingly I dared what I should not have dared.

Of my own free will misjudging. Or rather, not judging—not thinking. In vanity and stupidity and now I am lost.

Sometimes on my knees in a posture of prayer I am able to break through the "censor barrier"—to remember . . .

But my brain hurts so! It is a terrible effort like struggling against the gravity of Jupiter.

My Exile-status forbids me to speak to anyone here of my sentence or of my life before Exile and so I am doubly lonely.

Though rarely alone in this strange place I am very lonely and am not sure that I can persevere.

My sentence is "only" four years. It might have been "life."

Or, it might have been Deletion.

On my knees each night straining to remember, to recall my old, lost self, I try to be grateful, my sentence was not Deletion.

And I try to be grateful, no one in my family was arrested as a collaborator/facilitator of Treason, with me.

I
Valedictorian

The Instructions

1. In the Restricted Zone, the Exiled Individual (EI) is allowed a ten-mile radius of movement the epicenter of which is the official residence of the EI. This residence can be changed only by appeal to the Homeland Security Exile Disciplinary Bureau (HSEDB).

2. The EI is forbidden to question, challenge, or disobey in any way any local Restricted Zone authority. The EI is forbidden to identify himself/herself except as established by HSEDB. The EI is forbidden to provide "future knowledge" in the Restricted Zone and to search for or in any way seek out "relatives."

3.   The EI will be issued a new and non-negotiable name and an appropriate "birth certificate."

4.   The EI is forbidden to enter into any "intimate" or "confidential" relationship with any other individual. The EI is forbidden to procreate.

5.   The EI will be identified as "adopted" by "adoptive parents" who are "deceased." The EI will be identified as having no other family. This information will be the EI's official record in his/her Restricted Zone.

6.   The EI will be monitored at any and all times during his/her exile. It is understood that HSEDB can revoke the term of Exile and Sentencing at any time.

7.   Violations of any of these instructions will insure that the EI will be immediately Deleted.

Deletion

D I—"Deleted Individual."
If you are Deleted, you cease to exist. You are
"vaporized."

And if you are Deleted, all memories of you are
Deleted also.

Your personal property/estate becomes the possession
of the NAS (North American States).

Your family, even your children, if you have children,
will be forbidden to speak of you or in any way remember you, once you cease to exist.

Because it is taboo, Deletion is not spoken of. Yet, it is
understood that Deletion, the cruelest of punishments,
is always imminent.

To be Deleted is not equivalent to being Executed.

Execution is a public-lesson matter: Execution is not a state secret.

A certain percentage of executions under the auspices of the Federal Execution Education Program (FEEP) are broadcast via TV to the populace, for purposes of moral education.

(In a prison execution chamber made to resemble a hospital surgery, the CI [Condemned Individual] is strapped to a gurney by prison guards; then, in the clinical-white uniforms of "medics," prison staffers administer the lethal dose of poison into the CI's veins as tens of millions of home TV viewers watch.)

(Except us. Though Dad was already of MI [Marked Individual] status, and his Caste Rank [CR] vulnerable, neither Dad nor Mom allowed our TV to be turned on at Execution Hours which were often several times a week. My older brother Roderick objected to this "censorship" when he was still in school on the grounds that, if his teachers discussed the educational aspect of an execution in class, he would not be able to participate and would stand out as "suspicious"—but this plea did not persuade our parents to turn on the TV at these times.)

Deletion is a different status altogether, for while Execution is intended to be openly discussed, even to allude to Deletion is a federal offense punishable as Treason-Speech.

My father Eric Strohl had been MI since a time before I was born. As a young resident M.D. in the Pennsboro Medical Center he'd been under observation as a scientifically-minded individual, for such individuals were assumed to be "thinking for themselves"—not a reputation anyone would have wished to have. In addition, Dad was charged with associating with a targeted SI—(Subversive Individual)—who was later arrested and tried for Treason; Dad hadn't done more than *sympathetically listen* to this man address a small gathering in a public park when he and the others were caught in a Homeland Security "sweep"—and Dad's life was changed forever.

He was demoted from his residency in the medical center. Though he had an M.D., with special training in pediatric oncology, he could find work only as a lowly-paid medical attendant in the center, where there had to be maintained a bias against him, that he might never be allowed to "practice" medicine again. Yet, Dad never (publicly) complained—he was lucky, he often (publicly) said, not to be imprisoned, and to be alive.

From time to time MIs were obliged to restate the terms of their crimes and punishments, and to (publicly) express gratitude for their exoneration and current employment. On such occasions Dad took a deep breath and, as he said, *bartered his soul another time.*

Poor Dad! He was so good-natured in our household, I don't think I realized how terrible he must have felt. How *broken*.

Within the family it was understood that we didn't discuss Dad's status *per se*, but we seemed to be allowed—that is, we were not expressly forbidden—to allude to his MI status in the way you might allude to a chronic condition in a family member like multiple sclerosis, or Tourette's, or a predilection for freak accidents. Being MI was something *shameful, embarrassing, potentially dangerous*—but since MI was a (relatively) minor criminal category compared with more serious criminal categories, it wasn't a treasonable offense to acknowledge it. But Dad took risks, even so.

For one of the memories that comes to me, strangely clear and self-contained, like a disturbing dream suddenly recalled in daylight, was how one day when no one was home except us Dad took me upstairs to an attic room that had been shut up for as long as I could remember, with a padlock; and in that room Dad retrieved from beneath a loose floorboard, beneath a worn carpet, a packet of photographs of a man who looked teasingly familiar to me, but whom I could not recall—"This is your uncle Tobias, who was Deleted when you were two years old."

At this time I was ten years old. My two-year-old self was lost and irretrievable. In a quavering voice Dad explained that his "beloved, reckless" younger brother Tobias had lived with us while going to medical school and that he'd drawn the attention of the F.B.E./F.B.I. (Federal Bureau of Examiners, Federal Bureau of Inquisitors) after helping organize a May Day free-speech demonstration. At the age of twenty-three "your uncle Toby" had been arrested in this very house, taken away, allegedly tried—and Deleted.

That is, "vaporized."

What is that, Daddy?—"vaporized." Though I knew the answer would be sad I had to ask.

"Just—gone, sweetie. Like a flame when it's been blown out."

I was too young to register the depth of loss in my father's eyes.

For Dad had often that look of loss in his face. Exhausted from his hospital job, and his skin ashy, and a limp in his right leg from some accident after which a bone had not mended correctly. Yet, Dad had a way of smiling that made everything seem all right.

Just us, kids! We're hanging in here.

Except right now Dad wasn't smiling. Turned a little from me so (maybe) I wouldn't notice him wiping tears from his eyes.

"We aren't supposed to 'recall' Tobias. Certainly not provide information to a child. Or look at pictures! I could be arrested if—anyone heard."

By *anyone* Dad meant the Government. Though you would not say that word—"Government." You would not say the words "State"—"Federal Leaders." It was forbidden to say such words and so, as Dad did, you spoke in a vague way, with a furtive look—*if anyone heard.*

Or, you might say *They.*

You could think of *anyone,* or *they,* as a glowering sky. A low-ceiling sky of those large dirigible clouds rumored to be surveillance devices, sculpted shapes like great ships, often bruised colored and iridescent from pollution, moving unpredictably but always *there.*

Downstairs, in the vicinity of our electronic devices, Dad would never speak so openly. Of course you would never trust your computer no matter how friendly and throaty-seductive its voice, or your cell phone or dicta-stylus, but also thermostats, dishwashers, microwaves, car keys and (self-driving) cars.

"But I miss Toby. All the time. Seeing medical students his age . . . I miss how he'd be a wonderful uncle to you, and to Rod."

It was confusing to me. I'd forgotten what Dad had said—*Vaporized? Deleted?*

But I knew not to ask Dad more questions right now, and make him sadder.

Exciting to see photographs of my lost "Uncle Toby" who looked like a younger version of my father. Uncle Toby had had a frowning-squinting kind of smile, like Dad. And his nose was long and thin like Dad's with a tiny bump in the bone. And his eyes!—dark brown with a glisten, like my own.

"Uncle Toby looks like he'd be *fun*."

Was this a stupid thing to say? Right away I regretted it but Dad only just smiled sadly.

"Yes. Toby was *fun*."

He'd tried to warn his brother about being involved in any sort of free speech or May Day demonstrations, Dad said. Even during what had appeared to be a season of (relative) relaxation on the part of the Homeland Security Public Dissemination Bureau; during such seasons, the Government eased up on public-security enforcement, yet, as Dad believed, continued to monitor and file away information about dissenters and potential SIs (Subversive Individuals), for future use. *Nothing is ever forgotten*—Dad warned.

At such times rumors would be circulated of a "thaw"—a "new era"—for always, as Dad said, people are eager to believe good news, and to forget bad news; people wish to be "optimists" and not "pessimists";

but "thaws" are factored into cycles and soon come to an end leaving incautious persons, especially the young and naïve, vulnerable to exposure and arrest and—what comes after arrest.

After Uncle Toby's disappearance (as it was called) law enforcement officers had raided the house and appropriated his medical textbooks, lab notebooks, personal computer and electronic devices, etc., and all pictures of him either digital or hard copy that they could find; but Dad had managed to hide away a few items, at great risk to his own safety.

Saying, "I'm not proud of myself, honey. But I knew it would be wisest to 'repudiate' my brother—formally. By that time he'd been Deleted, so there was no point in defending him, or protecting him. I guess I was pretty convincing—and your mother, too—swearing how we didn't realize we were harboring an SI—a 'traitor'—so they let us off with just a fine."

Dad drew his sleeve across his face. Wiping his face.

"A devastating fine, actually. But we had to be grateful the house wasn't razed, which sometimes happens when there's treason involved."

"Does Mom know?"

"'Know'—what?"

"About Uncle Toby's things here."

"No."

Dad explained: "Mom 'knows' that my brother was Deleted. She never speaks of him of course. She might have 'known' that I'd kept back a few personal items of Toby's at the time but she's certainly forgotten by now, as she has probably forgotten what Toby looked like. If you work hard enough to *not think* of something, and wall off your mind against it, and others around you are doing the same, you can 'forget'—to a degree."

Brashly I was thinking *Not me! I will not forget.*

Touching one of my lost uncle's sweaters, soft dark-wool riddled with moth holes. And there was a yellowed-white T-shirt with a stretched neck. And a biology lab notebook with half the pages empty. And a wristwatch with a stretch band and a blank dead face forever halted at 2:20 P.M. that Daddy tried to revive without success.

"Now you must promise, Adriane, never to speak of your lost uncle to anyone."

I nodded *yes, Daddy.*

"Not to Mommy, and not to Roddy. You must not speak of 'Uncle Toby.' You must not—even to me."

Seeing the perplexed look in my face Dad kissed me wetly on the nose.

Gathering up the outlawed things and returning them beneath the floorboards and the worn carpet.

"Our secret, Adriane. Promise?"

"Yes, Daddy. Promise!"

———

So yes, I knew what Deletion was. I know what Deletion *is.*

I am not likely to emulate my uncle Toby. I am no longer interested in being "different"—in drawing attention to myself.

As I have sworn numerous times I determined to serve out my Exile without violating the Instructions. I am determined to be returned to my family one day.

I am determined not to be "vaporized"—and forgotten.

Wondering if beneath the floorboards in the attic there's a pathetic little cache of things of mine, gnarled toothbrush, kitten socks, math homework with red grade *91,* my parents hastily managed to hide away.

The Warrant

Hereby, entered on this 19th day June NAS-23 in the 16th Federal District, Eastern-Atlantic States, a warrant for the arrest, detention, reassignment and sentencing of STROHL, ADRIANE S., 17, daughter of ERIC and MADELEINE STROHL, 3911 N. 17th St., Pennsboro, N.J., on seven counts of Treason-Speech and Questioning of Authority in violation of Federal Statutes 2 and 7. Signed by order of Chief Justice H. R. Sedgwick, 16th Federal District.

"Good News!"

O r so at first it seemed.

I'd been named valedictorian of my class at Pennsboro High School. And I'd been the only one at our school, of five students nominated, to be awarded a federally funded Patriot Democracy Scholarship.

My mother came running to hug me, and congratulate me. And my father, though more warily.

"That's our girl! We are so proud of you."

The principal of our high school had telephoned my parents with the good news. It was rare for a phone to ring in our house, for most messages came electronically and there was no choice about receiving them.

And my brother, Roderick, came to greet me with a strange expression on his face. He'd heard of Patriot Democracy Scholarships, Roddy said, but had never known anyone who'd gotten one. While he'd been at Pennsboro High he was sure that no one had ever been named a Patriot Scholar.

"Well. Congratulations, Addie."

"Thanks! I guess."

Roddy, who'd graduated from Pennsboro High three years before, and was now working as a barely paid intern in the Pennsboro branch of the NAS Media Dissemination Bureau (MDB), was grudgingly admiring. I thought—*He's jealous. He can't go to a real university.*

I never knew if I felt sorry for my hulking-tall brother who'd cultivated a wispy little sand-colored beard and mustache, and always wore the same dull-brown clothes, that were a sort of uniform for lower-division workers at MDB, or if—actually—I was afraid of him. Inside Roddy's smile there was a secret little smirk just for *me*.

When we were younger Roddy had often tormented me—"teasing" it was called (by Roddy). Both our parents worked ten-hour shifts and Roddy and I were home alone together much of the time. As Roddy was the older, it had been Roddy's task to *take care of your little sister*. What a joke! But a cruel joke, that doesn't make me smile.

Now we were older, and I was tall myself (for a girl of my age: five feet eight), Roddy didn't torment me quite as much. Mostly it was his expression—a sort of shifting, frowning, smirk-smiling, meant to convey that Roddy was thinking certain thoughts best kept secret.

That smirking little smile just for me—like an ice-sliver in the heart.

My parents had explained: it was difficult for Roddy, who hadn't done well enough in high school to merit a scholarship even to the local NAS state college, to see that I was doing much better than he'd done in the same school. Embarrassing to him to know that his younger sister earned higher grades than he had, from the very teachers he'd had at Pennsboro High. And Roddy had little chance of ever being admitted to a federally mandated four-year university, even if he took community college courses, and our parents could afford to send him.

Something had gone wrong during Roddy's last two years of high school. He'd become scared about things—maybe with reason. He'd never confided in me.

At Pennsboro High—as everywhere in our nation, I suppose—there was a fear of seeming "smart"—(which might be interpreted as "too smart")—which would result in calling unwanted attention to you. In a True Democracy all individuals are *equal*—no one is *better than anyone else.* It was OK to get B's, and an occasional

A−; but A's were risky, and A+ was very risky. In his effort not to get A's on exams, though he was intelligent enough, and had done well in middle school, Roddy seriously missed, and wound up with D's.

Dad had explained: it's like you're a champion archer. And you have to shoot to miss the bull's-eye. And something willful in you assures that you don't just miss the bull's-eye but the entire damned target.

Dad had laughed, shaking his head. Something like this had happened to my brother.

Poor Roddy. And poor Adriane, since Roddy took out his disappointment on me.

It wasn't talked about openly at school. But we all knew. Many of the smartest kids held back in order not to call attention to themselves. HSPSO (Home Security Public Safety Oversight) was reputed to keep lists of potential dissenters/ MIs/ SIs, and these were said to contain the names of students with high grades and high I.Q. scores. Especially suspicious were students who were good at science—these were believed to be too "questioning" and "skeptic" about the guidelines for curriculum at the school, so experiments were no longer part of our science courses, only just "science facts" to be memorized ("gravity causes objects to fall," "water boils at 212 degrees F.," "cancer is caused by negative thoughts," "the average female I.Q. is 7.55

points lower than the average male I.Q., adjusting for ST status").

Of course it was just as much of a mistake to wind up with C's and D's—that meant that you were *dull-normal,* or it might mean that you'd deliberately sabotaged your high school career. Too obviously "holding back" was sometimes dangerous. After graduation you might wind up at a community college hoping to better yourself by taking courses and trying to transfer to a state school, but the fact was, once you entered the workforce in a low-level category, like Roddy at MDB, you were there forever.

Nothing is ever forgotten, no one is going anywhere they aren't already at. This was a saying no one was supposed to say aloud.

So, Dad was stuck forever as an ME2—medical technician, second rank—at the district medical clinic where staff physicians routinely consulted him on medical matters, especially pediatric oncology—physicians whose salaries were five times Dad's salary.

Dad's health benefits, like Mom's, were so poor Dad couldn't even get treatment at the clinic he worked in. We didn't want to think what it would mean if and when they needed serious medical treatment.

I hadn't been nearly as cautious in school as Roddy. I enjoyed school where I had (girl) friends close as sisters. I liked quizzes and tests—they were like games which, if you studied hard, and memorized what your teachers told you, you could do well.

But then, sometimes I tried harder than I needed to try.

Maybe it was risky. Some little spark of defiance provoked me.

But maybe also (some of us thought) school wasn't so risky for girls. There had been only a few DASTADs—Disciplinary Actions Securing Threats Against Democracy—taken against Pennsboro students in recent years, and these students had all been boys in category ST3 or below.

(The highest ST—SkinTone—category was 1: "Caucasian." Most residents of Pennsboro were ST1 or ST2 with a scattering of ST3's. There were ST4's in a neighboring district and of course dark-complected ST workers in all the districts. We knew they existed but most of us had never seen an actual ST10.)

It seems like the most pathetic vanity now, and foolishly naïve, but at our school I was one of those students who'd displayed some talent for writing, and for art; I was a "fast study" (my teachers said, not entirely approvingly), and could memorize passages of prose easily. I did not believe that I was the "outstanding" student in my class. That could not be possible!

I had to work hard to understand math and science, I had to read and reread my homework assignments, and to rehearse quizzes and tests, while to certain of my classmates these subjects came naturally. (ST2's and 3's were likely to be Asians, a minority in our district, and these girls and boys were very smart, yet not aggressive in putting themselves forward, that's to say *at risk*.) Yet somehow it happened that Adriane Strohl wound up with the highest grade-point average in the Class of '23—4.3 out of 5.

My close friend Paige Connor had been warned by her parents to hold back—so Paige's average was only 4.1, well inside the safe range. And one of the obviously smartest boys, whose father was MI, like my Dad, a former math professor, had definitely held back—or maybe exams so traumatized him, Jonny had not done well without trying, and his average was a modest/safe 3.9.

Better to be a safe coward than a sorry hero. Why I'd thought such remarks were just stupid jokes kids made, I don't know.

Fact is, I had just not been thinking. Later in my life, or rather in my next life, as a university student, when I would be studying psychology, at least a primitive form of cognitive psychology, I would learn about the phenomenon of "attention"—"attentiveness"—that is within consciousness but is the pointed, purposeful, focused aspect of consciousness. Just to have your eyes open is to be conscious only minimally; to *pay attention* is something further. In my schoolgirl life I was conscious, but I was not *paying attention.* Focused on tasks like homework, exams, friends to sit with in cafeteria and hang out with in gym class, I did not pick up more than a fraction of what hovered in the air about me, the warnings of teachers that were non-verbal, glances that should have alerted me to—something . . .

I would realize, in my later life, that virtually all of my life beforehand had been *minimally conscious.* I had questioned virtually nothing, I had scarcely tried to decipher the precise nature of what my parents were actually trying to communicate to me, apart from their words. For my dear parents were *accursed with attentiveness.* I had taken them for granted—I had taken my own bubble-life for granted . . .

So it happened, Adriane Strohl was named valedictorian of her graduating class. Good news! Congratulations!

Now I assume that no one else who might've been qualified wanted this "honor"—just as no one else wanted a Patriot Democracy Scholarship. Except there'd been some controversy, the school administration was said to favor another student for the honor of giving the valedictory address, not Adriane Strohl but a boy with a 4.2 average and also a varsity letter in football and a Good Democratic Citizenship Award, whose parents were allegedly of a higher caste than mine, and whose father was not MI but EE (a special distinction granted to Exiled persons who had served their terms of Exile and had been what was called 110 percent rehabilitated—Exile Elite).

I'd known about the controversy vaguely, as a school rumor. The EE father's son had not such high grades as I did, but it was believed that he would give a smoother and more entertaining valedictory address, since his course of study was TV Public Relations and not the mainstream curriculum. And maybe administrators were concerned that Adriane Strohl would not be entertaining but would say "unacceptable" things in her speech?

Somehow without realizing, over a period of years, I'd acquired a reputation among my teachers and classmates for saying "surprising" things—"unexpected" things—that other students would not have said. Impulsively I'd raised my hands and asked questions. I was not *doubtful* exactly—just curious, and wanting to know. For instance was a "science fact" always and inevitably a fact? Did water *always* boil at 212 degrees F., or did it depend upon how pure the water was? And were boy-students *always* smarter than girl students, judging from actual tests and grades in our school?

Some of the teachers (male) made jokes about me, so that the class laughed at my silly queries; other (female) teachers were annoyed, or maybe frightened. My voice was usually quiet and courteous but I might've come across as *willful*.

Sometimes the quizzical look in my face disconcerted my teachers, who took care always to compose their expressions when they stood in front of a classroom. There were approved ways of showing interest, surprise, (mild) disapproval, severity. (Our classrooms, like all public spaces and many private spaces, were "monitored for quality assurance" but adults were more keenly aware of surveillance than teenagers.)

Each class had its spies. We didn't know who they were, of course—it was said that if you thought you knew, you were surely mistaken, since the DCVSB (Democratic Citizens Volunteer Surveillance Bureau) chose spies so carefully, it was analogous to the camouflage wings of a certain species of moth that blends in *seamlessly* with the bark of a certain tree. As Dad said, *Your teachers can't help it. They can't deviate from the curriculum. The ideal is lockstep—each teacher in each classroom performing like a robot and never deviating from script under penalty of—you know what.*

Was this true? For years in our class—the Class of NAS -23—there'd been vague talk of a teacher—how long ago, we didn't know—maybe when we were in middle school?—who'd "deviated" from the script one day, began talking wildly, and laughing, and shaking his/her fist at the "eye" (in fact, there were probably numerous "eyes" in any classroom, and all invisible), and was arrested, and overnight Deleted—so a new teacher was hired to take his/her place; and soon no one remembered the teacher-who'd-been-Deleted. And after a while we couldn't even remember clearly that one of our teachers *had been* Deleted. (Or had there been more than one? Were certain classrooms in our school *haunted?*) In our brains where the memory of ——— should have been, there was just a blank.

Definitely, I was not aggressive in class. I don't think so. But compared with my mostly meek classmates, some of whom sat small in their desks like partially folded-up papier-mâché dolls, it is possible that Adriane Strohl stood out—in an unfortunate way.

In Patriot Democracy History, for instance, I'd questioned "facts" of history, sometimes. I'd asked questions about the subject no one ever questioned—the Great Terrorist Attacks of 9/11/01. But not in an arrogant way, really—just out of curiosity! I certainly didn't want to get any of my teachers in trouble with the EOB (Education Oversight Bureau) which could result in them being demoted or fired or—"vaporized."

I'd thought that, well—people liked me, mostly. I was the spiky-haired girl with the big glistening dark-brown eyes and a voice with a little catch in it and a habit of asking questions. Like a really young child with too much energy in kindergarten, you hope will run in circles and tire herself out. With a kind of naïve oblivi-ousness I earned good grades so it was assumed that, despite my father being of MI caste, I would qualify for a federally mandated State Democracy University.

(That is, I was eligible for admission to one of the massive state universities. At these, a thousand students might attend a lecture, and many courses were online.)

Restricted universities were far smaller, prestigious and inaccessible to all but a fraction of the population; though not listed online or in any public directory, these universities were housed on "traditional" cam-puses in Cambridge, New Haven, Princeton, etc., in restricted districts. Not only did we not know precisely where these centers of learning were, but we also had not ever met anyone with degrees from them.

When in class I raised my hand to answer a teach-er's question I often did notice classmates glancing at

me—my friends, even—sort of uneasy, apprehensive—
*What will Adriane say now? What is wrong with
Adriane?*

There was nothing wrong with *me!* I was sure.

In fact, I was secretly proud of myself. Maybe
just a little vain. Wanting to think *I am Eric Strohl's
daughter.*

The Arrest

The words were brisk, impersonal: "Strohl, Adriane. Hands behind your back."

It happened so fast. At graduation rehearsal.

So fast! I was too surprised—too scared—to think of resisting.

Except I guess that I did—try to "resist"—in childish desperation tried to duck and cringe away from the officers' rough hands on me—wrenching my arms behind my back with such force, I had to bite my lips to keep from screaming.

What was happening? I could not believe it—I was being *arrested*.

Yet even in my shock thinking *I will not scream. I will not beg for mercy.*

My wrists were handcuffed behind my back. Within seconds I was a captive of the Homeland Security.

I'd only just given my valedictorian's speech and had stepped away from the podium, to come down from the auditorium stage, when there came our principal Mr. Mackay with a peculiar expression on his face— muted anger, righteousness, but fear also—to point at me, as if the arresting officers needed him to point me out at close range.

"That is she—'Adriane Strohl.' That is the treasonous girl you seek."

Mr. Mackay's words were strangely stilted. He seemed very angry with me—but why? Because of my valedictorian's speech? But the speech had consisted entirely of questions—not answers, or accusations.

I'd known that Mr. Mackay didn't like me—didn't know me very well but knew of me from my teachers. But it was shocking to see in an adult's face a look of genuine *hatred*.

"She was warned. They are all warned. We did our best to educate her as a patriot, but—the girl is a born *provocateur*."

Provocateur! I knew what the term meant, but I'd never heard such a charge before, applied to me.

Later I would realize that the Arrest Warrant must have been drawn up for me before the rehearsal—of course. Mr. Mackay and his faculty advisers must have reported me to Youth Disciplinary before they'd even heard my valedictory speech—they'd *guessed* that it would be "treasonous" and that I couldn't be allowed to give it at the graduation ceremony. And the Patriot Democracy Scholarship—that must have been a cruel trick, as well.

As others stood staring at the front of the brightly lighted auditorium the Arrest Warrant was read to me by the female Arresting Officer. I was too stunned to hear most of it—only the accusing words *arrest, detention, reassignment, sentencing—Treason-Speech* and *Questioning of Authority.*

Quickly then, Mr. Mackay called for an "emergency assembly" of the senior class.

Murmuring and excited my classmates settled into the auditorium. There were 322 students in the class, and like wildfire news of my arrest had spread among them within minutes.

Gravely Mr. Mackay announced from a podium that Adriane Strohl, "formerly" valedictorian of the class, had been arrested by the State on charges of Treason and Questioning of Authority; and what was required now was a "vote of confidence" from her peers regarding this action.

That is, all members of the senior class (excepting Adriane Strohl) were to vote on whether to confirm the arrest, or to challenge it. "We will ask for a show of hands," Mr. Mackay said, voice quavering with the solemnity of the occasion, "in a full, fair, and unbiased demonstration of democracy."

At this time I was positioned, handcuffed, with a wet, streaked/guilty face, at the very edge of the stage. As if my classmates needed to be reminded who the arrestee Adriane Strohl was.

Gripping my upper arms were two husky Youth Disciplinary Officers from the Youth Disciplinary Division of Homeland Security. They were one man and one woman and they wore dark blue uniforms and were equipped with billy clubs, Tasers, Mace, and revolvers in heavy holsters around their waists. My classmates stared wide-eyed, both intimidated and thrilled. An arrest! At school! And a show-of-hands vote which was not a novelty in itself except on this exciting occasion.

"Boys and girls! Attention! All those in favor of Adriane Strohl being stripped of the honor of class valedictorian as a consequence of having committed treason and questioned authority, raise your hands— yes?" There was a brief stunned pause. Brief.

Hesitantly, a few hands were lifted. Then, a few more.

No doubt the presence of the uniformed Youth Disciplinary Officers glaring at them roused my classmates to action. Entire rows lifted their hands—*Yes!*

Here and there were individuals who shifted uneasily in their seats. They were not voting, yet. I caught the eye of my friend Carla whose face too appeared to be wet with tears. And there was Paige all but signaling to me—*I'm sorry, Adriane. I have no choice.*

As in a nightmare, at last a sea of hands were raised against me. If there were some not voting, clasping their hands in their laps, I could not see them.

"And all opposed—no?" Mr. Mackay's voice hovered dramatically as if he were counting raised hands; in fact, there was not a single hand, of all the rows of seniors, to be seen.

"I think, then, we have a stunning example of democracy in action, boys and girls. 'Majority rule—the truth is in the numbers.'"

The second vote was hardly more than a repeat of the first: "We, the Senior Class of Pennsboro High, confirm and support the arrest of the former valedictorian, Adriane Strohl, on charges of Treason and Questioning of Authority. All those in favor . . ."

By this time the arrestee had shut her teary eyes in shame, revulsion, dread. No need to see the show of hands another time.

The officers hauled me out of the school by a rear exit, paying absolutely no heed to my protests of being in pain from the tight handcuffs and their grip on my upper arms. Immediately I was forced into an unmarked police vehicle resembling a small tank with plow-like gratings that might be used to ram against and to flatten protesters.

Roughly I was thrown into the rear of the van. The door was shut and locked. Though I pleaded with the officers, who were seated in the front of the vehicle, on the other side of a barred, Plexiglas barrier, no one paid the slightest attention to me, as if I did not exist.

The officers appeared to be ST4 and ST5. It was possible that they were "foreign"-born/ indoctrinated NAS citizens who had not been allowed to learn English.

I thought—*Will anyone tell my parents where I am? Will they let me go home?*

Panicked I thought—*Will they "vaporize" me?*

Heralded by a blaring siren I was taken to a fortress-like building in the city center of Pennsboro, the local headquarters of Homeland Security Interrogation. This was a building with blank bricked-up windows that was said to have once been a post office, before the Reconstitution of the United States into the North American States and the privatizing and gradual extinction of the postal service. (Many buildings from the old States remained, now utilized for very different purposes. The building to which my mother had gone for grade school had been converted to a Children's Diagnostic and Surgical Repair Facility, for instance; the residence hall in which my father had lived, as a young medical student, in the years before he'd been reclassified as MI, was now a Youth Detention and Re-education Facility. The Media Dissemination Bureau, where my brother Roddy worked, was in an old brownstone building formerly the Pennsboro Public Library, in the days when "books" existed to be held in the hand—and read!) In this drafty place I was brought to an interrogation room in the Youth Disciplinary Division, forcibly seated in an uncomfortable chair with a blinding light shining in my face, and a camera aimed at me, and interrogated by strangers whom I could barely see.

Repeatedly I was asked—"Who wrote that speech for you?"

No one, I said. No one wrote my speech, or helped me write it—I'd written it myself.

"Did your father Eric Strohl write that speech for you?"

No! My father did not.

"Did your father tell you what to write? Influence you? Are these questions your father's questions?"

No! My own questions.

"Did either of your parents help you write your speech? Influence you? Are these questions their questions?"

No, no, *no*.

"Are these treasonous thoughts their thoughts?"

I was terrified that my father, or both my parents, had been arrested, and were being interrogated too, somewhere else in this awful place. I was terrified that my father would be reclassified no longer MI but SI (Subversive Individual) or AT (Active Traitor)—that he might meet the same fate as Uncle Tobias.

My valedictorian speech was examined line by line, word by word, by the interrogators—though it was just two printed double-spaced sheets of paper with a few scrawled annotations. My computer had been seized from my locker and was being examined as well.

And all my belongings from my locker—laptop, sketchbook, backpack, cell phone, granola bars, a soiled school sweatshirt, wadded tissues—were confiscated.

The interrogators were brisk and impersonal as machines. Almost, you'd have thought they might be robot-interrogators—until you saw one of them blink, or swallow, or glare at me in pity or disgust, or scratch at his nose.

(Even then, as Dad might have said, these figures could have been robots; for the most recent AI devices were being programmed to emulate idiosyncratic, "spontaneous" human mannerisms.)

Sometimes an interrogator would shift in his seat, away from the blinding light, and I would have a fleeting but clear view of a face—what was shocking was, the face appeared to be so *ordinary*, the face of someone you'd see on a bus, or a neighbor of ours.

My valedictorian address had been timed to be no more than eight minutes long. That was the tradition at our school—a short valedictorian address, and an even shorter salutatorian address. My English teacher Mrs. Dewson had been assigned to "advise" me—but I hadn't shown her what I'd been writing. (I hadn't shown Dad, or Mom, or any of my friends—I'd wanted to surprise them at graduation.) After a half-dozen failed starts I'd gotten desperate and had the bright idea of asking numbered questions—twelve, in all—of the kind my classmates might have asked if they'd had the nerve—(some of these the very questions I'd asked my teachers, who had never given satisfactory answers)—like *What came before the beginning of Time?*

And *What came before the Great Terrorist Attacks of 9/11?*

Our RNAS calendar dates from the time of that attack, which was before my birth, but not my parents' births, and so my parents could remember a pre-NAS time when the calendar was different—time wasn't measured in just a two-digit figure but a *four-digit figure!* (Under the old, now-outlawed calendar, my mother and father had been born in what had been called the twentieth century. It was against the law to compute birth dates under the old calendar, but Daddy had told me—I'd been born in what would have been called the twenty-first century if the calendar had not been reformed.)

NAS means North American States—more formally known as RNAS—Reconstituted North American States, which came into being some years after the Great Terrorist Attacks, as a direct consequence of the Attacks, as we were taught.

Following the Attacks there was an Interlude of Indecisiveness during which time issues of "rights"—(the Constitution, the Bill of Rights, Civil Rights law, etc.)—vs. the need for Patriot Vigilance in the War Against Terror were contested, with a victory, after the suspension of the Constitution and the Bill of Rights by executive order, for PVIWAT, or Patriot Vigilance. (Yes, it is hard to comprehend. As soon as you come to the end of such a sentence, you have forgotten the beginning!)

How strange it was to think there'd been a time when the regions known as (Reconstituted) Mexico

and (Reconstituted) Canada had been separate political entities—separate from the States! On a map it
seems clear, for instance, that the large state of Alaska
should be connected with the mainland United States,
and not separated by what was formerly "Canada."
This too was hard to grasp and had never been clearly
explained in any of our Patriot Democracy History
classes, perhaps because our teachers were not certain
of the facts.

The old, "outdated" (that is, "unpatriotic") history
books had all been destroyed, my father said. Hunted
down in the most remote outposts—obscure rural libraries in the Dakotas, below-ground stacks in great
university libraries, microfilm in what had been the
Library of Congress. "Outdated"/"unpatriotic" information was deleted from all computers and from all
accessible memory—only reconstituted history and information were allowed, just as only the reconstituted
calendar was allowed.

This was only logical, we were taught. There was
no purpose to learning useless things, that would only
clutter our brains like debris stuffed to overflowing in
a trash bin.

But there must have been a time *before that
time*—before the Reconstitution, and before the Attacks. That was what I was asking. Patriot Democ-

racy History—which we'd had every year since fifth grade, an unchanging core of First Principles with ever-more detailed information—was only concerned with post-Terrorist events, mostly the relations of the NAS with its numerous Terrorist Enemies in other parts of the world, and an account of the "triumphs" of the NAS in numerous wars. So many wars! They were fought now at long-distance, and did not involve living soldiers, for the most part; robot-missiles were employed, and powerful bombs said to be nuclear, chemical, and biological. In our senior year of high school we were required to take a course titled "Wars of Freedom"—these included long-ago wars like the Revolutionary War, the Spanish-American War, World War I, World War II, the Korean War, the Vietnam War, and the more recent Afghanistan and Iraq wars—all of which our country had won— "decisively." We were not required to learn the dates or causes of these wars, if there were actual causes, but battle-places and names of high-ranking generals, political leaders, and presidents; these were provided in columns to be memorized for exams. The question of *Why?* was never asked—and so I'd asked it in class, and in my valedictory address. It had not occurred to me that this was *Treason-Speech,* or that I was *Questioning Authority.*

The harsh voices were taking a new approach: Was it one of my teachers who'd written the speech for me? One of my teachers who'd "influenced" me?

The thought came to me—*Mr. Mackay! I could blame him, he would be arrested . . .*

But I would never do such a thing, I thought. Even if the man hated me, and had me arrested for treason, I could not lie about him.

After two hours of interrogation it was decided that I was an "uncooperative subject." In handcuffs I was taken by YD officers to another floor of Home Security which exuded the distressing air of a medical unit; there I was strapped down onto a movable platform and slid inside a cylindrical machine that made clanging and whirring noises close against my head; the cylinder was so small, the surface only an inch or so from my face, I had to shut my eyes tight to keep from panicking. The interrogators' voices, sounding distorted and inhuman, were channeled into the machine. This was a BIM (Brain-Image Maker)—I'd only heard of these—that would determine if I was telling the truth, or lying.

Did your father—or any adult—write your speech for you?

Did your father—or any adult—influence your speech for you?

Did your father—or any adult—infiltrate your mind with treasonous thoughts?

Barely I could answer, through parched lips—*No. No, no!*

Again and again these questions were repeated. No matter what answers I gave, the questions were repeated.

Yet more insidious were variants of these questions.

Your father Eric Strohl has just confessed to us, to "influencing" you—so you may as well confess, too. In what ways did he influence you?

This had to be a trick, I thought. I stammered—*In no ways. Not ever. Daddy did not.*

More harshly the voice continued.

Your mother Madeleine Strohl has confessed to us, both she and your father "influenced" you. In what ways did they influence you?

I was sobbing, protesting—*They didn't! They did not influence me . . .*

(Of course, this wasn't true. How could any parents fail to "influence" their children? My parents had influenced me through my entire life—not so much in their speech as in their personalities. They were good, loving parents. They had taught Roddy and me: *There is a soul within. There is "free will" within. If—without—the State is lacking a soul, and there is* no "free will" that you can see. Trust the inner, not the outer. Trust the soul, not the State. But I would not betray my parents by repeating these defiant words.)

At some point in the interrogation I must have passed out—for I was awakened by deafening noises, in a state of panic. Was this a form of torture? Noise-torture? Powerful enough to burst eardrums? To drive the subject insane? We'd all heard rumors of such torture-interrogations—though no one would speak openly about them. Shaken and excited Roddy would come home from his work at Media Dissemination to tell us about certain "experimental techniques" Homeland Security was developing, using laboratory primates—until Mom clamped her hands over her ears and asked him to please stop.

The deafening noises stopped abruptly. The interrogation resumed.

But it was soon decided then that I was too upset—my brain waves were too "agitated"—to accurately register truth or falsity, so I was removed from the cylindrical imaging machine, and an IV needle was jabbed into a vein in my arm, to inject me with a powerful "truth-serum" drug. And again the same several questions were asked, and I gave the same answers. Even in my exhausted and demoralized state I would not tell the interrogators what they wanted to hear: that my father, or maybe both my parents, had "influenced" me in my treasonous ways.

Or any of my teachers. Or even Mr. Mackay, my enemy.

I'd been taken out of the hateful BIM, and strapped to a chair. It was a thick squat "wired" chair—a kind of electric chair—that sent currents of shock through my body, painful as knife-stabs. Now I was crying, and lost control of my bladder.

The interrogation continued. Essentially it was the same question, always the same question, with a variant now and then to throw me off stride.

Who wrote your speech for you? Who "influenced" you? Who is your collaborator in Treason?

It was your brother Roderick who reported you. As a Treason-Monger and a Questioner of Authority, you have been denounced by your brother.

I began to cry harder. I had lost all hope. Of all the things the interrogators had told me, or wanted me to believe, it was only this—that Roddy had reported me— that seemed to me possible, and not so very surprising.

I could remember how, squeezing my hand when he'd congratulated me about my good news, Roddy had smiled—his special smirking-smile just for me.

Congratulations, Addie!

"Disciplinary Measure"

Next morning I was taken from my cell and returned to Youth Interrogation.

Half-carried from my cell, handcuffed and my ankles shackled, I was very very tired, very sick, scarcely conscious.

It was my hope that my parents would be waiting for me—that they'd been summoned to come get me, and take me home. I would accept it that I'd be forbidden to attend graduation—forbidden even to graduate from high school; I would accept it that I might be sent to a Youth Rehabilitation camp, as it had been rumored the boys at Pennsboro High had been, who'd been arrested by Youth Disciplinary. All I wanted was to see my parents—to rush at them, and throw myself into their arms . . .

Some months ago my parents had celebrated my seventeenth birthday with me. It had been a happy time!—but seemed now a lost, childish time. I had not felt like seventeen and now, desperate for my parents, I scarcely felt like a teenager at all.

Of course my parents were nowhere near. Probably they did not know what had happened to me. And I did not dare ask about them.

Instead I was being sternly informed: several Patriot Scholars had been arrested yesterday afternoon, simultaneous with my arrest, in a Youth Disciplinary "sweep." After a season or more of relatively few such sweeps and seizes, YDDHS was "cracking down" on "potential subversives."

These Patriot Scholars were graduating seniors from other high schools in the area. Their names, too, had been handed over to YDDHS by the principals of their schools. The question was put bluntly to me: Was I, Adriane Strohl, a collaborator with these students? Was I a co-conspirator?

Their names were told to me: I'd never heard of any one of them.

Their faces appeared on three overhead TV screens: I'd never seen any one of them before.

A camera was turned on me, in a blaze of blinding light. I had to assume that my frightened face was being beamed into other interrogation rooms, where the arrested Patriot Scholars were being held.

Repeatedly I was asked: Was I a collaborator with any one, or more, of these individuals? Was I a *co-conspirator*?

All I could answer was *No*.

Weakly, hopelessly—*No*.

CHEN, MICHAEL was a very young-looking Asian-American boy with sleek black hair worn to his collar and widened, very dark and alarmed eyes. He, too, had been named valedictorian of his graduating class, at Roebuck High School. A glance at CHEN, MICHAEL and you knew that this was a smart boy, probably ST3.

PADURA, LAUREN was a thick-bodied girl with a strong-boned if rather ashen face and damp eyes, probably ST2. She was sitting as upright as possible, though handcuffed and shackled at the ankles; she was a student at East Lawrence High. A glance at PARUDA, LAUREN, and you knew that this was a girl who thought for herself and very likely, in her classes, asked questions as I had.

ZOLL, JOSEPH JAY was a tall lanky dark-blond boy with a blemished face, thick glasses, and a small mustache on his upper lip, ST1 like me. He had been named salutatorian of his class at Rumsfeld High and looked like a math/computer whiz—one glance at ZOLL, JOSEPH JAY and you knew that here was a boy you wanted for your friend, whose kindness, patience, and computer expertise would be invaluable.

The four of us, on the TV monitors, were not looking great. Our eyes were bloodshot. Our mouths were trembling. Whatever we'd done, we regretted it. We didn't look *innocent*. We didn't any longer resemble high school seniors—we looked much younger. *Just kids. Scared kids. Kids needing their mom and dad. Kids without a clue what was happening to them.*

A panicked thought came to me—what if one of the Patriot Scholars suddenly confessed to "collaborating" with the rest of us? Would we all be executed?

A brisk voice informed us that we had thirty seconds to compose our confessions. At the end of these thirty seconds, if no one had confessed, one Patriot Scholar would be suitably "disciplined" with a Domestic Drone Strike (DDS)—on camera.

We were terrified—paralyzed. No one spoke.

Sleek-black-haired CHEN, MICHAEL opened his mouth and tried to speak, but no words came out.

There were tears, and agitation, in PADURA, LAUREN'S face—but no words issued from her mouth.

Then, I heard myself pleading, in a thin wavering voice, that we were not "collaborators"—we didn't know one another, we'd never seen one another before, we didn't know one another's names . . .

Indifferently the off-screen voice was counting: eleven, sixteen, twenty-one . . . Twenty-seven, twenty-eight . . .

My heart was pounding so violently, I thought that it would burst. My eyes darted from one TV monitor to the others—as the Patriot Scholars trembled and cringed in their chairs, narrowing their eyes, yet unable to shut their eyes entirely.

On one of the screens there was a blinding flash. The boy with the mustache on his upper lip—ZOLL, JOSEPH JAY—was slammed sideways as if he'd been struck with a laser ray, that entered the side of his head like liquid fire, exploded and devoured his head, and then his torso and lower body, in less than three seconds.

What was left of ZOLL, JOSEPH JAY fell to the floor, slithering and phosphorescent, and by quick degrees this, too, vanished . . . I had a glimpse of the other Patriot Scholars staring in horror at their TV screens before all four screens went dark and a roaring in my ears became deafening.

When I woke from a sick, dead faint, I was being lifted from my chair. Yet so terrified still, I didn't dare to open my eyes.

Exile: Zone 9

"Adriane. I am your Youth Disciplinary Counsel." She was a woman of about Mom's age. Her face was shiny and glaring, so that I could barely look at her. Or maybe my vision had become over-sensitive from the previous day's interrogations in blazing light.

Her name was S. Platz. Her manner was almost jovial, as if she and I shared a joke.

"Try to lift your head and look at me, dear. As if you have nothing to hide. We are being 'surveyed' and videotaped—you must know."

After the terror I'd been feeling, and the hopeless-ness, S. Platz was so astonishing to me, I couldn't at first believe her; I was sure that she must be another torturer. Each time I closed my eyes I saw ZOLL, JOSEPH JAY struck down like an animal—or an "enemy" figure in a video game.

I would never forget that horrific sight, I thought.

I would never want to forget, for the executed boy's sake.

S. Platz, unlike the other interrogators, did not continue to ask me the same questions, and she did not speak in a brisk impersonal voice.

She asked one of the uniformed officers to unshackle me—both my wrists and my ankles. She asked if my wrists and ankles hurt, and if I was "very tired" and would like to "sleep an uninterrupted sleep" in a real bed—to help with "healing."

Almost inaudibly I said *Yes.*

(Wondering if "uninterrupted sleep" meant something terrible?)

But S. Platz seemed so kindly! Tears flooded my eyes, I was so grateful for her sympathy.

Yes thank you. Oh yes—I would like to sleep . . .

"I have good news for you, Adriane. Youth Disciplinary has ruled that the discipline for your violation of the federal statutes is—Exile."

Exile! I had heard of Exile—of course. This form of discipline was often confused with Deletion because, so far as anyone knew, including the families of Exiled Individuals, the Exiled Individual simply—vanished.

It was said to be highly experimental, and dangerous. Exiled Individuals were *teletransported*—every molecule in their bodies dissolved, to be *reconstituted* elsewhere. (No one who was left behind knew where. A colony on another planet? This was a prevailing rumor, according to Roddy. But which planet? If any had been colonized by the Government, ordinary citizens knew nothing about it.) But often, the teletransportation failed, and individuals were injured, incapacitated, killed, or, in effect, "vaporized"—and no one ever saw them again.

Only if the Exiled Individual reappeared, years later, after having served out his sentence, could it be assumed that he had been alive all the while, but in a remote place. EIs were generally allowed to live but had to submit to a process of "Re-education" and "Reconstitution."

Exile was considered to be the "humane"—"liberal"—disciplinary measure, appropriate for younger people who had not committed the most serious crimes—yet.

In our Patriot Social Studies class we were taught that the "Re-educated" and "Reconstituted" individual, successfully having completed his sentence of Exile and returned to the present time, designated EI1, was often an outstanding Citizen-Patriot; several notable EI1's had been named to federal posts in Homeland Security Public Safety Oversight and Epidemic Control; and the most renowned of EI1's had risen to a high-ranking executive post in the Capitol, as an assistant to the director of the Federal Bureau of Interrogation.

There were rumors that the president was himself an EI1—a former "traitor"-genius now totally converted to NAS and its democratic tradition.

S. Platz was saying: "Your case was carefully adjudicated, Adriane, after several of your teachers entered pleas for you. Their claim was that you are 'naïve'— 'very young'—'not subversive'—and 'not radical'—and that, if you are separated from the influence of your MI-father and are allowed to Re-educate yourself, you would be of value to society. Therefore, we are transporting you to Zone Nine. There, you will attend an excellent four-year university to train yourself in a socially useful profession. Teaching is strongly suggested. Or, if your science grades are good, you would be allowed to apply to medical school. Zone Nine is not so 'urban' as our Eastern zones, nor is it so 'rural' as most of our North-Midwest zones. It is not on any

NAS map—it is a place that 'exists' only by way of special access, for, in our present time, in the North-Midwest States that now encompass what was known as 'Wisconsin' in the era of Zone Nine, things are very different." Seeing that I was looking confused and frightened, S. Platz said, "You need not concern yourself with any of this, Adriane—you will simply be transported to the university in Zone Nine, where you will be a 'freshman.' You will be given a new, abbreviated identity. You will be, as you are, seventeen years old. And your name will be 'Mary Ellen Enright.' If necessary, when you return to us your training can be brought up-to-date. Everything that you need to know is explained in The Instructions, which I will give you now."

Though S. Platz spoke clearly I was having difficulty understanding. Badly wanting to ask *But can I see my parents again? Just once before I am sent away . . .*

S. Platz handed me a sheet of paper stiff as parchment. When I tried to read it, however, my eyes filled with moisture, and lost focus.

"So there is really no need to ask me questions—is there?"

S. Platz paused, smiling at me.

And now I saw that the counsel's steel-colored eyes were not smiling, but only just staring, and assessing.

The realization came to me—*If I don't react properly, I will be vaporized on the spot. The woman has this power.*

With a numb smile I managed to murmur *Thank you!*

And not a word about my parents. Or the life I would be leaving—the life to which I would be "lost."

II
Zone 9

The Happy Place

*S*he was a strange girl. At first, we didn't like her. She never smiled at us. Her face was like a mask. She prayed on her knees—we'd seen her! She cried herself to sleep every night like us, only worse.

We were all homesick, our first semester at Wainscotia. Missed our parents and our families so! But this girl was sad in a way we weren't—like her heart was broken. And she would not be comforted—which does not seem natural.

We were Christian girls, mostly Protestant. We attended chapel on Sundays. (She never did—we noticed that.) We believed in prayer—seriously!

We believed in helping one another. We believed in smiling-through-tears. You cried, and then you laughed—you opened a box of brownies your mom *had sent to you, to share with your roommates, or anyone who showed up in the room.*

You cried, and wiped away your tears—and you were yourself again.

She was the girl who scorned our mothers' brownies, and scorned the opportunity to walk with us to class on the steep-hilly sidewalks leading into the campus, who almost never came with us to the dining hall and sat with us. She'd gone to freshman orientation alone, and slipped away alone. The only girl in Acrady Cottage who didn't participate in Vesper Song.

Probably the only person in the freshman class who claimed she'd "lost" her green-and-purple freshman beanie. Who paid no heed to upperclassmen ordering her to "step out of the way, frosh"—stared through them as if she didn't see them and kept walking in her stiff-hunched way like a sleepwalker you pitied and would not want to waken.

The girl-with-no-name we called her. For if you called out a cheery Hi there, Mary Ellen!—she didn't seem to hear, or to register the name, even as she quickened her pace hurrying away.

We knew little about her. But we knew that she was a scholarship girl, like us.

Acrady Cottage was a residence for freshman scholarship girls—meaning that most of us couldn't have afforded Wainscotia State except for financial aid and part-time jobs on campus.

(She had a part-time job in the geology library.)

Scholarship girls were thrifty girls! Most of our text-books were used—some of them pretty badly battered.

We wore hand-me-down clothes and clothes sewn by our mothers or grandmothers—or by us.

Quite a few of us were 4-H girls. We were three Wisconsin State Fair blue-ribbon winners, in Acrady Cottage.

Acrady wasn't a residence hall like the ivy-covered stone buildings elsewhere on campus—it was just a house, plain weathered-gray shingle board, where freshman girls lived who could not afford to live any-where else.

But Acrady Cottage had spirit!

At Vesper Song, Acrady excelled though we were one of the smaller residences on campus—twenty-two girls.

Twenty-two girls including "Mary Ellen"—the girl who kept to herself like someone in quarantine.

First week at Wainscotia we were all homesick. But trying to be cheerful—"friendly."

Not her—"Mary Ellen Enright."

She'd avoid us if she could. Her own roommates!—that isn't easy.

Four of us in the third-floor room. Cramped space and just two (dormer) windows.

She'd taken the bed that was farthest, in a corner. And her desk jutted out from the wall, to partially hide the bed from the rest of the room. No window in that corner.

She'd shrink from us. Trying to smile—a weird bright smile that didn't reach her eyes.

And then, when she thought we were asleep and wouldn't see her, on her knees in the corner, praying.

And crying herself to sleep.

She looked *like someone who has traveled a long journey and has not fully recovered.*

We'd wondered—Is she foreign?

But what kind of foreign?

Even the way she spoke was strange. If you cornered her to say hello and ask how she was and she couldn't escape or avoid answering she would stammer a reply that was almost—but not quite—intelligible. We could recognize in her speech the rhythms and vowel-sounds of English, so if we didn't exactly know what she was saying, we could guess.

And she spoke so fast and nervous! Like none of the other girls of Acrady Cottage.

Of course, we were all from the Midwest. Most of us from Wisconsin. Where Mary Ellen was from was— one of the eastern states, we'd been told. Evidently people talked faster there.

Our part of the U.S., it's generally known as the Happy Place. (Midwest!) And Wainscotia is a very special university at the heart of the Happy Place.

This girl Mary Ellen, we had to wonder: Was she a Christian?

Was she—Jewish?

None of us from Wisconsin had ever seen a Jewish person, before coming to Wainscotia. But there were Jewish people here—professors, it was said, as well as students. A few.

There was even a Jewish fraternity, and there was a Jewish sorority. So they could live with their own kind. This was amazing to us!

In large cities in Wisconsin, like Milwaukee, and Madison, there were Jewish people—we knew that. But we were mostly from upstate Wisconsin, or rural counties. German, Scandinavian, Scots and Irish backgrounds—and English of course.

Also, "Mary Ellen" did not look like us. This was difficult to explain, but we all agreed. Her hair was darkish blond, spiky like it hadn't been combed or brushed properly; never curled or waved, and not washed often enough. It needed cutting, and trimming. And she went to bed without hairpins or rollers. Ever.

Didn't do anything for her hair. Didn't even seem to recognize what rollers were!

(Like she didn't seem to know how a phone worked—the way you dial with your forefinger. Of all of us in Acrady Cottage, only Mary Ellen would shrink from answering the phone when it rang near her, so we had to wonder—was it possible her family didn't own a telephone?)

(And she didn't smoke! And was forever coughing from our cigarette smoke—coughing in fits, until her eyes watered—though she never complained as you'd have expected a nonsmoker to complain. You could see the misery in her face but it was what you'd call long-suffering misery.)

She might have been pretty—almost—except she never wore lipstick. A guy looking at her would look right past her, there was so little to catch the male eye. (We all wore red—very red—lipstick!) She didn't even pluck her eyebrows which is about the least a girl can do, to make herself attractive.

She looked like a convalescent. Some wasting disease that left her skinny, and her skin ashy-pale and sort of grainy as if it would be rough to the touch like

sandpaper. Her eyes would have been beautiful eyes—
they were dark-brown, like liquid chocolate—with
thick lashes—but they were likely to be narrowed and
squinting as if she were looking into a bright, blinding light. And she did not look you in the eye—like a
guilty person.

Along with not smoking, she also didn't eat potato
chips, glazed doughnuts, Cheez-bits, M&M's, and
those little cellophane bags of Planters peanuts that
were our favorite snacks while we were studying, that
left salt all over our fingers. She didn't eat any kind of
chewy meat like beef or pork or even chicken, sometimes. She'd eat fish casseroles.

Which was why she was so skinny. Flat-chested, and
her hips flat, like a guy's, she didn't have to struggle
into girdles like the rest of us.

Didn't even know what a "girdle" was—just stared
at Trishie's when she was getting dressed for a frat
party, like she'd never seen anything so scary!

Scholarship girls in Acrady Cottage studied, hard.
We worked long hours at our desks for we had to retain
B averages or lose our scholarships. But Mary Ellen
Enright worked harder, and longer than any of us—so
far as we knew, Mary Ellen did almost nothing else
except her schoolwork, and her part-time job in the
geology library!

At her desk with her back to the room, and to her roommates, she was unnaturally still, concentrated upon her work motionless as a mannequin but so tense, you could see the tension in her neck and shoulders.

As if she was holding back a scream, or a sob.

Yet she remained at her desk, with the crook-necked lamp shining a halo of light onto the desktop, for as long as she could endure it—if none of her roommates objected to the light.

(At first we did not object. We had no trouble sleeping with a single light on in the room. But as time passed, and we grew less patient with our misfit-roommate, we did object, and Mary Ellen took her work downstairs to the work-study lounge where she would disturb no one, and no one would disturb her. And sometimes she slept there, on a couch. And we did not have to hear her sob herself to sleep!)

It was hard to say what was wrong with Mary Ellen. The way she'd stare at us, and look away—like she'd seen something scary—made us think there was something wrong with us.

We hoped (sort of) that she would drop out of school. Or transfer. This was cruel of us, and not very Christian—we were not proud of such thoughts. But we were girls who'd only just graduated from high school a few months before and maybe Mary Ellen scared us,

so close to the edge. Close to mental and physical col-
lapse as we'd sometimes felt ourselves away from home
for the first time and at the University of Wisconsin–
Wainscotia where 9,400 students were enrolled.

A certain percentage of freshmen dropped out in
the first several weeks of their first semester at Wainscotia. You'd hear of someone—mostly girls, but there
were boys, too—who just "broke down"—"couldn't
sleep"—"cried all the time"—"felt lost."

But Mary Ellen seemed determined not to be one of
these. She was deeply unhappy and seemed to us—(to
some of us, at least)—on the verge of a nervous col-
lapse but there was something willful about her—like
a cripple who doesn't seem to know she's a cripple,
or a stutterer who doesn't seem to know that she's a
stutterer.

Another strange thing: alone among the girls of
Acrady Cottage Mary Ellen Enright received no mail.

And yet stranger: Mary Ellen Enright seemed to
expect no mail, for she walked by the mailboxes without glancing at her own.

We asked our resident adviser Miss Steadman what
she thought we could do to make Mary Ellen less
lonely and Miss Steadman suggested leaving her alone
for the time being, for "Mary Ellen" had traveled a
long distance—from one of the eastern states like New

York, New Jersey or Massachusetts—and was feeling a more acute homesickness than we were feeling, whose families lived in the state and whom we could visit on weekends by bus.

Is "Mary Ellen" Jewish? we asked.

Miss Steadman said she did not think so. For "Enright" was not known to be a Jewish name.

But she seems like she's from—somewhere else. Like she's not an American—sort of.

Miss Steadman frowned at this remark which clearly she did not like.

Miss Steadman would tell us only that Mary Ellen Enright was the sole resident of Acrady Cottage whose complete file hadn't been made available to her, as our resident adviser. She'd received a file from the office of the dean of women for Mary Ellen but it was very short, and some of it had been blotted out with black ink.

Hilda McIntosh described how in the first week of classes she'd come into her room on the third floor one afternoon—and there was her roommate Mary Ellen Enright standing in front of Hilda's desk staring at her typewriter.

This was Hilda's portable Remington typewriter, one of her proudest possessions which she'd brought to

college. Not everyone in Acrady Cottage had a typewriter, and those who didn't were envious of Hilda!

And there was Mary Ellen staring at the typewriter
with some look, Hilda said, "way beyond envy."

Like the girl had never seen a typewriter before!
Like it was some new invention.

So Hilda said, speaking softly not wanting to startle
Mary Ellen—(but startling her anyway, so that she
jumped, and quivered, and her eyelids fluttered)—You
can try it, Mary Ellen, if you want to. Here's a piece of
paper!

Hilda inserted the paper into the typewriter. Hilda
indicated to the girl how she should type—striking
several keys in rapid succession.

The girl just stared blank-faced.

Like this, see? Of course, you have to memorize the
keyboard. That comes with practice. I learned in high
school—it isn't hard.

The girl touched one of the keys, lightly. Like she
hadn't strength to press it down.

In a faint voice she said, It doesn't w-work . . .

Hilda laughed. Of course it works!

The girl peered at the back of the typewriter, as if
searching for something missing.

In a faint voice saying, But—there's nothing con-
necting it to—to . . .

Hilda laughed. This was like introducing a rural relative to, well, an indoor toilet! Funny.

Look here, *Hilda said.*

Hilda sat down at her desk and the keys clattered away like machine-gun fire:

SEPTEMBER 23, 1959
ACRADY COTTAGE
WAINSCOTIA STATE UNIVERSITY
WAINSCOTIA FALLS, WISCONSIN
USA
UNIVERSE

The new girl Mary Ellen stared at this display of magic—the flying keys, the typed letters that became words and sentences—and could not seem to speak. As if her throat had shut up. As if the clattering typewriter frightened her. As if she couldn't bear the sight of— well, what was it? Hilda couldn't imagine.

Hilda encouraged Mary Ellen to try the typewriter again but Mary Ellen backed away as if it was all too much for her. And suddenly then, her eyes rolled back in her head, her skin went chalky-white—and she fell to the floor in a dead faint.

Typewriter

"Mary Ellen?"

One of them was speaking to me. She'd come up behind me.

I was very frightened. I knew there were informers like my brother Roddy—of course. But I could not comprehend if I was behaving like a guilty person or whether, in my EI status, I was behaving in a manner appropriate to my circumstances.

The girl was the one called "Hilda McIntosh." She had a round bland moon-face and a very friendly smile. Her hair was a chestnut-colored "pageboy." I could not bring myself to look her in the face, still less in the eyes, for fear of what I would see.

The empty gaze. The iris in the eye the size of a seed.

I wondered: Was this person an informer? Did she know who *Mary Ellen Enright* really was? *Had she followed me?*

It was often the case, here in Zone 9, that individuals followed me. Yet in such practiced ways, I could not be certain that they were following me by design or by coincidence.

I'd had to escape from—wherever it was—the lecture hall in the building near the chapel—Hendrick Hall—as oxygen was being sucked from the room by the others—(I'd counted sixty-six student-figures seated in steep-banked rows)—and the professor-figure at the podium continued lecturing on the rudiments of logic. *Some Y is X. X is M. What is the relationship of M to Y?*

I did not cross the green. The open, vulnerable expanse of the green. Making my way like a wounded wild creature close beside buildings and through narrow passageways in order not to attract attention.

Not daring to glance up, to see who was "seeing" me.

The EI will be monitored at any and all times during his/her exile.

Violations of these Instructions will insure that the EI will be immediately Deleted.

In a sequence of hills, mostly downhill, approximately

one mile to Acrady Cottage where I would hide in the third-floor room assigned to "Mary Ellen Enright."

It was the epicenter of the Restricted Zone 9. It was my imprisonment. Yet, I felt safe there.

I entered the cottage by a side door. Made my way up the back stairs hoping not to be detected by any girl-figures and I avoided the resident adviser's suite on the first floor where the door was always flung open in a way to suggest *Welcome!* but which I worried might be an informer's trick.

It had been a blade twisted in my heart, that my brother Roddy had informed on me. I could not recall much of those terrible hours of interrogation at YDDHS but I did recall this revelation and my shock and yet my unsurprise for *Of course, Roddy always hated me. He would wish me Exiled—or worse.*

I wanted to think that one day I would see Roddy again—and I would forgive Roddy. Tears stung my eyes for I could not bear to think that Roddy did not want my forgiveness.

But if I confronted Roddy, it would mean that I would see my parents again. Desperately I wanted to think this!

It was a time, early afternoon, when the freshman residents of Acrady Cottage were mostly out.

I was counting on being invisible. I could not breathe normally, if I knew myself *visible.*

In these early days in Zone 9 I did not think of those others who might be in Exile here—for surely there were others like myself. Like one trapped in a small cage who has no awareness of others similarly trapped, and in her desperation no sympathy to spare, I could only think of my own situation.

Hurrying up the stairs. Panting, and sweating. For it was a hot dry September in this place, and Acrady Cottage was not air-conditioned.

In Zone 9 very few buildings were air-conditioned. Evidently in this era air-conditioning was rare. And what air there was, to my dismay and disgust, was often polluted by cigarette smoke.

Astonishing to me, my roommates smoked! Each one of them. As if they knew nothing about cigarettes causing cancer, or did not care. Worse, I saw their annoyed expressions when I coughed and choked and yet—how could I help myself? Smoking had been banished in NAS-23 for as long as I'd been alive. (Intravenous nicotine was promoted in its place.)

Thinking *Is this my punishment? Secondary smoke inhalation.*

Had to wonder who my roommates really were. Why I'd been assigned to room 3C of Acrady Cottage, with these individuals. In NAS-23 it was said—"No accidents, only algorithms." I could not think that there were coincidences in the stratagems of Homeland Security. I could not think that at least one and perhaps all of my roommates were informants assigned to *Enright, Mary Ellen.*

Possibly, one of them was a robot. But which one?

Such relief, when I was alone in our room.

(But was I ever "alone" in our room?)

That prevailing odor of cigarette smoke like body odor made my nostrils pinch.

Here was my opportunity to examine a clumsy black machine with a keyboard on the desk of one of my roommates—a "typewriter."

I'd heard of typewriters of course. I'd seen photographs of typewriters and my parents had spoken of owning a typewriter, I think. (Or had it been my grandparents?) But I had never seen an actual typewriter, from an era before computers.

In a kind of trance I stared at the strange machine. Something about it that made me uneasy.

So badly I missed my laptop computer, I felt almost faint. I missed my cell phone, that fitted so comfortably in the palm of my hand it was like a growth there, a rectangular luminous eye.

Could not comprehend the logic of this machine. Could it be so crude, only just—*typing*?

No Internet? No e-mail? No texting? Only just—*typing*?

There was nowhere to look in or about the type-writer! There was no *screen*.

Profound to think that this clumsy machine connected with no reality beyond itself. Just—a *machine*.

You were trapped in yourself, at a typewriter. You could not escape into cyberspace. In Zone 9, you could not access cyberspace.

Hard to comprehend: in 1959 cyberspace *did not exist*.

And yet, that was not possible—was it? For one of the great accomplishments of the twenty-first century— we'd been told and retold—was the establishment of cyberspace as an entity separate and distinct and (presumably) independent of human beings, thus independent of constraints of time and space.

Not that I'd ever understood this. To truly understand you'd have to know math, physics, astrophysics, the most advanced computer science that was in fact, in NAS-23, classified information . . .

"Mary Ellen?"—the voice was close behind me.

The smiling girl had crept up silently behind me— "Hilda" was her name. She'd scared me so, my heart leapt in my chest like a shot bird.

Hilda was very friendly of course. They were all very friendly.

Their eyes eating at me, like hungry ants. Memorizing, assessing. Planning the words they would use in their reports to Homeland Security.

In her flat midwestern voice that seemed mocking to my ears Hilda was saying that the machine was her "almost-new Remington," of which she seemed to be proud.

"You can try it, if you want to. Here's a piece of paper!"

Hilda inserted a sheet of paper and rolled it into position. She indicated to me how I should type, striking several keys in succession—random keys, with her deft fingers.

But I just stared. I was feeling light-headed.

I would have tried to speak but my tongue felt like cotton batting too big for my mouth.

Hilda said, "Like this, see? Of course, you have to memorize the keyboard. So that your fingers type without you having to think. That comes with practice. I learned in high school—it isn't hard."

I touched one of the keys. Nothing happened.

"It doesn't w-work . . ."

Hilda laughed at me. Not maliciously but as an older sister might laugh at a naïve younger sister.

"Of course it works, Mary Ellen! Like this."

Mary Ellen. Was this name uttered in a friendly way, or in a mocking way?

I wanted to think that the girl-figure "Hilda" was actually a girl like myself, who was being sincerely friendly. I did not want to think that the girl-figure was a registered agent of Homeland Security or (possibly) a virtual representation of an undergraduate girl manipulated on a screen by a (distant) Homeland Security agent teasing me in my Exile in Zone 9.

It was distracting to me, that Hilda stood so close. Many of the girls of Acrady Cottage stood close to me, and caused me to back away. Our way of behaving with one another in NAS-23 was noticeably different: the unspoken rule was *do not come close.* Since the arrest, and the terrible sight on the TV monitor of the boy executed, I was in dread of strangers coming too close. My skin prickled with the danger.

Hilda was so very friendly, so *nice,* she seemed entirely oblivious of my wariness. It would be said of Hilda that she was a "pretty" girl—(as it would be said of me, I was sure, that I was a "plain" girl). Shorter than I was by at least two inches, and plumper. Where my body was lean almost like a boy's her body was shapely as a mature woman's. Like the other girls Hilda wore a sturdy brassiere—a "bra"—that might have stood by itself, made of firm, metallic-threaded fabric; beneath her clothes, this "bra" asserted itself like an extra appendage. Half-consciously I shrank away hoping that Hilda would not, seemingly unconsciously, brush against me with her sharp-pointed breasts.

Hilda sat at her desk with an exaggerated sort of perfect posture like a young woman in an advertisement and typed, rapidly and flawlessly, to demonstrate to me how easy "typing" was:

SEPTEMBER 23, 1959
ACRADY COTTAGE
WAINSCOTIA STATE UNIVERSITY
WAINSCOTIA FALLS, WISCONSIN
USA
UNIVERSE

"See? Now you try it, Mary Ellen."

September 23, 1959! It could not be true—could it?

This was Zone 9—of course. This was my Exile. I must accept my Exile, and I must adjust. Yet—

The horror swept over me: this was eighty years into the past, and more. I had not yet been born. My parents had not yet been born. There was no one in this world who loved me, no one who even knew me. No one who would claim me. I was utterly alone.

"Mary Ellen? What's wrong?"

With a look of genuine—sisterly—concern, Hilda reached out for me, even as I shrank away.

"Don't t-touch me! No . . ."

I was terrified, nauseated. Yet too weak to escape—a black pit opened at my feet, and sucked me down.

The Lost One

Help me! Help me—Mom, Daddy . . .
I miss you so much . . .

It was a ravenous hunger in me, to return home. A yearning so strong, it seemed almost that a hand gripped the nape of my neck, urging me forward as in a desperate swooning plunge.

I am all alone here. I will die here.

They'd strapped me down. Wrists, ankles, head—to prevent "self-injury."

A painful shunt in the soft flesh at the inside of my elbow, through which a chill liquid coursed into my vein. It was a mechanical procedure they'd done many times before.

In a flat voice the pronouncement: *subject going down.*

I saw myself as a diminishing light. A swirl of light, turning in upon itself and becoming ever smaller, more transparent.

Abruptly then—I was gone.

Dematerialization of the subject. Teletransportation of the subject's molecular components. Reconstitution in Zone 9.

"'Mary Ellen Enright.' This is she?"

The question was put to someone not-me. Yet I could observe the lifeless body from a slightly elevated position and felt pity for it.

Like a zombie. Exiled.

I would wonder—*Does a zombie know that it is a zombie? How would a zombie comprehend.*

This was funny! But laughter caught in my throat like a clot of phlegm.

In this very cold place. Where blood coursed slow as liquid mercury.

I was very confused. I could not clear my head. My brain had been injured. I had heard them joking.

NSS it was called—*Neurosurgical Security Services.* Rumors had circulated in high school. The subject was taboo.

Before *teletransportation* they'd inserted a microchip into a particular part of my brain called the hippocampus, where memory is processed before being stored elsewhere in the brain. At least, I thought this must have happened. I did not think it had been a dream.

Part of my scalp had been shaved, a pie-shaped wedge of skull removed, the microchip installed. (Evidently) I felt no pain. A zombie does not feel pain. Even the sawed-out portion of the skull and the lacerated scalp were cold-numb and remote to me. And yet I felt such a powerful wave of gratitude, I could have wept— *They did not remove my parents from me. They left me my parents at least.*

For that part of my brain might have been removed, which contained all memory of my parents.

In Exile you cling to what you have, that has not (yet) been taken from you.

From this cold place I was carried, with others who'd been *teletransported,* in a vehicle resembling an emergency medical van.

The vehicle did not move rapidly. There was no siren.

This was not an emergency but routine.

The vehicle made stops at several destinations, before mine. In my semiconscious state I had little awareness of what was happening. I was trying to speak to my parents whose faces were vivid to me in their concern for me. I was trying to say *In four years I will see you again. Don't forget me!*

I could not have said if I was seventeen years old, or seven years old.

I could not have said which year this was. I had no idea where I was.

We had left the lights of a city and were traveling now in a vast rural night. It was astonishing to me, stars in the night sky overhead were large and luminous as I had never seen stars before in my old, lost life.

The air was purer here, in Zone 9. So sharp to inhale! The night sky was not obscured by the scrim of pollution to which we were all accustomed in the old, lost life.

We who were being carried in the van in the night were strapped to stretchers and could not turn our heads to regard one another. We were very tired, for we'd come a long distance.

It might have been the case, not all of the *teletransported* had made the journey fully alive. It was not clear to me initially whether I was fully alive.

One of the other *teletransported* was hyperventilating in panic. Something must have gone wrong with his medication. I could not turn my head to see. Or, my head was strapped in place. I held myself very still and breathed calmly as Dad would instruct me in the presence of the Enemy. I thought—*They will vaporize him.* It was a desperate thought—*They will vaporize him, and not me.*

At the next stop, I was taken from the van.

Unstrapped from the stretcher, and made to stand.

"Use your legs, miss. There is nothing wrong with your legs. Your brain sends the signal—left leg, right leg. And your head—lift your head."

I was able to walk a few yards, before I collapsed.

In the morning I woke beneath a thin blanket, on a lumpy cot. The bandages were gone from my head. The straps were gone from my wrists and ankles. Most of the grogginess had faded.

It would be explained to me: I was a freshman student at Wainscotia State University in Wainscotia Falls, Wisconsin. I had arrived late the previous night, feverish. I had been brought to the university infirmary and not to my residence. And now, in the morning, since my fever had disappeared, I was to be discharged.

"Your things have been delivered to your residence, Miss Enright."

"Yes. Thank you."

"Your residence is Acrady Cottage, on South University Avenue."

"Thank you."

Acrady Cottage. South University Avenue. It was up to me to find this place, and I would do so.

I was feeling hopeful! Small gulping waves of wonder would rush over me from time to time, amid even the paralysis of fear.

For the crucial matter was: my parents were living, and I would return to them, in four years. My parents had not been "vaporized" even in my memory.

And the crucial matter was: "Mary Ellen Enright" was evidently a healthy specimen. She had not died in *teletransportation*. If her brain had been injured, it was not a major injury.

If it was a minor injury, maybe it would heal.

When I tried to rise from the cot, however, I felt faint, and would have lost my balance—but the strong-muscled young woman in the white nurse's uniform reached out to catch me.

"There you go, 'Mary Ellen'! On your way."

She laughed. Our eyes locked, for a fleeting second.

She had pinned-back blond hair, so pale it was almost white. Above her left breast, a little plastic name tag—IRMA KRAZINSKI.

She knows who I am. Yet, she is not an Enemy.

Later I would think—*Maybe she is one like me and will pity me.*

At the residence a large cardboard box awaited M. E. ENRIGHT in the front foyer.

"You are—'Mary Ellen'? This just arrived."

The box measured approximately three by four feet. It was so crammed, one of its sides was nearly bursting.

And the box was badly battered, as if it had come a long distance, in rainy weather. Transparent tape covered it in intricate layers crisscrossing like a deranged cobweb. Even with a pair of shears provided by the resident adviser of Acrady Cottage it was very difficult to open.

"My! Someone took care that this box would not rip open in delivery!"

Inside were clothes: several skirts, blouses, sweaters, a pair of slacks, a navy-blue wool jumper, a fleece-lined jacket, flannel pajamas, white cotton underwear, white cotton socks, a pair of sneakers, and a pair of brown shoes identified by the resident adviser as "penny loafers." There were also "Bermuda shorts" and a "blazer"— clothes of a kind I had never seen before. And sheer, long "stockings"—I'd never seen before. All these items were secondhand, rumpled, and smelled musty.

I was staring inside the box. I felt dazed, dizzy. I thought—*These are castoff clothes of the dead.*

"Shall I help you carry these upstairs? It might be more practical just to leave the box here and take your things up in our arms . . ."

"No. I can take them by myself. Thank you."

The resident adviser, Miss Steadman, was being very kind. But I did not want even to look at her. I did not want to speak with the woman more than necessary and I did not want to be alone with her in the room to which I was assigned for even a few minutes.

I did not want her to see these clothes close up. I did not feel comfortable with her registering that, to me, some of these things were unfamiliar. Nor did I want her to smell the sour, stale odor that lifted from them, any more than she already had.

I did not want her to feel sorry for me. *That poor girl!—indeed, she is* poor.

Also, Miss Steadman's words, her manner of speech, were strange to me. It was clear that she was speaking English yet so slowly, with such odd nasal vowels, it made me anxious to listen to her.

At the bottom of the box was an envelope with M. E. ENRIGHT stamped on it. I would not open this envelope until I was alone in room 3C when I would discover that it contained five twenty-dollar bills that were crisp as if freshly printed, and a stiff sheet of paper headed THE INSTRUCTIONS.

There was no personal note. I felt a small stab of disappointment for I had thought—I mean, I'd wanted to think—that *S. Platz* had taken a personal liking to me.

In my arms I carried my new belongings upstairs to room 3C. I grew short of breath quickly for I had not recovered from my long journey. Miss Steadman watched me with concerned eyes but did not attempt to help me another time.

Freshmen would be arriving on the Wainscotia campus the next day. I'd been sent into Exile at the perfect time and I did think that S. Platz must have had something to do with this timing.

Room 3C was at the rear of the cottage. A large room with two dormer windows and a slanted ceiling. Bare floorboards, bare walls with scattered holes for picture hanging and small nails.

Four beds, four desks: four roommates!

It was surprising to me, I would be rooming with three other girls and not alone.

But a relief, the room was ordinary. Except for the slanting ceiling that, if I wasn't alert, would bump against my head.

Quickly my eyes glanced about. It would be an involuntary reaction in Zone 9: establishing that a new space held no (evident) danger. Nothing in it (that I could see) to frighten, threaten, or disorient.

Nothing unique to Zone 9. Rather, a room that could be *anywhere*.

I took the bed in the farthest corner, beneath the slanted ceiling. I would leave the windows, the better-positioned beds, and the largest closets for my room-mates for I did not want them to dislike me.

"'Mary Ellen'! Are you sure, you want that bed way off in a corner?"—so my roommates asked when they arrived, with evident sincerity.

These were nice girls. (Were they?) Staring at me with curious eyes but they were not rude, or did not mean to be rude.

Though they were enough alike to be three sisters they were strangers to one another. "White" girls—ST1. All were from rural Wisconsin and had gone to Wisconsin high schools. Their broad flat northern-midwestern accents were identical. Their names were immediately confused in my head like a buzzing of insects.

I thought—*One of them may be my executioner.*

"When did you arrive, Mary Ellen? Last night?"

"Where're you from, Mary Ellen?"

"Did your parents bring you? Are they still here?"

"Sorry, Mary Ellen! We're taking up a lot of room, I guess . . ."

Much of the day the room was crowded with parents, relatives, young children, helping my roommates move in.

I went away to hide. The sounds of strangers' voices, loud, assured, happy-seeming, those broad flat vowels, were oppressive to me. But I did not cry.

At evening I returned to the room at the top of the stairs for I had nowhere else to go. Acrady Cottage was my home now.

Eventually, when I began to wear the clothes that had come in the box, I would discover that only a few items fitted me.

Some things were too small, too short, too tight—most were too large.

Faint half-moons of stains beneath the armpits of sweaters. Loose buttons, missing buttons. Broken zippers. Dark-smeared something, possibly food, I hoped not blood, on a skirt.

The girls of Acrady Cottage would whisper among themselves, to see me so badly dressed—like a pauper, with clothes from Goodwill—but I never minded for I was grateful for what had been given to me.

My favorites were a pleated Black Watch plaid skirt (as it was identified for me by a roommate) with an oversized ornamental brass safety pin holding the skirt together—ingeniously; a dark-rose turtleneck sweater that reminded me of a sweater back home, though this sweater was much larger; a long-sleeved white blouse with a "lace" collar that fitted me, and gave me a serious, somber look, that I particularly liked because it seemed to suggest *This is a good girl, a nice girl, a shy girl, a girl who would never, ever be subversive or raise her voice. Please be kind to this girl thank you!*

In my old, lost life I had never worn blouses. I had never worn "lace"—or known anyone who had.

I had never worn skirts, dresses. I had worn only jeans. In fact, just two or three pairs of jeans, that had not cost much and that I wore all the time without needing to think.

In Zone 9 girls wore skirts to classes, sometimes dresses. They wore "sweater sets"—cardigans over matching short-sleeved sweaters. Sometimes they encased their legs in *nylon stockings* which I did not think I could manage without tearing, though I would try.

How my friends would laugh, to see me in a lacy blouse. In nylon stockings. In the Black Watch plaid skirt with the big brass safety pin holding the pleated material together—*Oh God what has happened to Addie. Is that even her?*

Not a pleasant sight. Electrodes in my roommates' heads.

Well, not *electrodes.* I knew better.

"Like this, Mary Ellen. I can't believe you've never 'set' your hair!"

Laughing at me. Not unkindly. (I wanted to think.)

But I could not manage it: putting my hair in plastic "rollers" before going to bed.

First, you wetted your hair with some special smelly setting-solution. Brushed and combed your hair. Separated your hair into numerous strands, and rolled these strands onto "rollers" (three sizes: largest pink, medium blue, smallest mint green) which were secured to the scalp as tightly as possible with bobby pins.

Yes, your scalp might hurt from the pins and from having to lie with your head on a pillow, on rollers.

You might even get a little headache! But it was worth it, for the effect of the smooth glossy pageboy the next day.

Tried just once. Awake half the night. Drifting off to sleep and waking in a nightmare sweat of electrodes in my brain. And in the morning most of the rollers had come out, and when I brushed out my hair it was as limp and straggling as ever, or almost.

Hilda said, "Next time, Mary Ellen, I'll set your hair in rollers. Don't you dare say *no*."

Coed

So lonely! It was as if my body had been gutted from within.

As if, in the place where my heart had been, there was an emptiness that nothing could fill.

Other freshmen were homesick, and other girls in my residence cried from time to time in this new place. But their homesickness was a kind of exquisite torture, a way of measuring their love for their families. They called home, often on Sunday evenings (when the rates were lower) and received calls from home. They wrote home, and received letters from home. Their mothers sent them baked goods to share with their roommates and friends. And their homes were accessible to them— just a few hours away by car.

I began to be ashamed, as well as despondent, that I received no mail from home—no calls, no packages. I could not bear it, the girls of Acrady Cottage pitied me and spoke of me wonderingly behind my back.

Yet, there must be genuine orphans in the world, with no families and no relatives. The category into which *Enright, Mary Ellen* had been placed could not have been so empty of inhabitants.

I wondered if I would discover someone like myself? Or—someone like myself would discover *me*?

A "coed" at the State University at Wainscotia, Wisconsin, enrolled in the College of Liberal Arts with the likelihood of an education major, Class of 1963.

If this was Exile, it was not the cruelest Exile.

I knew this: the cruelest Exile would be death.

Badly wishing I could let my parents know that I was (still) alive. (But was I alive? Often I wasn't sure.)

Wishing that I could know that my parents were (still) alive in NAS-23 and that we would be together again, in four years.

Wainscotia State University covered many acres of land in semi-rural Wainscotia Falls in northeastern Wisconsin, a day's drive from the city of Milwaukee in the south. Most of its nine thousand students were from small Wisconsin towns or farms. One of the largest colleges was Agriculture and Animal Husbandry.

Other prominent colleges were the School of Education, the School of Business, the School of Nursing, and the School of Engineering.

So many thousands of people linked by a single sprawling campus! Though much of the time the campus looked calm—in the morning, on the hilly paths, students hurrying to classes, in small groups, in pairs, alone—as the chapel bell sounded sonorously. *You must move along. You must take your place. You have your name, your identity. You have no choice.*

There was a thrill in this! There was the solace of the impersonal.

I was enrolled in five courses, three of them "introductions"—to English literature, to psychology, and to philosophy. These were large lecture courses with quiz sections that met once weekly. It was possible to be invisible in large lecture halls and to imagine that no one was observing me.

If I saw, on campus, or in one of my classes, a girl from Acrady Cottage, my vision blurred and didn't register what I saw. If a girl waved to me, or smiled at me—I did not seem to see. Wherever it was possible, I was invisible.

Eventually, they would leave me alone, I believed. I would learn in Intro to Psychology the phenomenon of *operant extinction: when reinforcement is no longer forthcoming, a response becomes less and less frequent.*

All my determination was to survive. To get through the challenge of the first weeks, the first semester, and the first year; to get through four years; to complete my Exile, and be *teletransported* back home.

I did not want to think that absolute obedience to The Instructions might not save me. I did not want to think about the future except in the most elemental terms: *behavior, reward.*

Almost it seemed to me, S. Platz had personally promised me—my Exile would end, one day.

In the meantime I was obliged to obey The Instructions. I had immediately memorized them though I did not quite understand what was meant by the admonition against providing "future knowledge" in the Restricted Zone.

So far as I had been informed the microchip in my brain blocked many memories of my past (that were, of course, in 1959, anticipations of the "future"). I could not confidently "foresee," still less predict. When I tried to recall classic discoveries of the intervening decades—

the discovery of DNA, for instance—the development of molecular genetics—brain "imaging"—any modern history apart from Patriot History—it was like trying to peer through a frosted glass window.

You can see shadowy shapes beyond, maybe. But you cannot *see*.

How ironic it was, I'd been, for those few cruel days, *valedictorian of my high school class*!

As for the admonition against seeking out "relatives"—I would not have known how to begin.

In the Cultural Relocation Campaign that swept the country when I was in middle school, hundreds of thousands—millions?—of individuals were evicted from their homes, to be settled in relatively depopulated areas which the Government wanted to "reconstitute"; among these were Mom's and Dad's parents—Roddy's and my grandparents—who were evacuated to western Nebraska and northern Maine, respectively; but I had no idea where they'd lived previously, still less where they might have been living in 1959.

And I would not have dared leave the ten-mile radius of the "epicenter."

I would be the ideal student—the ideal "coed." I would attract no unwanted attention. I would never betray or even feel the mildest curiosity. I would never enter into any "intimate" relationship with anyone—hardly! This was my resolve.

During the first week of classes instructors took attendance by reading off names. It was exciting to hear a cascade of strangers' names in which there was secreted, like a cuckoo egg in a nest of unsuspecting birds, the name to which I'd been assigned: *Enright, Mary Ellen*. This seemed to me so wholly a fictitious name, so totally unconvincing a name, I steeled myself as shyly I raised my hand and murmured "Here." But no one took any notice. Most of the names were, like "Enright," immediately forgettable. Though scattered amid these were odd nasal-sounding names that turned out to be, as I would later discover, Swedish, Norwegian, Germanic.

Instructors were not likely to linger over *Enright, Mary Ellen*.

Virtually all of my fellow students, indeed all of my professors, were ST1: "Caucasian." Exceptions were staff workers (cafeteria, janitorial, grounds) who were likely to be ST5 or darker.

I wondered if in any of my classes there were other Exiled Individuals. Could we recognize one another? Did we dare recognize one another? But how? At what risk?

We would all be in disguise. In secondhand clothes, with secondhand names, determined to survive.

I took a kind of grim pride in my own disguise: sweaters and skirts from out of the battered cardboard box, fleece-lined jacket in cold weather, sneakers, even "penny loafers" with white cotton socks darned at the toes, but not darned very substantially. My textbooks and anthologies were all secondhand, their spines stamped USED. In the campus bookstore I'd bought a spiral notebook whose cover was speckled black and white, and on the pristine lined pages of this notebook I took fanatic notes in a kind of miniature handwriting, to save on space. In lecture halls I was the faceless girl in the first row hunched over her notebook, rapidly writing as the professor spoke, scarcely daring to look up.

How strange to be *writing*. This was a so-called hand-eye coordination skill that had nearly vanished by the time I was born—though Mom and Dad had insisted upon teaching Roddy and me how to *write*. And strange to be *reading* in a book, on paper "pages" which you had to turn with your fingers, and which, if you wanted, you could tear out; but you needed no "power" to maintain the book, and no electronic medium.

Strangest of all, the university library—a vast brownstone building of numerous floors descending even into the earth, filled with row upon row of "stacks" containing "books" to be touched, and opened, *by hand.* And in reading rooms, high ceilings, myriad lights, and polished floors—and students!

Just to climb the stone steps to this building, like some ancient temple, left me dazed, and apprehensive.

Often in Zone 9 I found myself out of breath. My heart beat erratically as it had beat—(I remembered this amid so much that had been wiped from my memory)—when I'd witnessed the Domestic Drone execution of—(but what was the boy's name? *Zoll-* was the first syllable)—in a time that seemed to me now long ago, and fading. My head ached somewhere behind my eyes, where the microchip had been inserted. If I tried to think of—(was the word *home*? *parents*?)—there emerged a barrier like Plexiglas. Against this barrier I would strain and strain—like a trapped creature trying to press through a wall.

Yet, if I gave up this effort, and turned my concentration upon my work, reading passages of print in textbooks and anthologies, underlining, taking notes, making outlines, writing first drafts of papers—in the way of a "normal" undergraduate in Zone 9—the pressure in my brain relaxed, and my breathing grew calmer.

This is your life now. What you must be, now.

Lost Friends

Sometimes I woke with a sob, and it wasn't my parents I was missing but my friends.

And it came to me in a rush of emotion—I loved my friends! I'd taken them for granted sometimes, for which I was sorry now.

Trying to recall their names: Carla, and Melanie, and Deborah, and . . . was it Paige?

Like trying to peer through something clotted. A thick gauze. Strength was required to remember. My eyes ached in their sockets with the effort of trying to see my friends' faces that were beginning to fade.

We'd been together since middle school. We'd become closer in high school under certain stresses and pressures. *To be like everyone else. But—how is that possible? No one is like anyone else.*

At Pennsboro High there'd been a vicious social hierarchy about which no one was supposed to speak: the sons and daughters of Government officials at the top, and the rest of us spread out beneath. With my father an MI, my social caste had been determined from the first day my mother had brought me to preschool.

There'd been a time in tenth grade when Carla had been deeply sad and anorexic, and her friends had helped her through the crisis; there'd been a time in our junior year when Glenna had been in a perpetual state of anxiety, when her research-scientist father had been removed from his laboratory on a charge of *Science-Treason*. And there was the terrible ten-month period when Deborah's father was in custody at Homeland Security Interrogation, and no one knew if he'd ever be released. (Eventually Mr. Albright was released, but in a perpetual benign zombie-state, so it was as if Deborah had lost her father after all.) Using a text-code we'd invented for ourselves, which we were shrewd enough to change every few weeks, we'd texted one another continuously, day after day, for years. We were closer in some essential ways than we were with our parents who did not speak openly to us, and certainly we were closer with each other than with any of our male classmates. ("Female" and "male" were expected to distrust each other. It was not considered good behavior to have close friends of the opposite sex before high school graduation.)

Somewhere in my damaged memory was the vague knowledge that my friends had tried to warn me about the valedictorian address—Paige had advised me to work with our English teacher on the speech, which, she thought, should have been modeled after previous valedictorian addresses, that had not antagonized the Youth Disciplinary censor, but I'd ignored her suggestion totally—in fact, I'd been insulted and hurt by it.

How stupid I'd been! Paige had wanted to protect me, and I'd been heedless.

I wondered what graduation at my high school had been like. The boy-athlete whom Mr. Mackay had wanted to give the valedictory address would have given it, in my place. Someone else would have been named salutatorian. No one except my friends would miss me.

Wasn't someone else supposed to be valedictorian?

Someone else? Who?

That girl . . . What was her name . . .

What girl? I don't remember any girl.

You know, the one with—I guess brown hair . . .

Oh gosh! I remember her—sort of . . .

She was arrested for Treason. She's gone now.

Gone—where?

Gone.

He, Him

And then, in this place of utter loneliness, I fell in love.

He was not the first person who looked kindly upon me in Zone 9. Or protectively. Or even curiously.

He was the first person who *knew*. Staring at me, in an instant he knew who I was. What I was.

And I thought—*There are two of us now. Him, and—Mary Ellen.*

Wolfman

"'Enright, Mary Ellen'"—the eyes moved onto me curiously, coolly.

I could scarcely breathe. Digging my nails into the palms of my hands.

Our instructor was returning midterm exams. He was smiling, though not with his eyes. His eyes moved restlessly over us, impersonal and detached, calculating.

I wondered: were we "subjects" to him? Wolfman was a research psychologist, an assistant professor in psychology.

After several weeks of class he knew the names of certain individuals in our class but not, until now, mine.

Hesitantly I'd risen from my seat to take the little blue booklet from Wolfman. He had not known me before. I had not distinguished myself in the quiz section by raising my hand, answering his questions or asking questions of my own, as a scattering of other students had, more aggressive than Mary Ellen Enright. But now, Wolfman was looking at Mary Ellen Enright.

"Good work, Miss Enright. You've been reading Skinner outside the textbook?"

"Y-Yes."

Continuing to stare at me, just a moment too long.

In class Wolfman was brusque and sunny and sharp-witted—a knife-blade that has been honed razor-sharp, you would not carelessly reach out to touch. Now his ironic smile faded. His expression seemed one of surprise—genuine surprise. As if about to ask me something further but changed his mind, quickly looking away and calling the next name.

A sensation of faintness enveloped me. But I managed to return to my desk, clutching the blue book without daring to open it.

Does he know?

Does he—somehow—recognize me?

Is he in Exile too—like me?

For the remainder of the hour I remained in a state of something like suspended animation. I could not bring myself to look at the quiz section instructor at the front of the room, casually sitting at the edge of a table; meekly I leaned over my notebook, to take notes. Nor did Wolfman glance at me. Through a roaring in my ears I could barely hear his voice expounding upon some principle of psychology and by the end of the period, when the bell sounded, I remained benumbed in my desk as others trooped out of the room. When at last I dared to raise my eyes Ira Wolfman had departed.

Only when I was safely alone did I open the blue book. Extravagant, exclamatory, the grade was in red ink—99%.

And in red ink the witty scrawl below—*No one is perfect.*

The EI is forbidden to identify himself/herself except as established by HSEDB.
The EI is monitored at all times.

A soul in Exile. I was convinced, I'd come into contact with a kindred soul.

Those of us who'd been assigned to Wolfman's quiz section were considered both lucky (Wolfman was *fun*) and not-so-lucky (Wolfman was *tough*). He could be intimidating as well as entertaining. He was, to midwestern eyes and ears, "different"—even "foreign."

Wolfman spoke more fluently, more rapidly and on the whole less patiently than most other adults in Zone 9 whom I'd encountered. His hair was thick and dark and lifted from his forehead in wayward curves that reminded me of the thick swirly feathers of an owl. (Thinking of the handsome great horned owl specimen in the Natural History collection.) Though Wolfman was clean-shaven you could see the shadow of a beard darkening his jaws and beneath his jaws, on his throat. Most days for our class he wore a sport coat, dark trousers and a white or pale blue shirt. Often, not always, a necktie. His eyes were dark, of the hue of wet slate, quizzical and restless. You did think that, at times, Wolfman's attention—his deepest and most profound attention—was elsewhere.

I am here but not truly here. You have no idea who I am.

It was Wolfman's custom to fling out questions as one might fling out a handful of coins to underlings—some students responded alertly, others held back suspecting a trick. Others were confused, disoriented. We were likely to be cautious of Ira Wolfman despite his genial and inviting smile.

There were twenty-five students in the quiz section of whom three were female. Rarely had I tried to answer the instructor's questions for I feared his possible sarcasm, the stroke of a razor-sharp blade across the knuckle of an unsuspecting undergraduate.

The week's subject was "neurobehavioral analysis"—a

Skinnerian postulate that the nervous system is inactive most of the time and roused only by stimuli from the environment, that result in "reflexes." It was a behavioral premise that an animal is, essentially, a machine. A human being is an animal and is therefore, essentially, a machine. Individual, group, and mass behavior can be programmed, conditioned, predicted and controlled. Radical behaviorism is a science: you can graph the consequences of experiments. A human being is not *inward* but *outward*—the sum of (measurable) behavior. A human being *is* behavior, to be observed and charted by others. What the environment can't control is the genetic self. But this too is determined. Zombies come in all shapes, sizes, and types.

I did not want to think that this was true. But in Zone 9, in the psychology department of Wainscotia State University, such "truths" prevailed.

The lecture course taught by Professor A. J. Axel—Introduction to Twentieth-Century Psychology—was one of the most popular and revered in the College of Liberal Arts, with an enrollment of more than two hundred students. Many were pre-med, for this was a requirement. Wolfman's quiz section met on Friday mornings when it was his task to explicate Professor Axel's often abstruse lecture for us, to shine a beacon of clarity into the dark patches of our ignorance. You could see that the youthful Wolfman took pleasure in befuddling us further, before enlightening us. He took pleasure in scribbling graphs—"learning curves"—on the blackboard, to illustrate the professor's argument. It was a pleasurable task to explain experiments in detail to which Professor Axel only alluded.

Occasionally, always very subtly, Wolfman corrected Professor Axel. *As Professor Axel meant to say . . .*

A. J. Axel was claimed to be one of the most distinguished academic psychologists in the United States, a former Harvard collaborator with the greatest experimental psychologist of the twentieth century, B. F. Skinner. He had been a protégé of the famed Dr. Walter Freeman as well, assisting Freeman in performing a number of lobotomies in the Midwest, in the early 1950s. He was the director of the Wainscotia Center for Social Engineering. Tall, white-haired, gentlemanly, invariably dressed in a tweed coat, white shirt and tie, Axel was a figure of dignity and erudition. Yet, Axel was not always comprehensible to his audiences for his vocabulary was highly specialized, as in a secret code. Such mysterious terms as *operant conditioning, schedules of reinforcement, law of effect, reinforcers, punishers, escape learning, avoidance learning* were predominant.

To undergraduates Wolfman was "Dr. Wolfman,"

for he had a Ph.D. To Wolfman, we were "Miss"—
"Mister."

He was unfailingly courteous with us, if often slightly
ironic; he seemed not to trust us to quite understand
his jokes. And he seemed to have many jokes. He was
quick-witted, funny. With the acuity of one swatting a
fly while his attention seemed to be elsewhere, he could
rebuke a skeptical student.

Wolfman attended Professor Axel's lectures on
Tuesday and Thursday mornings at 10:00 A.M., seated
in the front row of the lecture hall with several other
assistant professors and departmental graduate students.
With few exceptions among the graduate students, they
were all male: there were virtually no female faculty
members at Wainscotia.

Of Professor Axel's young assistants Ira Wolfman
must have been the most trusted, for when the professor was forced to miss a lecture Wolfman took his
place. On those mornings there was a quickened sense
of anticipation in the lecture hall, for most of the
students preferred dashing young Ira Wolfman to
the renowned A. J. Axel.

Sometimes following Wolfman's lectures there was
a scattering of applause in the lecture hall. Unobtrusively in my seat I clapped with the others, thrilled and
breathless.

In our class Wolfman described psychology experiments in which he'd participated: the systematic
precipitation of "learned helplessness"—a term for
"breakdown"—in pigeons, rats, and small primates
(monkeys) after a volley of stimuli followed by random
and unpredictable consequences. Initially, the subject
tries to make sense of the stimuli, to perceive a pattern
amid randomness; the subject tries to "control" the
situation, but of course fails, and eventually suffers a
breakdown.

After the "learned helplessness," the subject can
be reconstituted through a volley of new stimuli, with
predictable consequences.

*Like animals, human beings require order, coher-
ence, predictable consequences. If they fail to experience
these, they suffer breakdown.*

It was a fact of behavioral psychology. No one could
contest this (cruel) fact.

I thought—*That is our condition. If we are lucky.*

Lonely

Before Wolfman I'd been so lonely: I had done something reckless.

It was foolish, futile—I'd known this beforehand. And it was reckless.

Kneeling in the shadowy corner of my room, beside my bed, and pressing my forehead against the wall, in an effort to summon back memory—memories—of my old, lost life—biting my lower lip to keep from crying—and I could not, *could not remember*—my mother's face, or voice; my father's face, or voice; my own face, in the bureau mirror in my room that I'd had since I had been a little girl, when Daddy had painted my room a pale rose color, and Mommy had painted the frame around my mirror a color she called creamy-white . . . And I felt that my head might explode with the effort; for the microchip in my brain was blocking the very memories that would nurture me, like a kind of mental asthma, suffocating . . .

You can't. You are forbidden. You are in Exile. This is your punishment.

And so I gave up. Several times in succession, I gave up.

And one day when I'd given up trying to remember, when loneliness was choking me, I threw on my fleece-lined jacket and went out again in the late afternoon, at a time when other students were leaving campus, returning to their residences for dinner; and hiked over to the university infirmary on the far, eastern edge of the campus; and there, I searched for the nurse whom I'd seen in my first hour at Wainscotia, in the immediate aftermath of the *teletransportation*—I didn't remember the woman's name but I remembered her face, her darkish blond hair brushed back behind her ears, her eyes that were kindly but wary—*Don't ask me any questions, Mary Ellen Enright. Just go away.*

I asked the receptionist if there was a nurse who fitted that description, in her early thirties maybe; and the receptionist shook her head *no;* she had no idea whom I meant. And I said, "But could I look around for the nurse—there's really something I need to ask her."

The receptionist told me that at the present time no one else was on duty in the infirmary except her. The resident doctor was "on call"—but not on the premises.

I glanced about the waiting room, which was empty. It was a small, cramped space with just three chairs. (Curious to see ashtrays in the infirmary waiting room!) There was a close, stale, congested smell of something medicinal and sickly, as well as cigarette smoke, and in the near distance, in the adjoining ward, a sound of despondent coughing. I remembered now—some sort of sickness was sweeping the campus, "Asian flu"—several girls in Acrady Cottage were stricken.

Since I seemed so indecisive the receptionist said again that she didn't know whom I meant, and she knew all of the nurses in the infirmary.

Hearing this, I simply chose not to absorb it. No.

"Are you sure? Could I—look around? Is there a nurses' station?"

The nurse-receptionist looked at me as if I had to be joking.

"Nurses' station? *Here?*"

"Her name might have been"—I was straining to remember, despite something knotty in my brain that blocked my thoughts—"something like Imogene?—Irma?"

"'Imogene'—'Irma.' No."

Quickly the nurse-receptionist spoke. Too quickly, I thought.

And I thought—*Is this the nurse? This woman, who is speaking to me?*

I saw, now. She was older than I'd remembered—about my mother's age. Her (dark blond) hair was all but hidden behind a nurse's starched white cap. She was wearing a bulky cardigan over her white nylon nurse's uniform for it was cold in the infirmary, and her plastic name tag was hidden beneath the sweater. I saw that she was the woman—the nurse—who'd helped me wake up, in my first, terrified hour in Zone 9.

"I think you know me? 'Mary Ellen Enright'? You were kind to me, when I was brought here . . ."

Now the receptionist spoke sharply, with a mirthless laugh. "Miss, I said *no.* I've never seen you before, and you've never seen me. And now it's time for you to leave."

"But—aren't you 'Imogene'—or—'Irma'? Please—"

"*Now.*"

"—'Irma Kazinski'—'Krazinski'—"

"If you don't leave, miss, I'm going to call—security. You've been warned."

Her eyes on my face, and not friendly. The way in which she enunciated the word *security* allowed me to know that it wasn't *security* she meant but something far more devastating—*Deletion, DDS, vaporization.*

For a moment I stood paralyzed, unmoving. I could not contemplate leaving the infirmary and returning to Acrady Cottage, alone.

"There is no one here who—knows me. I was—I am—Adriane Strohl—I am not 'Mary Ellen Enright'—I was sent here—brought here—from NAS-23—do you know anything about me? Anything at all—you could tell me?"

Nurse Irma's face was shut tight. The irises of her eyes were tiny as peppercorns, as if sightless. Her mouth was an angry scrawl.

"You're raving. You must be feverish. But we can't take you here—we're filled up with flu patients. Don't you know there's flu sweeping the campus? Better for you to get out of here while you can. While you can walk. Before you get sick. Before you get very sick. Miss Enright—is that your name?—be sure to shut the door firmly when you leave. Do you understand?"

"Please—anything you could tell me, just—anything . . . About what is happening there—in NAS-23? Has anything changed? Is there still Homeland Security, and the president? And the Army, and the Wars for Freedom? Do you know anything about my parents—Madeleine and Eric Strohl? We live—lived—in Pennsboro, New Jersey. Don't send me away, I'm so lonely . . ."

Nurse Irma was furious now.

"I said, miss—*Do you understand?*"

I did not understand but yes, I retreated. I obeyed and left the infirmary. I shut the door firmly behind me. And I thought despite my disappointment, and my hurt, that another time, the nurse named Irma with the dark blond hair, the nurse who'd tended to me in my first hour in Zone 9, had been kind to me: she had not reported me to the authorities in lethal violation of The Instructions.

The proof was, I was still alive.

Possibly

Possibly, in my terrible loneliness I had loved Ira Wolfman for weeks. Before our exchange at midterm.

Possibly, forever.

It was a feeling much more powerful than anything I could feel for Nurse Irma Krazinski.

From the first time I'd seen him in our classroom in Greene Hall. Entering the room briskly, dropping his briefcase on the table at the front of the room, casting his eyes like a fine-meshed net out over the rows of desks, our attentive faces . . . *Hello! My name is Ira Wolfman, I am your section instructor for Psychology 101.*

And there was the man striding to the podium in the lecture hall when he substituted for Professor Axel. For a young professor taking the place of a much-esteemed elder, Wolfman had not seemed hesitant, or lacking in confidence. Happily he'd smiled out at his audience like a diver on a high board before he executes a perfect dive. This acknowledging of an audience as if we were companions together, embarking upon an exciting journey, was not the custom of white-haired Professor Axel who more or less read his lecture notes without troubling to glance out at us, to establish that we were there.

Before it was revealed to me that Wolfman was an Exile like myself, I'd seemed to have known—something.

He is the one. He will save me from Zone 9.

As I did not appear to be susceptible to the flu sweeping the campus, so I was not so susceptible to *falling in love* like girls my age. I could take pride in this.

My roommates at Acrady Cottage talked excitedly, tirelessly of boys they were dating, or hoped to date; *fraternity men* with whom they were already in love, or were desperate to hear from, their happiness depending upon the next telephone call . . . But I was not one of these, for I was not that young any longer.

My feeling for Wolfman was different. Mine was the desperation of the drowning who will clutch at one who comes near, who has the power to save her from a terrible death.

Dean's List

"Mary Ellen?"—the voice was startlingly near. Miss Steadman.

It was the seventh week of classes, just after midterm. Early November. A late, dark, sleet-lashed afternoon. The resident adviser appeared to be waiting for me as I hurried into the residence in my hooded fleece-lined jacket, bound for the stairs, past the wall of mailboxes at which I rarely glanced.

No mail ever came for Mary Ellen Enright of course. But often there were flyers and announcements in my mailbox which cruelly resembled mail.

I wasn't envious of the other girls' letters. I never thought of it, any longer.

My daytime anxiety was concentrated on my course

work. There were five courses: five instructors. That one of them was Ira Wolfman was a coincidence.

I tried not to think of anything else. I shrank from the attention of others. Except, I could not be rude to any adult. I could not rush past Miss Steadman in her doorway, smiling at me.

Silently begging the woman—*Leave me alone, will you! All of you! Please.*

Such fierce thoughts raced through my head. It seemed amazing to me, that others could not hear them and recoil from me.

"Mary Ellen? May I speak with you—briefly?"

I could not turn from Miss Steadman with a muttered *No.* Meekly I followed her into her apartment: into her sitting room which opened out onto the smaller of two lounges in Acrady Cottage, where there was a console-model television, a "Philco"—the smallest television I had ever seen, with a miniature screen, a picture in tremulous shades of gray, broadcast over just three channels.

In the evenings, some of the girls of Acrady Cottage watched this ridiculous little television set! And Miss Steadman who seemed to crave company sometimes watched, too.

Ardis Steadman was a tall rangy woman with sand-colored hair, eyebrows, skin. She was plain-faced, earnest. Her eager smile revealed pale-pink gums. Her eyes were large, brown, brimming with sincerity. She'd introduced herself to us at the first meeting of Acrady Cottage as an assistant in the office of the dean of women. She was a Ph.D. candidate in Public School Administration, in her mid-thirties perhaps, or perhaps younger, for Miss Steadman was one of those women who, as a young girl, is already praised as "mature"—"responsible"—"a leader." My roommates spoke of trying to avoid Miss Steadman who was *really nice, but bor-ing.*

Especially, they pitied her as unmarried: *spinster.*

(Such words as *spinster, old maid* were new to me, for in NAS-23 marriage was hardly more common than divorce. But I understood the meanings of these words, and something of the panic that underlay them in Zone 9.)

Miss Steadman smiled happily at me. In her warm eager voice she asked how I was?—how my classes were going?—and I murmured polite replies. I tried to sound cheerful, upbeat: it was a phenomenon of Wainscotia—"upbeat." But I was not very skilled at "upbeat" and I could see that Miss Steadman was not deceived.

She asked me in some detail about my courses. For I

was a "scholarship girl"—and so of particular interest to her. (I'd learned that, at Wainscotia, I was a University Scholar—and not a Patriot Scholar. Evidently, in 1959, "Patriot Scholar" did not yet exist.) Miss Steadman had heard of most of my instructors, and was enthusiastic about them; particularly, she was enthusiastic about Professor A. J. Axel who'd collaborated with the great B. F. Skinner at Harvard—"Professor Axel has developed his own experimental project, with the aim of curing antisocial behavior—the 'aberrant,' the 'perverse,' and the 'subversive.' Wainscotia is to establish a center for this new field—'The Wainscotia Center for Social Engineering.' Each October, we expect Professor Axel to receive a Nobel Prize. This will happen soon, I predict!"

I asked Miss Steadman what sort of "aberrant," "perverse," and "subversive" behavior did she mean?

Miss Steadman paused. A faint blush rose into her face. With a frown she said, "Oh—the kind of shameful behavior you can imagine, Mary Ellen. Or, rather—you can't imagine. And I can't, either." She shook her head vigorously. "It's mostly among men, I think. Between men. But Professor Axel will change all that."

How would Professor Axel change such behavior? I asked.

"Oh, I think—electric shock treatment." Miss Steadman spoke vaguely.

I wondered if Wolfman was involved in this Center? I had to suppose he was, as an assistant to A. J. Axel.

But how ironic, an Exiled Individual enlisted to cure *antisocial behavior!*

Miss Steadman had much praise for the chairman of the philosophy department, Professor Myron Coughland, whose theory it was that the history of philosophy and linguistics from the Greeks onward had been a steady progression to present time, mid-twentieth-century Christian United States—"It has something to do with 'practical'—'pragmatic'—ethics, and with 'democracy'—'the greatest good for the greatest number'—plus Christianity of course. Our American beliefs in the age of Sputnik, which are very different from the beliefs of Soviet Russia! Professor Coughland has a hundred-thousand-dollar grant from the National Science Institute to pursue his research. He's been on the front page of the student newspaper, I'm sure you must have seen the articles."

Vaguely I murmured yes. Maybe I'd seen the articles. Since my exile in Zone 9 I had tried to fill in the considerable gaps in my knowledge of history—there'd been very little in our Patriot Democracy History courses about the Soviets' early success in sending a small, unmanned satellite ("Sputnik") into space, and their development of nuclear weapons, for most of high school Patriot Democracy History focused upon continual threats to American democracy, and the triumphs of American democracy over its countless "terrorist" enemies around the world.

"It is obviously true that our American philosophy is the culmination of thousands of years, and that human beings are 'more civilized' than ever before—don't you think? Who could possibly disagree, who has listened to Professor Coughland? He argues that our American presidency is the 'high point' of political history, and that Dwight Eisenhower is the greatest world leader so far."

I knew little of the presidency of 1959, except that the blandly smiling, golf-playing president had been a general in World War II, and was a popular favorite with the American people, like our president of NAS-23, whose approval ratings in the polls, posted every morning on the Internet, was in the range of 95 to 99 percent.

In 1959, there appeared to be two major political parties, Democrats and Republicans, that struggled with each other for dominance; by NAS-23 there was just the Patriot Party, funded by NAS's wealthiest individuals, which appointed all political leaders as well as the judiciary. CVs—"Citizen Voters," a rank determined by income—could cast ballots for the Patriot Party candidate, represented by a smiling emoji, to which a name was affixed, in an election that was both preliminary and final, for the Patriot Party candidate, with no opposition, was inevitably the president. (Dad had said that within his memory there'd been elections with not just one emoji but two emojis on the ballot. The voter, in the privacy of the voting booth, was "free" to vote his choice.)

(It had been explained to us in Patriot Democracy History that, in past decades, hundreds of millions of dollars had been spent on "campaigning"—a largely useless gesture since the presidency invariably went to the candidate with the largest campaign fund; so election procedure was modified to determine which Patriot Party member could amass the most money, and this individual was presented on the ballot as the party candidate, with no need to actually spend the money.)

Badly I wished that I could trust Miss Steadman, to confide in her something of my lost life in what was, to her, the "future"; but even if I'd dared to violate The Instructions, Miss Steadman would not have believed me, and would have thought that I was *mentally ill.*

Already in 1959, as I'd learned in my psychology lecture class, it had become a technique to discredit "rebellious" individuals by suggesting that they were *mentally ill—emotionally unstable.*

"Borderline personality"—which made me wonder who controlled and defined the border.

In her pleasant but dogged manner Miss Steadman was asking if I found logic "difficult—a brainteaser," as she had as an undergraduate, and I said yes, very difficult. Miss Steadman said: "Logic isn't a course of study for women. Like math, physics, engineering— our brains are not suited for such calculations."

Did I believe this? Such thinking was self-destructive, as it was mistaken. In NAS-23 it was axiomatic that "all sexes are equal"—which is to say, no sex is allowed to be "handicapped"—no individual of any sex merited special consideration. But my objection wasn't very convincing, and Miss Steadman ignored my remarks.

In fact since coming to Zone 9 I'd often felt that something was wrong with my brain. The microchip and the *teletransportation* had injured my ability to think. Laboring on the problems in my logic textbook I felt a visceral misery, as if "logic" were a kind of virus that had infected me, from which I couldn't be purged; after a few hours I was left fatigued, despondent. I had noted that not one professor in the philosophy department was a woman, and that not one philosopher in the Intro to Philosophy anthology was a woman. *It was as if the female did not exist.* I wondered if an immersion in logic might result in a strong wish to commit suicide.

I could not tell Miss Steadman this but I did tell her that, of the several courses I was taking, it was logic I was most worried about failing.

"Oh, Mary Ellen—*you* won't fail! I'm sure."

(It was probably so, I wasn't likely to fail the course. My lowest grade in our several quizzes had been A–. Yet still, I anguished over the possibility of failing, for, in logic, there is much unhappiness that is possible, beyond the range of the merely probable.)

Miss Steadman went on to speak, with the breathy enthusiasm of an administrator, of Wainscotia in the "forefront" of academic research. Philology, mathematics, sociology, physics—"You've heard of Amos Stein? Originally of the Institute for Advanced Study in Princeton? No?" Miss Steadman seemed disappointed in me. "Professor Stein was also featured in the student newspaper recently. He's the director of the 'Hoyle project'—a team of first-rate physicists and mathematicians working on a rebuttal of Einstein's theory of relativity. And there is something called the 'Big Bang' theory—the universe began with an explosion, and is 'rapidly expanding.' But our Wainscotia team believes that the universe is infinite and unchanging—a 'steady state.' No beginning and no end. If you believe in God, only the 'steady state' is sensible. For after all—what could precede God? All the professors need is mathematical proof. It's said that they're working on the problem virtually day and night—and that they have enlisted a computer in the project, in Greene Hall. The computer is so large, it takes up half the ground floor of Greene Hall! Everyone in the intellectual world is eagerly awaiting their findings—we're hoping that Wainscotia will be a site for world-renowned physicists and mathematicians to work together in the future. Einstein also argued that 'all things are relative'—that 'time can bend'—obviously impossible. As if God could 'bend'! Professor Stein says such reasoning is 'Jewish logic'—to confound, and not to illuminate." Miss Steadman spoke so vehemently, her lips were damp with spittle.

Yet, her remarks were exciting to me. I did not understand anything of Einstein's theories—though I had heard of the "steady-state universe"—(I wondered if it had originated in the Midwest?)—I didn't understand it either. But I felt Miss Steadman's hope, that Wainscotia State would be so rewarded.

I recalled S. Platz describing the university to which I would be sent as "excellent"—she had sounded so positive, and hopeful for me! When I returned from

Exile, I would be well trained; if I received high grades I might qualify for a good job, and could help out my parents financially.

My life-after-Exile loomed before me like a mirage at the horizon. If my present life was difficult, and lonely, I had only to think of this life—this mirage—to feel more hopeful.

Miss Steadman was speaking of Wainscotia's "pre-eminent" biologist Carson Lockett II, who'd been trained at Oxford in "life sciences"—a world expert in the work of Alfred Russel Wallace, the Victorian scientist who had anticipated Charles Darwin's evolutionary theory; but had gone beyond Darwin in hypothesizing a "special creation" for the human brain which, Wallace argued, could not have possibly emerged from "natural selection" over millions of years—"Dr. Lockett and his colleagues are engaged in a refutation of Darwinian atheism in the most objective, scientific, 'evolutionary' terms." And Miss Steadman was speaking of Wainscotia's resident poet H. R. Brody—did I know his work? Had I seen his photograph?—"H. R. Brody has white hair like Robert Frost. His poems are rhyming poems, about nature—like Frost's. They are not those strange little lower-case-letter poems by the man 'cummings'—'c. c. cummings'—or is it 'e. c.'?—who doesn't even try to rhyme. I don't understand much of contemporary poetry but H. R. Brody's poetry is *beautiful,* and *wise.*"

I tried to remember if I had ever heard of H. R. Brody as a poet, in our English classes in NAS-23. I didn't think that I had. Eighty years later, H. R. Brody had been totally forgotten.

"Are you interested in poetry, Mary Ellen? I think you must be."

Why would Miss Steadman say this? All I could stammer was *no.*

In fact I'd tried to write poetry in high school. In our English class we were given poetry-formulas, with rhymes to fill in—

I'm Nobody! Who are ____?
Are you—Nobody—___?

And

I think that I shall never see
A poem as lovely as a ___.

Poems are made by fools like ___,
But only God can make a ___.

My own poems were not so smoothly composed. A twenty-line formula-poem, for me, might spill over into thirty lines, or end prematurely at eighteen.

I'd also tried to write what were called "stories"— following the pattern of the Nine Basic Plots we were provided, along with vocabulary lists and recommended titles.

We were not allowed to take books out of the public library marked *A*—for Adult; we were restricted to *YA*, Young Adult, which had to be approved by the Youth Entertainment Board, and were really suitable for grade school. My parents had had Adult Books at one time, but I had never seen them.

I did try to compose a graphic novel with animals, not people. My illustrations were clumsy and childish and the project, that had begun with much enthusiasm, gradually dwindled away like ice melting.

I remembered that my brother Roddy had gone through a phase in middle school when he'd built kites out of papier-mâché. These were sort of amazing kites, dragons, eagles, giant butterflies, you'd never expect from Roddy.

For a while I'd helped him make the kites. It had been exciting to do something with Roddy instead of mostly trying to avoid him. Our parents were impressed, too. But eventually he lost interest, or became discouraged for some reason saying with a shrug *Who cares? Making stuff is a waste of time.*

Miss Steadman was smiling at me as if in the expectation that I might share with her something of my "poetic" nature but I knew better than to reply. She then asked how I was getting along with my roommates?—and I told her that they were very nice, and I liked them very much.

"Well, good! They are very different from you, Mary Ellen, I think."

I should hope so! My roommates are zombies.

To hide my surprise I smiled. (In the Happy Place, I was smiling nonstop!) For this had been an unexpected remark of Miss Steadman.

"Your roommates are religious girls," Miss Steadman said, "like most of the girls in Acrady, I believe. But you—some of us have wondered—what is the church of your choice?"

Church of your choice. A strange and coercive phrase.

"I—I don't go to 'church'—actually. But I am a—a—what you'd call a—'religious believer.'"

"Well, I thought so, Mary Ellen." Miss Steadman frowned thoughtfully as if the issue (was Mary Ellen Enright "religious") had been gravely pondered. "And you are—a Christian?"

This was blunt! No one had ever asked me such a question before. In NAS-23 it was assumed that all citizens were "Christian" but that "Christian" did not mean much more than "NAS-citizen." Certainly, no one ever spoke of "Christian values"—doing good, helping the less fortunate, being "selfless."

"Sometimes, Mary Ellen, you seem just slightly"— Miss Steadman searched for the appropriate word— "sad. Your roommates have said that you've been homesick."

"No."

"Well—good! That's good to know."

It was disconcerting that my roommates would speak about me to the resident adviser behind my back, but equally disconcerting that the resident adviser would allow me to know that they had.

"You've come a distance to Wainscotia, I think?"

What did Miss Steadman mean by this? I was becoming very uneasy.

(How much information had Miss Steadman been given about me?)

"We're all homesick in new places. Even those of us who've lived away from home for years."

Miss Steadman spoke gently, warmly. Encouraging me to share my feelings with her. Of course, I would not!

At the front of the residence there were voices, laughter. It was mysterious to me what my roommates and the other girls found so hilarious, so often.

Gathering by the mailboxes, loitering in the foyer. Drifting upstairs to their rooms. Such hilarity! From a little distance I could not decipher a word they said. Some of them brayed loudly, some were convulsed with giggles. It was nearing 6:00 P.M.: soon they would troop off to the dining hall for the evening meal. (Acrady Cottage was too small to provide meals for residents. The deafening-loud dining hall to which we were assigned was two blocks away, and served both male and female students.) Usually I sat alone in the dining hall at a table with solitary individuals like myself, engrossed in a textbook and pretending not to notice girls from Acrady who might have invited me to join them. My invisibility was like a magic coat that kept me warm but also compounded my loneliness.

I was wearing the navy-blue jumper that was too large for me, over a gray turtleneck sweater with a stretched neck; the rubber boots, which were scruffy and stained. I wondered if Miss Steadman could see that the clothes in the box had been secondhand? Not mine, only just addressed to me? And did she know about me? Nurse Irma had known about "Mary Ellen

Enright"—to a degree. Certain key administrators at Wainscotia had to know.

But possibly not. Possibly inhabitants of Zone 9 knew nothing about NAS-23 and its procedures. It was likely that they were given minimal information: an Exiled Individual, an individual with no past, no background, no family, no history, appearing among them by government decree.

For all they knew, "Mary Ellen Enright" was an orphan whose parents had died in a natural disaster, or in some act of war. Why would they have questioned this?

As Miss Steadman spoke of homesickness I began to think— *She wants me to confess to her, and then she will report me.*

Or, maybe—*She wants me to confide in her, and then she will comfort me.*

Or—*Miss Steadman is in Exile herself!*

Except I did not believe this. Miss Steadman was hardly the Treason-type.

Oh, I hated this! Trapped in my thoughts.

Exile means you can't free your mind to think of anything except Exile. While others never question the terms of their existence you question the terms of your existence constantly. *Why am I here, when will I be taken from here, who is watching me, who is moni-*

toring me, is it this person who invites me to trust her? What will she report of me? What will be the summary and the judgment?

Miss Steadman was asking where I was from. A quite natural/friendly question yet I stammered trying to give a plausible reply. Trying to recall The Instructions—what was not forbidden, and was therefore allowed.

"I—I'd rather not say, Miss Steadman."

Miss Steadman stared at me, surprised. "But—why not?" Her manner was guileless, innocent. I had truly surprised her.

"It makes me sad to think about it. I'm sorry."

"Well! I'm sorry that this is upsetting to you. I'd been told that you have a scholarship from out of state, I'd had the idea it was one of the eastern Atlantic states like New York, New Jersey . . ."

"I'm an 'orphan,' Miss Steadman. I'm not from any-place really. And my parents—my parents who adopted me—are both dead."

These words were shocking to me. I had never spoken them aloud before. Yet, I'd rehearsed them. I thought—*If this is being recorded, I have not said anything wrong.*

Miss Steadman's manner seemed to suggest that my remarks were utterly unexpected. If she had a file on me, it was incomplete. Or, she wanted me to think so.

(I wondered, too: were tape recorders available for ordinary individuals, in 1959? Was it likely that Miss Steadman could be recording this conversation? There were few electronic devices in this primitive culture but agents of the State might be equipped for surveillance.)

More girls had entered the residence and were congregating around the mailboxes like a flurry of squirrels. Ordinarily Miss Steadman would appear at the front of the house around this time in the hope of waylaying a few girls to chat with her, but not this evening.

"Did you say that you have no family, Mary Ellen? Is that what I understood you to have said?"

"Yes. I mean no—I have no family. I was adopted and—my 'adoptive parents' died."

These words came glibly. Almost, I wanted to laugh at the solemn expression on Miss Steadman's face.

"That's so very sad, Mary Ellen! When did this happen?—I mean, when did your parents die?"

When? I had no idea. The Instructions had not prepared me for such an interrogation. Like an actor who has been handed only a skeletal script I would have to improvise.

"A long time ago—I think. I don't really remember."

"Well—that's very sad . . . And very unusual."

Unusual that an orphan's parents have died, or *un-usual* that the orphan seems not to remember when they died?

"So, did no one bring you here to Wainscotia? Did you come alone?" Miss Steadman seemed embarrassed by my faltering words yet persevered in her questioning. In her plain earnest face was a look almost of hunger.

"Yes. Alone."

"So young, to be traveling alone! I didn't think I'd seen anyone with you, that first night. You seemed very—independent."

Independent! I smiled inanely.

"I wanted to help you with your steamer trunk, but you told me you didn't want help. Yes, you were very—precociously, I'd thought—independent."

Steamer trunk? What was this woman remembering?

Somehow confusing a badly wrapped cardboard box with something called a *steamer trunk*. Had there been, over the years at Acrady Cottage, more than one "Mary Ellen Enright"?

Miss Steadman was assuring me that she, too, had been homesick when she first went to college—not at Wainscotia but a smaller college, in northern Wisconsin. But she found her friends, eventually—"As you will also, Mary Ellen."

To this cheerful remark I had no reply. Trying to envision "friends" hiding on the Wainscotia campus whom it would be my task to discover and if I did not, it would be a failing of mine.

Somehow, I'd missed the transition, Miss Steadman was speaking of food. Dining hall? Home-cooked?

Often, I forgot to eat. Or, I had no appetite for the food in the dining hall. (Much fried food, greasy fatty meat, vats of lumpy mashed potatoes, "fruit cup" and Jell-O desserts.) My roommates had noticed—at first— and offered to bring back food for me from the dining hall, but I hadn't encouraged them.

"Would you like to have dinner with me, Mary Ellen? I mean—tonight?"

Stammering thanks, but—"I don't think so, I have so much homework . . ."

"I mean in my apartment here. I like to cook. I specialize in simple meals." Miss Steadman smiled shyly. "You're welcome to join me, Mary Ellen, if you wish."

"Thanks, but—I guess I can't."

"Well. Another time perhaps."

With an air of disclosure Miss Steadman went on to say that she'd had an "advance report" from the dean's office regarding my midterm grades.

Grades? Now I was concerned.

In my stressed state the very mention of grades made my heart trip.

"Oh dear, don't look alarmed, Mary Ellen! You've done very well. The dean makes it a point to go over reports from the faculty at midterm to see if anyone is having problems, and to offer help with these problems before it's too late. And I hope you will keep the news to yourself, as it is confidential."

Trying now to feel relief instead of acute anxiety.

"Your instructors have reported that you've earned straight A's, it seems. Well—one A minus, in logic. Wonderful work, Mary Ellen! Congratulations." Miss Steadman smiled at me. If I had not drawn away she would have seized my hands and squeezed them in an outburst of girlish enthusiasm. "You are currently at the very top of Acrady Cottage, and Acrady is usually at the top of the freshman women's residences."

At the top. What did this mean? I was beginning to perspire, for it seemed that once again without thinking I had insufficiently *held myself back.*

But the situation was different. Now it was good to be praised, not a warning. If but by this friendly stranger who had no idea who I was.

I thought *My parents would be proud of me.*

"Oh, Mary Ellen! You aren't crying—are you?"

"N-No."

My face was very warm. By now I was desperate to escape.

At the doorway of her sitting room Miss Steadman asked if I liked chamber music and I said yes, yes I did like chamber music, for it seemed a reasonable reply; though really I knew little about chamber music, and might have thought that this was music played on instruments like organs, pianos, and harpsichords, in special music-chambers. If I was interested, Miss Steadman said, there was a chamber music quartet recital at the music school on Friday evening, playing compositions by Bach, Brahms, and Ravel; she was going, and had an extra ticket if I would like to join her.

"We could have dinner before at a restaurant on Moore Street."

Seeing how alarmed I looked at the prospect of a restaurant dinner, Miss Steadman said quickly that she would pay for both our meals—"If you're interested, Mary Ellen. But I know you spend most of your time on your courses."

I told her yes, I would be interested. For I wanted to learn all that I could, and "chamber music" was new to me.

At the same time I did not want to spend time with Miss Steadman. I did not want to risk intimacy with another person. And I did not trust Miss Steadman, finally.

"Good night, Mary Ellen! It was good to talk to you, at last."

At last. What did that mean?

I ran away upstairs. So grateful to have escaped without saying a wrong thing that might be used against me.

Fell onto my bed, exhausted. Thank God my roommates were at the dining hall.

Thinking—*She wants to be my friend. Why can't I trust her!*

The Spell

Truth was: I had no time in my emotional life for anyone except Ira Wolfman. I had not time to *fantasize* about anyone but Ira Wolfman.

Like a small comet in the wake of a larger comet, helpless to resist its gravitational field, I fell under Wolfman's spell.

The microchip in my brain blocked me from summoning my parents. I could not summon my closest, lost friends. And during my sleepless nights I began to think of Wolfman compulsively.

He knows me. He will acknowledge me, soon.

But when? A week passed after midterm. And another week.

In Professor Axel's lecture Wolfman sat in the front row, to the far left as you entered the hall from the rear.

I did not want to distract Wolfman by sitting near him, or in his line of vision if he turned his head, so I sat several rows behind him, with a clear view of his profile. In fact I stared mesmerized at Wolfman's profile, as A. J. Axel lectured of the distinction between Pavlovian and Skinnerian "conditioning," and the significance of "operant reinforcement" in terms of a "social utopia." I saw that Wolfman was glancing around, into the audience of mostly undergraduates—as he hadn't done previously, that I could recall.

Was Wolfman looking for me? In my naïveté I wanted to think so.

Here was a purely classical, Pavlovian response: when Wolfman turned to glance back into the audience, my heart gave a painful leap, and a sense of alarm tinged with acute pleasure, or acute pleasure tinged with alarm, ran through my body like an electric current. At once I felt faint, and very happy.

Yet, if Wolfman's eyes moved over me—quickly, with a pained expression—he did not seem to wish to see *me*. This was a clear rebuff. My physiological symptoms abated at once, like air escaping a balloon.

A Pavlovian response, involuntary.

Also, I noted that while Wolfman was courteously friendly to other students in our quiz section, whose names he certainly didn't know, he seemed never to notice me if we happened to encounter in the lecture hall, or in the corridor outside. He seemed stubbornly blind to the physical fact of *Enright, Mary Ellen*.

This had to be voluntary. Deliberate.

In our class Wolfman was not so composed as he'd appeared at the start of the term. Though always prepared for the class, with notes, much-annotated texts, and a seemingly endless supply of anecdotal experimental-psychology material, he often appeared distracted, like one in the presence of—who? What? An enemy? A spy? He was edgy, uneasy. He lit cigarettes and smoked hurriedly. (In Zone 9 it was common for professors to smoke in classrooms; students smoked everywhere, as if by natural right. A dull-blue haze drifted freely. Did no one know of the hazards of smoking? Secondary smoke? Did no one associate lung cancer with all this smoke? After a few days in these barbaric circumstances I'd learned to arrive early in my classrooms to take a seat near a window if possible, or near a door that might be opened a crack. I would never learn to stifle my coughing as clouds of toxic smoke drifted languidly in the air in which for fifty minutes nonsmokers were trapped. It was a symptom of Zone 9 that nonsmokers never dared complain of smoke. If we waved smoke from our faces it had to be with an air of apology, for our silent protests antagonized smokers and smokers were the great majority.)

Wolfman was an energetic instructor, always on his feet. As he lectured he wrote decisively and dramatically on a "blackboard." He paced about the room which was wider than it was deep, with long rows of seats stretching the width of the space; as Wolfman faced the class he had no need to see me for my seat was far to the left, in what would be the periphery of his vision.

Virtually everything Wolfman said was fascinating to me. Yes including the words *the, and, a*. It's as if he were lifting a flap of human skull and peering into the workings of the brain coiled inside. He spoke of animal and plant characteristics that had "several times evolved" through the millennia—"bioluminescence," for instance. ("Obviously, 'bioluminescence' is important," Wolfman said. "Without it, fireflies would have to mate in less exciting ways.") Wolfman spoke of Darwin's initial bewilderment at the extravagant display of the male peacock's tail before Darwin had "got it" that such showy behavior had to be linked to natural selection—"Smart as Darwin was, he hadn't taken a clue from eighteenth-century male attire in England and Europe—wigs, lace, satins and silks, even makeup. He was too Victorian to make the identification." Enchanting to me, who'd had dull, careful, cautious, not-very-intelligent or well-educated teachers in high school, to hear a man of Wolfman's intelligence speak—about anything.

"It's a phenomenon of mental life," Wolfman said, one memorable hour, "that the dreamer is always convinced that he is awake, no matter how surreal a dream may become. There's one test, though. See if you can remember it when you're dreaming, when you believe you're wide awake. Look into the distance, if you can. Out a window, if there's a window. In a dream you won't see the detail you see right now, looking out this window—the foliage, for instance; the intricate network of leaves. I'm sure there are no 'cloud formations' in dreams. And if you're trying to read something in your dream, you will discover that you can't—instead of print there's just a jumble of hieroglyphics, or nothing at all. Go to a mirror, if you can—you'll see, there is no reflection in it. There is no *you* in a dream, just firing neurons. These are ways you can be absolutely certain if you're asleep, or if you're awake—which is the state you are in now: awake." Wolfman snapped his fingers, loudly.

In the lecture hall students laughed uneasily. Was

Dr. Wolfman serious, or joking? Somehow, Wolfman's jokes were only funny if you didn't think about them too carefully.

Another time Wolfman told us: "There are no jokes, students. When you laugh, ask what are you laughing at?"

From time to time I began to raise my hand, to volunteer answers to Wolfman's questions. Sometimes Wolfman called upon me—"Yes, Miss Enright?"—and sometimes Wolfman ignored me. Each time I raised my hand, each time I spoke, was terribly exciting to me. Each time, my voice faltered. Sometimes, I choked and could scarcely speak. Yet, I persevered, I plunged forward. I felt like the valedictorian of my class—I *would not be discouraged.*

In the lecture hall, it did not seem quite right that a girl should speak so frequently, or rather so— impressively. Even Wolfman sometimes frowned. *Enough! For now.*

I wondered when Wolfman would ask to speak with me after class in his office? I did not want to appear in his doorway without an invitation.

I thought—*He is frightened of me. We are both at risk.*

I thought—*But he knows me! He is the only one.*

Initially, at the start of the term, Wolfman had ignored me. Hadn't seemed to see me.

Not because he recognized me as an Exile like himself. But because he'd had little interest in me, as a "coed."

His manner toward the three girls in our class had been courtly, condescending. He hadn't been malicious, or cruel. Unlike other instructors of mine who made casual sexist remarks in their classes—("sexist" was a concept unknown in Zone 9, I'd quickly come to realize, for "sexism" prevailed everywhere here, like the atmosphere: it was degrees of "sexism" that mattered)—Wolfman wasn't insulting. It was just that the category *female* was freighted with a kind of comic irrelevance in the field of psychology—(except for abnormal psychology, in which female degenerates were given nearly as much attention as male degenerates, though for different reasons). In our psychology textbook examples of representative psychological subjects were exclusively male; the behaviorist model was male. Professor Axel's lectures alluded incidentally to male experimental subjects and only once did the professor discuss a specifically female phenomenon: the failure of "good mothering" that was thought to cause autism in children.

In our quiz section the next morning I raised my hand to ask Wolfman —"Is there any scientific proof for saying such a thing? That 'bad mothers' cause autism in children?"

Wolfman was taken by surprise. Class had scarcely begun. He had no choice but to look at me.

Tried to smile his genial smile. But his manner was stiff.

He said that frankly, he wasn't an expert. Child development wasn't his field. And "Freudian theory" wasn't his field. He'd like to think that there was proof for Professor Axel's casual remark—but he couldn't personally swear to it.

"However, it's a good question, Miss Enright."

Others in the class glanced at me, curious. It must have seemed to them preposterous, that a freshman girl might question the great authority A. J. Axel.

"It's just that I can't imagine an experimental situation in which 'mothering' was observed by these psychologists, over a period of time. Aren't they just inferring it? Wouldn't there be simultaneous 'fathering' too? I think that psychologists must select autistic children, or children they label as 'autistic,' and try to determine if their mothers had been 'good mothers'— but how would they know? Unless they lived in people's houses with them on a daily basis . . ."

Now this was going too far. Saying too much!

There was a kind of ripple in the room, of discomfort, disapproval. You could see that Wolfman was surprised by my remarks, and the length of my remarks, so unlike those of other students when, not very frequently, they spoke in class.

Yet I'd taken care, for this was Zone 9, "1959," to speak in a soft, unassertive, "feminine" tone, to avoid blatantly offending the professor.

Wolfman acknowledged that this was a good point—

"Autism is a poorly understood mental condition that is presumably 'caused' by something—so, an agent is hypothesized. Why not a neurological deficit? Why blame the mother? You are right. The circumstances don't lend themselves to experimentation, like Skinner's work. Which is why Skinner, and not Freud, is the great scientist of the twentieth century."

This was an odd thing for Wolfman to say. Like wiping away an equation on the blackboard with his sleeve, to change the subject.

"But—but—behaviorism doesn't even try to measure 'subjectivity'—does that mean that 'subjectivity' isn't a proper study for psychology? Ever?"

"It means that 'subjectivity' is 'subjective'—it can't be objectively demonstrated. Behaviorism concentrates on what is objectively available, what *works*."

Wolfman spoke curtly. It was the standard Skinner line. He'd had enough of our exchange for now.

He might have said *Come see me after class, Miss Enright. If you are interested in discussing this further.*

Instead Wolfman turned to another subject. For the remainder of the class he didn't call upon me, and I didn't volunteer to speak.

Nevertheless I went away elated—*He respects me! I'm more than just a "coed" to him.*

Like a little balloon, elated. Filled with helium but not quite enough helium, the little balloon doesn't soar only just bobs along the ground. Blown a bit by the wind.

Finally stuck somewhere in a bush. Little balloon pierced of helium, reduced to just rubber.

Unidentifiable as a balloon.

Where do elation, happiness, hope *go*?

B. F. Skinner had not a clue.

Dear Professor,

I love you.

Sincerely,
"Mary Ellen Enright"

PS. No need to reply!

Alone I was assailed with thoughts of Wolfman. *Of course* Wolfman wanted me to see him: he was waiting for me to make the first move.

Composing absurd little love-notes to Wolfman. Such pleasure in writing these notes, folding them up into tiny squares and hiding them at the rear of my desk drawers.

The Wolfman-spell was like a narcotic. In such a state you are not unhappy for you are under the spell and to be under the spell is to be incapable of being unhappy.

But my devotion to Wolfman wasn't selfless. No. Always I was thinking, if Wolfman too were in Exile, he could help me—somehow . . . This I wanted to believe.

The wariness in his eyes, when he saw me—this, I tried to ignore.

He doesn't want a special relationship with you.

Can't you see, he doesn't even want to "see" you.

Where in the past I'd never lingered after class to speak with other students, or to hear their remarks, now I yearned to hear comments on Ira Wolfman. Oh, anything! I liked even to hear the name—*Dr. Wolfman.* Or, just *Wolfman.* The name alone mesmerized.

It was astonishing to me, Wolfman was not universally admired. In fact, Wolfman seemed to be resented.

His grading, his sarcasm, his "fancy" vocabulary. Wolfman wasn't *down-to-earth* like certain other professors who told jokes, teased their students and didn't expect them to know much.

Of course, in some quarters Wolfman was much admired. "Brilliant guy"—"brainy"—"cool." (It was notable, "cool" had been a term of admiration way back in 1959.) Even the foolish remarks of some girl classmates were prized by me, comments on Wolfman's looks, clothes, style—"He's from New York City, you can tell. Real smart."

"He'd be a dreamboat if he didn't act so snooty . . ."

"Snotty."

(Not funny. Though others laughed I did not laugh.)

"Obviously, Wolfman is Jewish."

"Oh—that's a *Jew*? Him?"

"Bet you. They're supposed to have little horns on their foreheads—just bumps, by now. After so many thousands of years."

Jewish! I had not thought of this.

Wolfman. Ira Wolfman. My love.

Therefore I could not be anything less than the very best student in Wolfman's quiz section. My hope was to be the very best student in Psychology 101—to earn the highest grades among the more than two hundred students enrolled in the course.

Miss Enright! Dr. Axel and I are—well, frankly impressed . . . We would like to encourage you to major in psychology.

How many times I dared to approach Wolfman's office during his office hours. Invariably there was a student inside: the frosted-glass door was closed. Badly I wanted to press my ear against the window, to determine if the visitor was a boy or a girl.

Feeling a kind of disappointed relief, that I was spared making a fool of myself.

The corridor was a busy one, on the first floor of Greene Hall. I was jostled by students hurrying to classes. To give myself some purpose I stared at a bulletin board festooned with posters and announcements of psychology department events: lectures, symposia, applications for summer fellowships, advertisements for graduate programs at other universities. I thought—*I could apply for one of these. Could I?*

I wondered if I really might excel in psychology. If I might go to graduate school, someday. (But when? And where?) If there was any hope for me, in Exile, to do anything worthwhile with my life.

I clung to S. Platz's words: Wainscotia was an "excellent" university. After I graduated, and was returned from Exile, the State would arrange for me to receive additional training, to prepare me for employment in NAS. I wanted to believe this.

Yet, in the corridor outside Wolfman's office, I felt a sense of hopelessness. What had brought me here? What did I think I might acquire from Wolfman? His respect, his friendship? His love? His assistance, in escaping from Exile? (But—where? "Adriane Stohl" had not yet been born.) There was no *his;* I had no true idea of the man, beyond his charismatic classroom personality which (I had to know) was a public performance. I felt dazed, uncertain. Abandoned. If a stranger had tapped me on the shoulder and said *Come with me. Your sentence has been altered, you will now be Deleted* I would have come unresisting.

I wasn't sure if I was waiting to see my quiz section instructor, as others enrolled in Psych 101 were, or just standing there in the corridor hoping not to be jostled. My insomniac nights and protracted workdays left me in a paralysis like a ball that has been thrown hard, has rolled far, but has lost momentum and has come to a stop . . .

A student emerged from Wolfman's office, somber-faced, clutching at a paper, and departed. And there came Wolfman to the doorway yawning, to see if another student awaited him.

His eyes moved onto me, startled. I saw a look of pained recognition. "Miss Enright. Hello."

Wolfman's usually ebullient voice was wary, flat.

Pleading with me—*No. Go away please.*

I nodded hello. I felt very shy, suddenly. Stricken with shyness like a physical disability.

"Did you want to see me, Miss Enright?"

"N-No. Thank you."

"You don't? Didn't?"—Wolfman was vexed but amused.

Quickly I turned away. Fled. The part-deflated little balloon, the rubber ball given a kick by Wolfman—there it goes!

Afterward the encounter left me shaken. I had to wonder if it left Wolfman shaken, too.

Orphan

Embarrassing to confess: how I followed Ira Wolf-man, at (what I hoped was) a discreet distance. I did not want to upset him—or anger him—but I could not stay away from him.

I was convinced: he'd recognized me. We were two of a kind in Zone 9: Exiles.

In English literature class we read poetry of the Romantics. We learned of the Romantic concept of *soul-mates*. It was clear to me, Ira Wolfman was my *soul-mate*.

Once Ira Wolfman left Greene Hall by the side door near his office, in the company of two other men—young men—had to be psychology colleagues. In our class he often spoke of his "lab"—an experimental laboratory under the direction of A. J. Axel—and these two might have been laboratory coworkers. So long as Wolfman was with them he appeared to be relaxed and jovial; he did most of the talking, and the others laughed; for Wolfman had a dominant personality, in such circumstances. But as soon as he left his companions and walked on alone his expression reverted, like ice melting, to an expression of sobriety, brooding.

Like one who is in Exile. One who is far from home.

In an entranceway I stood just far enough away so that Wolfman wasn't likely to see me. Badly I wanted to call to him—"Dr. Wolfman, hello! Let me walk with you."

Never would I have spoken so recklessly. Of course.

Observing how Wolfman made his way to a bicycle stand behind Greene Hall where he tossed his briefcase into a wire basket, unlocked the bicycle and straddled it and pedaled away.

He didn't own a car? Was that possible?

Without breaking into a run I followed a block or so. Watching the cyclist disappear into traffic on University Avenue.

In Zone 9 bicyclists never wore safety helmets. Yet it surprised me that one who knew so much about the human brain, its fragility as well as its mysteries, should so expose his head to injury, as Wolfman did.

This was troubling. This made me wonder whether

Wolfman was of this time, after all. Was I imagining everything about him? Was I losing my mind?

Blindly I turned away. Stepped in front of a vehicle and was nearly run over amid a skidding of brakes.

Rawly a male voice yelled: "Look where you're going, stupid!"

The shout was a rebuke to my naïve yearning. But it would not dissuade me from yearning.

Tried to look up *Wolfman, Ira* in the Wainscotia telephone directory but there was no listing under that name. No listing under the name *Wolfman*.

Which meant: Wolfman didn't have a telephone. Or, Wolfman had a private number.

How strangely isolated people were, in 1959. If you could not "look up" someone in a telephone directory you could not locate him at all.

If I wanted to know where Wolfman lived I would have to follow him on foot. How I could manage that, I had not the slightest idea. And if I followed Wolfman home, what then? Could I have knocked at his door? Waited for him in the street?

How long, in the street?

I was becoming desperate, feverish. At the same time with a part of my mind I understood how irrational I was being. How like a rat in a maze, running, darting, always forward, never turning back, driven by appetite that was never filled. Yet the conviction that Wolfman was my *soul-mate* could not be shaken.

Wolfman had to live somewhere fairly close to the university campus, probably in a rented apartment. For he seemed to have no car, or anyway no car that I'd seen.

I wondered if he lived with someone? A chill passed over me at the prospect of his living with a woman. Or worse, his being married.

A husband? A father? Yet—an Exile?

This did not seem likely.

Certainly, not likely. *Procreation* was forbidden.

(But what a cold clinical term—*procreation!* Thinking of my mother who'd had Roddy and me, *had babies,* how much warmer a way of speech, how much more maternal.)

(Thinking of Mom with a sensation of such loss, sadness. Wanting to cry—*Mom! Dad! I am so sorry, I let you down.*)

(Did they even know if I was alive? I wondered. Maybe Roddy knew, and could tell them. Or hint to them.)

In Zone 9 there were limited ways in which one could learn about another person. Ira Wolfman wasn't a public figure, wouldn't have been listed in the university library catalogue probably. Still I decided to search there, in long clumsy wooden drawers, under the heading PSYCHOLOGY, 20TH CENTURY. To my surprise discovering that *Wolfman, Ira* was one of several authors listed for journal articles written under the direction of A. J. Axel. But there was no personal information about Wolfman.

How strange it was to me, this enormous building filled with *books*! In my former life everyone used eBooks of one kind or another, rarely "paper"-books; in NAS-23 the State controlled all electronic communications and transmissions and so it was not possible to access any title of any book that had not been approved by HSIB—Homeland Security Information Bureau. What would have been "magazines" and "newspapers" that had passed through the censor-filter were exclusively online in NAS-23—unlike the thousands of publications here in Zone 9, in 1959.

How strange, and how wonderful: the Government could not possibly control all these publications! Yet it seemed mysterious to me, that there was, in Zone 9, so much *freedom*—that, in Zone 9, did not feel like *freedom*.

As a university student I was often in the library—a building that stored books. There were no longer "libraries" in NAS-23—these old buildings had been put to more practical uses.

The university library was an old pinkish-red sand-stone building with a rotunda, stately columns, and wide stone steps descending to a broad flagstone path; from a distance the lighted rotunda could be seen for miles. The library faced the chapel, the administration building, and the Hendricks Humanities Building across the campus green: this was the so-called his-toric campus, originally established by a land grant from the federal government in 1831. Nearby was the McCabe Science Building with its several new wings for physics, chemistry, math, psychology—in the post-Sputnik era, the fastest growing departments at the university.

Everywhere were trees for which I was learning names: oak, elm, pine, birch. A particularly beauti-ful tree, with a beautiful name: juniper pine. Paths through the trees were sometimes concrete, some-times earthen. At the edge of the campus was the arboretum—a hilly place of many acres. (My room-mates never visited the arboretum—why would they? Too far away, and nothing to do but walk. They got enough walking up steep hills on campus! And I was afraid to walk a mile or so to the arboretum, out of an irrational concern that I would stray too far from my "epicenter" and draw unwanted attention from my invisible monitors.)

More than nine thousand students were enrolled at Wainscotia State yet the atmosphere of the campus was rural at its edges. In the early morning deer were seen grazing on lawns. There were sightings of wild turkeys, pheasants, foxes, raccoons. There were rumors of black bears.

Creatures of which I knew, but which I'd never seen except in facsimile, or as "virtual" images.

When I'd first come to Wainscotia this setting had seemed like a dream to me—unreal, disorienting. I thought—*This is a virtual place, this is not real.* In Media Dissemination, where my brother worked, there were skilled hackers who'd been co-opted by the Government to work for them, to create such utterly realistic VVS—(Visceral Virtual Settings)—that you could not believe they were not real. An entire subfield had emerged in VVS research, to establish a way in which "virtual" sounds could be made to seem as if they were coming from outside the human skull, and not inside; I had to suppose that the same was true for "virtual" sights. (Since the devastation of so much of the landscapes of North America, there had been perceived a practical need for virtual landscapes; even higher castes invested in these.) At Wainscotia I could not shake off the feeling that when I turned away from the "historic" campus it dissolved like ink fading in water.

Wondering if, in time, this unreal place would begin to seem "real" to me. And whether it might ever give comfort.

At first, books had seemed very strange to me.

Objects made of paper and cardboard designed to be *read*. How wasteful and clumsy it seemed—an *object* you had to hold in your hand (for reading was dependent upon turning the pages of a book). You could carry only five or six books easily, while on any eBook, you could access thousands of books. But then I realized that if there was a power outage you could continue to "read"—as the book you held in your hand would not vanish but continue to exist. The curiosity of the book was that, as you held it, and "read" it, you felt an intimate connection with it as with a living thing, which you did not feel with an eBook; as soon as you were finished with the eBook, you stored it, or deleted it; you felt no sentiment or particular ownership. You could not *see* it on a shelf or a table, you could not admire its design. In effect, it had been Deleted.

Badly I wanted to ask Ira Wolfman what he thought about these matters. Was there ever to be *comfort, happiness* in this place?

"Oh, Dr. Wolfman! Yes. He is"—lowering her voice so that no one could hear except me—"a *special case*."

Under the pretext of inquiring about part-time employment in the psychology department I filled out an application form for one of the department secretaries, a friendly young married woman named Bethany. I marveled to Bethany that it must be wonderful to work in a department with such distinguished professors as A. J. Axel and his assistant Wolfman; I asked her about Dr. Wolfman, who was my quiz instructor, and Bethany told me that Dr. Wolfman was generally considered to be the most promising of the younger faculty, who'd published papers with Dr. Axel and gave talks at conferences.

In a confiding tone, as if she didn't think it was curious that I should be asking about Wolfman so much, and Axel so little, she told me that Wolfman had been at Wainscotia, in the psychology department, for five or six years; that he lived alone, and was said to "work all the time"; he was invited to staff parties but rarely came. "I know for a fact that Dr. Axel invites him to dinner at his home sometimes, and Dr. Wolfman accepts—he wouldn't dare turn Dr. Axel down!" Bethany paused, lowering her voice. "He isn't engaged. He's never with anyone except other people in the department. He's always *alone*."

It might have been clear to Bethany that I was in love with my psychology instructor. Such emotions are hard to disguise in a seventeen-year-old. I'd seen the

young woman glance at my (ringless) left hand with a
look of sisterly solicitude.

And so I dared ask about Ira Wolfman's background:
where did his family live? Had she—or anyone—ever
seen them? And Bethany said solemnly, "That's just
it! Ira Wolfman is so *sad*. He was an orphan, I've been
told—he never knew his mother—and the saddest thing,
the wonderful people who adopted him were both killed
in a car crash, also. He's from somewhere far away in the
East—maybe New York City. But he doesn't have any
home, he says. He's just—here."

Suddenly

And that night, a powerful dream-memory.

After I'd learned that Ira Wolfman was an orphan-in-Exile like me.

For there sometimes came, in Zone 9, at unpredictable times, sudden memory-surges like heat lightning that illuminates the night sky for a split second—then vanishes, in silence.

And that night there came a sudden memory of a long-ago time when I'd been a child of three or four and my parents were walking with me outdoors in lightly falling snow. And Mommy was gripping one of my mittened hands, and Daddy was gripping the other hand, and there came snowflakes to tickle my face, and make me laugh. And there was a gust of wind, and Daddy cried *Whoa!* and stooped to shelter me. And

Mommy adjusted a wool cap on my head. *Hold still, honey! Let Mommy fix this strap.*

And I stood very still, and lifted my head, and—

(What came next? Nothing!)

(The memory ended abruptly, like a switch turned off.)

(And there was no way to return. No way back. Waking in my bed on the third floor of Acrady Cottage, in a darkened room with three other girls sleeping nearby, snoring faintly or murmuring in their sleep. And I bit my lower lip to keep from crying. Telling myself that I had lost my parents but only temporarily. And in the meantime I have found Ira Wolfman my *soul-mate.*)

The Denial

"My name isn't 'Mary Ellen Enright.' My name is—"

"No. Don't tell me."

Wolfman pressed his fingers against his ears. This was a gesture that reminded me of my father—a gesture that was both playful and serious simultaneously.

"You don't want me to tell you?"

"No. I don't want you to tell me."

We were in Wolfman's office. At last, after an exchange in class, he'd asked me to see him.

(This was not unusual. Wolfman often invited students to speak with him following class, when they had questions. But he'd avoided inviting *me*.)

I thought—*He will acknowledge me now.*

I was very excited, and apprehensive. For The Instructions were clear: the Exiled Individual is *forbidden to identify herself.*

Violations will insure that the EI will be immediately Deleted.

After Professor Axel's lectures this week Wolfman had taken up the subject of "schedules of reinforcement" in behavioral psychology—how acts (of human beings as of monkeys, rats, and pigeons) can be formulated along lines of behavioral responses to stimuli. On the blackboard Wolfman had drawn graphs. He'd scrawled equations. For it was not enough to demonstrate that the living being was a kind of automaton, when it came to "operant conditioning," but the terms of conditioning could be reduced to formulae.

Why does the (hungry) rat press the lever that will bring him food pellets? Not because the rat is "hungry"—("hunger" is an internal state, thus not measurable)—but because its response to stimuli has been sufficiently "reinforced."

Why does the (addicted) gambler continue to press the slot machine levers that sometimes, though not frequently, bring him rewards in the form of coins? Not because the gambler is "happy" when he wins—("happiness" is an internal state, thus not measurable)—

but because his response to stimuli has been sufficiently "reinforced."

Why does any individual—animal, human—behave as he does, over a period of time? Not because he has chosen to behave in these particular ways, but because his response to stimuli has been sufficiently "reinforced."

There was something wrong with this logic. My heart beat hard in opposition to it, though I could not have articulated my objection.

In our quiz section were undergraduates who had to be, like most of the residents of Acrady Cottage, Christians. Yet not one of them raised his or her hand to object to this mechanical, soulless view of consciousness. Instead, they took notes.

At last I said, trembling, whether with nerves or with indignation, "Dr. Wolfman? Do *you* think that human beings are machines, without 'free will'?"

Wolfman turned to me, politely. His slate-colored eyes were narrowed and wary. "It's a behavioral postulate that mental states can't be examined, so the scientific approach is to examine what is 'objective'—behavior. B. F. Skinner doesn't believe that there is no 'mind'—as his detractors claim—but that, given the principles of behaviorism, what is 'mind' is irrelevant to our understanding of behavior."

This seemed to me an oblique answer to a direct question.

"But—what about 'free will'? Don't human beings have 'freedom' in their choices for themselves?"

Wolfman said, with a shrug, "'Free will' is just a term. It's just speech. A habit of speech. It has no specific referent, thus no specific meaning. And it is not amenable to scientific proof or disproof."

I wanted to cry *My parents taught me there is free will. There is a soul, within.*

Wolfman continued, dryly: "'Free will' is a delusion, for most of us. It's a pleasant delusion, like the anticipation of Heaven which, though it never arrives, is comforting to contemplate. More realistically, 'free will' is like suggesting to a paraplegic that he has the choice of getting up and running in an Olympic competition—what's stopping him?"

This was not right. This was not the same thing at all. But I could not explain. I felt a thrill of sheer dislike of Wolfman, in that instant—the man was not my friend in Exile, but my enemy.

I could hear my parents' voices, objecting—but I could not hear their words clearly.

Trust the inner, not the outer. Trust the soul, not the State.

I was trembling now with emotion. I felt my eyes

sting with tears. Ira Wolfman was my only hope—yet, with these harsh words, he was pushing me from him.

Around me, my classmates were yawning, and taking notes.

Seeing the look in my face, Wolfman relented.

"All right, Miss Enright. Come see me after class."

And so: I told him.

As I'd so long rehearsed. As I'd excited and frightened myself, imagining.

I told him that *Enright, Mary Ellen* wasn't my name.

And he stopped me from telling him my true name.

"But—why?"

"'Why'? You know perfectly 'why,' Miss Enright."

His pained expression. His narrowed eyes, that would not confront me.

"I—I think—I want to tell you, Dr. Wolfman. Please."

"To what purpose?"

Wolfman's face flushed with heat. He kept glancing behind me, at the opened door to the corridor.

His question was cruel, unanswerable. *To what purpose?—so that I would be less lonely, and less desperate.*

And because I love you.

If Wolfman was in Exile, like me, he'd made a substantial place for himself in Zone 9. Maybe he'd been exiled as a young man, a student—in the intervening years, he'd accommodated himself to his new life, and had acquired a degree of conspicuous success in a competitive academic world. He had an appointment at Wainscotia State University. He was a trusted assistant of the revered A. J. Axel, formerly of Harvard. His office was small and had to be shared with another assistant professor, but it was an office in distinguished old Greene Hall with its high ceilings, elaborate moldings, interior carved staircases, hardwood floors.

Wolfman's desk was near the room's single window. In a bookcase beside the desk were many books, both hardcover and paperback; predominant were the names *Darwin, Pavlov, Watson, Thorndike, Skinner.* On the other side of the desk on the wall was a mesmerizing art poster, at which I'd been glancing, which I would one day recognize as a reproduction of Vincent van Gogh's *The Starry Night.*

(A strange art-choice for a behavioral psychologist, such beauty and such mystery!)

Half-pleading now Wolfman said, "Look. I don't have any idea what you're talking about, Miss Enright. And for your own good, I think you might just leave my office now, and forget about this conversation. Do you understand? For your own good."

The pleading was in Wolfman's eyes. The words were terse, unfriendly.

Wolfman was a young man, not yet thirty. He was much younger than my father. Yet I saw something of my father in his face—the faint, furrowed lines in his forehead, the anxious eyes that tried to deceive with levity, sardonic humor. And the smile that came and went, fleeting.

"'For my own good'—that's why I'm here, Dr. Wolfman. I need to—know—from you . . . Who you are, and if—if you are—anyone like myself."

"No. I am not 'anyone like yourself.'"

"But—"

"*No.*"

And I wondered then: Was Wolfman my delusion? Had I imagined—everything? Out of my loneliness and sorrow, had I imagined a savior in Ira Wolfman?

Yet, I was convinced that he knew me, deeply. He recognized me. Though he would not acknowledge it, as perhaps, in similar circumstances, to protect me, my father would not have wished to acknowledge the bond between us.

Wolfman wiped at his warm face with a tissue. His hands were strong and protective-looking, his fingertips stubby. His nails were cut short and rounded and reasonably clean.

No ring on the third finger of his left hand. But I knew that already.

Wolfman took up a ballpoint pen and scribbled something on the palm of his left hand. He held up the palm to me, as he touched the forefinger of his right hand to his lips:

GO AWAY PLEASE

Then, he shut his hand into a fist.

I understood. He did not want to speak to me, even to order me away. He had reason to believe that we were being overheard—we were *under surveillance*.

In a level voice, the voice of a reasonable university instructor confronted with a problematic student, Wolfman was saying, "Thank you for dropping by, Miss Enright. Be assured that your work in Psychology 101 is exemplary and that your ideas, though irreconcilable with Skinnerian behaviorism, will not endanger your grade—provided you continue to excel on our exams and know all the right answers to our questions. But we won't need any more personal conferences this semester, I think. And don't speak to anyone about this conversation—of course."

My legs were leaden. My head was heavy, and my heart.

I was shaky on my feet, but would leave Wolfman now.

"Who would I tell, Dr. Wolfman? You're the only person in Zone Nine to whom I could speak."

At the mention of *Zone 9*, Wolfman's face went rigid.

At the door I said, in a lowered voice, defiant, reckless—"And my name, which is not 'Mary Ellen Enright,' is, in fact, 'Adriane Strohl.'"

Now, he *knows. He knows with certainty. And I know him, with certainty.*

And what will happen to me, to us, now?

The Wall

There followed then a feverish time. The Asian flu that had been sweeping Wainscotia struck me at last. Days passed into nights, nights into days. I missed Wolfman's Friday morning class. I began to miss other classes. For I was too ill to get out of bed. I was often despondent. Only waiting until my roommates were gone from the room and then kneeling in a corner pressing my forehead against the wall was a solace of a kind.

Push push push—but the wall was unyielding.

My roommates whispered to themselves. They believed that their *strange, sad roommate* from out-of-state was praying.

They were pitying. They were concerned. They were beginning to be impatient.

For they believed that I was still homesick, and that I was kneeling in prayer to their Christian God, after so many weeks.

Wolfman would regret that he'd sent me from him! I wanted to believe this.

Miss Steadman tried to encounter me, in the front of the house. But I went invisible, and slipped past her.

On my bare knees on the floorboards. Pushing against the wall.

If I tried hard enough, the censor-barrier could be penetrated—flash-memories came through like the blinks of an eye.

Pushing a door open, hesitantly. My old, lost home!

It was our shingle board house on Mercer Street, Pennsboro.

Seeing my parents in the kitchen, at the table. Mom's bench containing geraniums by a window—stunted plants that didn't bloom much through the winter but, when they did bloom, yielded beautiful bright-red flowers.

It had been one of my duties as a child to keep Mom's plants watered. And to pinch off brown, desiccated leaves.

As Mom said sadly *A leaf that has turned brown will never be green again.*

So vivid was this memory, it seemed to me to be happening *now.*

As I knelt pressing my forehead against the wall to ease the tiny snarl in my brain, *now.*

Daddy was whistling. Brightly Daddy was whistling an old favored tune—"Battle Hymn of the Republic." (Daddy had explained to me: this was a famous abolitionist/antislavery hymn of the 1850s, of the old U.S.A.) So many times I'd heard Daddy whistling this tune, it came back to me now, as if I'd heard it only yesterday.

Yet, there was something strange about the tune. It was recognizable immediately—and yet, not quite right.

Daddy was whistling brightly, loudly. In a way to annoy (?) my mother as, preparing coffee, he annoyed my mother by brushing too close to her at the stove.

Mom murmured something to Daddy that I couldn't hear. Daddy laughed, mirthlessly.

(What was wrong with Daddy? His face was hidden from me, like half a moon cloaked in shadow. He was dressed in his hospital-attendant uniform, his slave-uniform as he'd called it, an orderly's white pullover and coat, white work-trousers and white rubber-soled sneakers.)

Mom was setting bowls down on the table—cereal bowls.

Dad's bowl was at one end of the little rectangular

Formica-topped table, Roddy's and my bowls to either side of his, and Mom's bowl nearest the stove.

Oh!—My mouth watered: I could smell the oatmeal Mom was preparing which was our favorite breakfast.

Steel-cut oatmeal cooked with raisins, brown sugar, and milk.

Mom had made this breakfast since I'd been a little girl. I hadn't realized how I had missed it.

There was Roddy in the doorway. Short-cut hair, nondescript clothes of a low-level "intern." His face lean and sullen and the eye sockets shadowy like a death's-head.

It was my childish wish that my brother might not be there, in this memory. If this was *my memory.*

There was something cruel that Roddy had done to me—I couldn't remember what it was. When news had come of my Patriot Democracy Scholarship he'd stared at me for a moment without any reaction—then, a clumsy forced smile.

Congratulations, Addie!

A smirk of a smile.

Badly I wished that just Mom and Dad were there, in this memory that was so precious to me.

But I could not dictate the memory—could I? If I tried, I was in danger of losing the memory altogether.

Softly I said *Hello! It's me—Adriane . . .*

Daddy didn't hear me. Mom didn't hear me. If Roddy heard me, he gave no sign.

They were talking about—I couldn't hear what they were talking about. It was a familiar problem—it was not-new—boring, humiliating. Probably, it was a financial problem. Or some problem of Roddy's? Some complaint of Roddy's? Or—Mom was having difficulty with her supervisor at work. Or—(maybe this was more likely)—Dad was having difficulty with his supervisor at the medical center. (It was an old humiliation of Eric Strohl's, that since he'd been demoted from staff resident M.D. to hospital attendant, his income had been decimated; yet, to keep this miserable job, he had to advise ever-younger and more career-minded physicians, and often he had to do minor surgical procedures for them, like the installing or removing of "ports" [portable, catheter-like artificial veins] in chemotherapy patients. He was also on hand to draw blood and assist in radiology. Yet, it wasn't like Dad to complain even jokingly—so this was strange.)

(And strange too: where was I, in this memory? Why wasn't I sitting at the kitchen table with my family? Judging by Roddy's age, I must have been about sixteen at this time. *But where was I?*)

Pressing my forehead against the wall of the third-

floor room of Acrady Cottage, Wainscotia, Wisconsin—
Zone 9.

Saying, begging—*Mom? Dad? Can't you see me?
It's—Adriane. Please—look at me.*

But they weren't looking at me. They were oblivious
of me.

Then I saw something that chilled me: my father's
face was coarser than I'd ever seen it. Not just that
Daddy hadn't shaved, but Daddy was looking di-
sheveled like a man you'd see on the street, homeless,
feral: his gray thinning hair uncombed, furrows in his
cheeks, a self-pitying downturn to his mouth. And
small, bloodshot eyes . . .

And my mother: What had happened to *her?*

Mom who'd always been so slender had definitely
gained weight. Her face was fleshy, peevish. A sardonic
smile on her lips. And her face heavily made-up, with
exaggerated arched eyebrows.

Mom's gaze was sulky, dissatisfied. An expression of
barely suppressed rage in Mom's face I had never seen
before.

*Mom, Dad—don't you love me? Don't you miss me?
It's your daughter Adriane—don't you remember me?*

Carelessly, as if she resented waiting on my father
and brother, Mom brought the pan from the stove, to
spoon out oatmeal into bowls. And now I saw that there

were only three bowls on the table. And I saw that their breakfast wasn't oatmeal after all—greedily they were eating some sort of gelatinous substance that was sticky, quasi-transparent, of a sickening fleshy-pink color, quivering in their bowls. This was no breakfast food that I could identify—horribly, it seemed *alive*.

Roddy glanced in my direction, as if he could see me!

Roddy said with a mean little smirk *Where she's gone to now, it serves her right.*

And Mom said *She thought she was too good for us.*

And Dad said *Good riddance!*

They laughed. It was a crude, hellish laughter. There was a swirl of light in the kitchen, as if the Plexiglas barrier were reflecting something shiny, interrupting the scene. I saw with horror that something was very wrong—these people were strangers to me.

The crudely imagined figure meant to be my father was not my father. The crudely imagined figure meant to be my mother was not my mother. And my brother Roddy . . .

It isn't Roddy, either. They have taken away Roddy, and substituted this person for him.

I wondered if this was so: if it hadn't been my brother who'd informed upon me but the other in his place, who'd sent me into Exile.

Suddenly the smell of the quivering jelly-like "oatmeal" was nauseating. Suddenly, I was gagging. The Plexiglas went opaque. The memory was shuttered, gone. I was left alone in a corner of the room, on my knees, pressing my forehead so hard against the wall that the impress of the wood would leave welts in my skin.

"Mary Ellen!"—someone was calling me.

That ridiculous name, that name I hated—someone was calling it, and pulling at my shoulder.

I woke, astonished and frightened. Where was this? What time was this? I must have fallen asleep, or lost consciousness, on the floor beside my bed, on my knees, and one of my roommates had found me slumped against the wall.

"Mary Ellen, what's wrong? You've been crying—you're upset. It must be the flu. Let me help you up."

My roommate whose name was—(Betsy?)—helped me up, onto my bed. She sat beside me, holding my hands that were like ice. She spoke comfortingly to me, soothingly. I was confused but knew not to say anything incriminating about where I had been. Where my remembering had taken me.

Another roommate came into the room, and joined her. What was wrong with Mary Ellen? What had so upset Mary Ellen? A nightmare? A bad memory?

The second girl was—Hilda? I remembered her last name, which was a charming name: McIntosh.

Betsy and Hilda conferred about "Mary Ellen"— what was wrong with "Mary Ellen," and what might be done with "Mary Ellen."

I was thinking: the ugly memory had been a false memory. The microchip was programmed to interfere with my memory. To provide me with a cruel, false, ugly memory. *To punish.*

Yet, it was hard not to think that the father in my memory, the mother in my memory, and the brother in my memory were "real."

It is terrifying, to lose memory. To lose trust in memory.

What is a human being except the sum of her memories? *Look inward, not outward. The soul is inward.*

I believed this. And yet, if my memories were taken from me, what would happen to me? What would happen to my soul?

My roommates argued with one another: Should I be put to bed, or should I be taken to the dining hall, to eat a proper dinner with them? Betsy and Hilda believed that I was seriously undernourished, and didn't sleep enough; Carly thought that I had "some kind of flu-virus." My skin was clammy, not feverish. But my face was oddly flushed, and my eyes were bloodshot.

My third roommate had come into the room, and joined us.

I told them that I wasn't sick—I didn't want to be put to bed. I had homework to do that evening, I was behind in my work. So Betsy, Hilda, and Carly walked me into the bathroom, ran cold water and washed my face that was streaked with tears. They brushed my hair—("Oh gosh, look—it's coming out in the brush. She needs to drink more milk!"). They insisted that I apply makeup: foundation, powder. And lipstick, which Carly lent me. They were enthusiastic about my looks—"If you'd just smile more, Mary Ellen. If you weren't so tired, and sad-looking."

"We're homesick, too—or anyway we *were*. But Wainscotia is so wonderful, it's time you were over missing home."

Carly lent me a sweater to wear to the dining hall: a soft-woolen heather-colored cardigan, far more beautiful than any of my secondhand clothes. Hilda lent me an actual coat—not a jacket—to wear to the dining hall. And leather boots, instead of my ugly rubber boots.

They sat with me, and watched me eat. They took my plate back for seconds. We talked together, and laughed. Other girls from Acrady Cottage joined us. After a while I was feeling better. That is, Mary Ellen was feeling better.

We returned to Acrady Cottage. There was a light snowfall, an icy crust of snow crackled underfoot. In the near distance, the rotunda of the library glowed with a bluish interior light. I thought—*I have no one now. But I will survive. And I will return home, one day.*

I gave back the leather boots, and the deep-forest-green wool coat, but when I tried to give back the heather cardigan Carly said, with a sweet, pained smile, "Oh no, Mary Ellen! It looks nicer on you than it does on me. It's *yours.*"

(**But I** could not be their friend. Because I was not "Mary Ellen"—I was someone else whom they had never met.)

GO AWAY PLEASE

I had only to close my eyes and the red-inked words hovered before me.

In melancholy moods, I didn't have to close my eyes. In the very air before me I seemed to see Wolfman's uplifted hand, the palm of his hand, the admonition that had sent me from him—

GO AWAY PLEASE

The gesture was playful—but desperate-playful. Wolfman had been sincere in wanting me gone.

He'd acknowledged me as one like himself, in Exile. And in the same gesture Wolfman had repudiated me.

Of course I understood: he was under a sentence of potential Deletion, like me. He had to follow the Instructions, as I did. He could not be reckless as I was.

Ira Wolfman had adjusted to his Exile-life, evidently. Or he'd learned to give that impression. He was older than I was, much more intelligent, and wiser as well—he knew that there was no way back home for us.

We could be *brought back home*. But we could not *make our way home*.

This was the curse of Exile: you are powerless to change your life, except for the worst. Others can change your life for you, unpredictably.

When I'd been sick, I'd missed some classes. But just one of Wolfman's classes, which met on Friday morning. Since the flu was said to have affected so many students at Wainscotia, instructors were understanding, and hadn't penalized us for absences or late papers. I was determined to make up for my lost classes for I was determined to be an excellent student at Wainscotia State University.

In all my courses but particularly in Psychology 101.

I went to meals with my roommates more frequently. I was friendly with other residents of Acrady Cottage. I did not avoid Miss Steadman. (Though I'd disappointed our resident adviser at Thanksgiving by hiding away in the university library, and then upstairs in my room in the near-empty residence, with the excuse that I had too much work to do and couldn't co6me to dinner with her and other lonely left-behind Wainscotia girls.) I wore the heather-colored cardigan sweater. I wore the Black Watch plaid pleated skirt. I even wore a strand of pale pink "pearls"—a dime-store necklace I'd found on a sidewalk on campus. In Wolfman's quiz section I was an attentive student but I did not raise my hand for Wolfman to call upon nor did Wolfman, in his coolly courteous way, call upon "Miss Enright." In a lapse of good judgment I even agreed to "double-date" (a term new to me) with Betsy and her Sigma Nu boyfriend; my date was a fraternity brother of his whose friends called him "Hedge," from a small town in northern Wisconsin. Hedge was taciturn and blushed easily. It was difficult to know if Hedge was chronically embarrassed or chronically irritated. He seemed not to know how to talk to me, and I certainly didn't know how to talk to him. He was a mechanical engineering major whose grades were mostly C's.

He'd been drinking beer before he'd come to Acrady Cottage to pick me up, and, at the Sigma Nu "keg party," in the basement of the sprawling red-brick fraternity house with its carpet stained from years of rough usage, he continued to drink with his friends, like one determined to get drunk as quickly as possible. The evening passed in a blur amid deafening music, voices and laughter, a smell of pizza and spilled beer. It wasn't surprising but it was dismaying to see Betsy drinking so much, "necking" with her date, and dancing drunkenly with him; after an hour or so, Betsy disappeared into the crowd, and I never saw her again that night. Hedge, flush-faced, seemed to want me to dance with him, too—or at least, he wanted to show his frat brothers that he was dancing with me, or clumsily pressing himself against me. He was very drunk: his belches stank of beer like popped balloons. At one point I hid away in a lavatory marked GIRLS ONLIE. I comforted freshman girls who were very drunk, and vomiting. I thought—*If Wolfman would love me. If Wolfman would just acknowledge me.* I wondered if, if I behaved recklessly, in violation of The Instructions, I would be "vaporized" by a Domestic Drone Strike here in Zone 9, and disappear before I felt pain or even fear. When I had the opportunity, and Hedge was nowhere in sight, I slipped

away from the fraternity house through the wide-
opened front door, and ran stumbling back to Acrady
Cottage.

How wonderful it was, to have escaped my first—
(and last)—fraternity keg party! How wonderful to be
alone, but not now lonely, running through a lightly
falling snow back to my residence, my breath steam-
ing! My roommates were all out on "dates"—I could
have wept with relief in the room.

Relief is happiness for those who, otherwise, would
have no happiness. But relief can be an exquisite
happiness, even in Exile.

Betsy never spoke to me about the keg party at
Sigma Nu.

Betsy did not speak to me very frequently, or very
warmly, about anything at all, for the remainder of the
time we roomed together.

(Though I'd overheard Betsy complaining bitterly
about me, for I'd embarrassed her with my "selfish"
behavior, in front of her Sigma Nu friends; and I would
learn sometime later that the night of the keg party had
not been a lucky night for Betsy, who would withdraw
from Wainscotia during winter break, and would not
return.)

When, all too often, I saw Hedge on campus, and Hedge saw me, we quickly looked away from each other.

The sudden, cruel thought came to me—*What does it matter if they hate me? They are both in their seventies by now, if they are still alive.*

This was the terrifying secret of Zone 9, of which its inhabitants were blissfully unaware: in the time that, to me, was present-tense, in the twenty-third year of the Reconstituted North American States, their lives were nearly over. If they were alive at all.

The Museum of Natural History

In December, I began part-time work at the Van Buren Museum of Natural History which was a sepulchral stone building adjacent to the Greene science building.

The Museum of Natural History was a shadowy hushed place which few people visited. In its dark interior, Time seemed to have stopped decades ago; in the rooms where fossils and ancient bones were displayed, thousands of years ago.

My work was carding and shelving books, for the museum included a special collection of rare natural-history books. My work was typing letters, documents, labels identifying items in glass display cases.

In Zone 9, much of work-life was reiteration. Office work was mechanical, robot-like. A typist was a kind of robot. You typed words directly onto a sheet of paper—the words were formed by (black) ink on a "ribbon" that wound through the typewriter on twin spools. Often you used a "carbon copy" to make a second copy, for there were no photocopying machines—there were no personal computers and printers. Everything was done *by hand.*

Everything was one-time-only, and yet would have to be repeated, usually. It was a kind of madness that could not have been explained in NAS-23. Office work inched slowly along deep-rutted grooves. It was commonplace to be required to type a second "ribbon" copy. There was terror in such repetition to no purpose save a replication of the original which might have been achieved by merely mechanical means—except, in 1959, these means did not yet exist.

Much of my part-time work involved (re)typing labels for exhibits. In NAS-23, such labels would be printed out within minutes, or seconds. Yet the task occupied hours of my time. My salary was one dollar an hour—before taxes.

In NAS-23, currency had been "reconstituted" in order to combat inflation. Still, everything was much more expensive than it had been in my parents' memory, they'd said—while their salaries, which were modest salaries, had been frozen for years. It was a profound surprise to me to receive so small a salary from the university—(equivalent to approximately one-half of a cent in NAS-23 terms)—and yet more of a surprise when I discovered that, after taxes, I was earning less than sixty cents an hour!

When I realized this, I burst into tears. My supervisor Miss Hurly said curtly, "Every one of us is taxed, Mary Ellen." She meant to encourage me by saying that if I continued to work well I might receive a raise of as much as twenty cents in the next semester.

Twenty cents! I laughed.

This was training, however. This was "experience."

Though the term did not exist in Zone 9 as it existed in the twenty-first century I was an "intern"—of sorts—I was accumulating skills, and a résumé, and, if I needed them, references for future employment. On Hilda's borrowed typewriter I had learned to type competently; in fact, it was not a very different sort of typing from what I'd been doing since the age of two at a computer. And then, I'd learned to operate the somewhat fantastical "office-model" Remington in the museum, which must have weighed twenty-five pounds. This was an enormous black machine with steel keys that could be made to fly through the air in arcs of about three inches, striking white paper and "printing" black-ink letters. Miss Hurly had taught me to remove old, used-up ribbons and replace them with new ribbons; these ribbons, amazingly, came equipped with both black ink (top) and red ink (bottom); it was not possible to remove a typewriter ribbon without getting my fingers smudged with ink, but I was proud of myself for having learned at all. Miss Hurly taught me also to clean the keys of gummed-up ink until they shone as if new.

Of my lost world of computers, cell phones, electronic pads and "readers"—I could have explained very little to any inhabitant of Zone 9. Even my memory of what these had meant to me, how I'd been habituated and addicted to them, seemed to be fading, like memories of my family and friends.

(And I wondered: Can you still love someone whose face you are forgetting? Whose voice you can no longer hear?)

(And I had to concede: If I had my cell phone here in Wainscotia, whom would I text or call? There was no one.)

Unexpectedly, I was beginning—almost—to like the typewriter. I could see why Hilda was so proud of her portable model, set beside which the massive office-Remington at the museum was high-tech. The most extraordinary fact regarding both was that they did not have to be *plugged in*—here were machines so primitive they didn't require power. I had learned to "set margins"—to "backspace"—to anticipate, like a subject in a behavioral psychology experiment, a tiny bell ringing near the end of a line. Most importantly, my fingers that had been accustomed to the light touch of a computer had learned with surprising alacrity to strike the keys down, hard. In the more popular keys, *a, o, s, t,* you could see the faint indentations of typists' nails.

Ghost-typists had preceded me in the shadowy interior of the Museum of Natural History.

My supervisor was a white-haired woman in her mid-fifties named Ethel Hurly who spoke in a hushed but stern voice as one might speak in a mausoleum. She had a large soft descending bosom and wore polka-dot blouses with bows at the throat. Her superior was the museum director, Professor Morris Harrick, whose Ph.D. was from Princeton in the field of "classical science" and whom I rarely saw. (Like so many of the higher-regarded Wainscotia faculty, Professor Harrick was from what had used to be, until the controversial Reconstitution of Higher Education in NAS-20, an Ivy League university.) I perceived that Miss Hurly was in love with Professor Harrick, who was himself white-haired, and in his fifties; with polished glasses, a distracted look, and a habit of blowing his nose loudly into white cotton "handkerchiefs." (These were actual clothes, small squares of cloth, invariably white, which men of a certain caliber or class used conspicuously, to signal, it seemed to me, that they had in their power or in their hire, in private, a female so trained that she would not bridle at laundering and "ironing" them, for his one-time use. Fortunately, for the rest of us, paper tissues had been invented by 1959.) Professor Harrick seemed to be married, for he wore a wedding band on the third finger of his left hand, and on the desk in his office there were small framed photographs of family members including young children. So Professor Harrick was a father, too! And very likely a grandfather.

It was touching to me that Miss Hurly adored Professor Harrick with no hope of his returning her feeling, or even becoming aware of it. I felt sorry for her even when she was impatient with me, surprised at my lack of skills and my general naïveté. (Once she'd said to me, "Mary Ellen, were you born in the United States? Sometimes you don't seem like an *American*.")

Morris Harrick was a dignified gentleman who not only carried a freshly ironed white cotton handkerchief in his vest pocket, but also wore a vest, a tweed jacket with leather elbow patches, a white cotton shirt and proper necktie, each day he appeared in the museum, or taught A History of Western Science in Greene Hall, immediately following Professor A. J. Axel's psychology lecture. Professor Harrick rarely spoke to me directly and scarcely "saw" me at all—he'd several times called me "Dolores," which was the name of another under-graduate girl–employee in the museum, whose work-hours didn't overlap with mine.

As I loved Wolfman at a distance, or consoled myself in my loneliness with the possibility of loving Wolfman, so Miss Hurly loved distracted Professor Harrick, for whom she was always typing letters, doc-uments, and manuscripts to be sent to learned journals in the professor's field. Miss Hurly showed me Pro-fessor Harrick's publications in these journals, which were impressive, and all but unreadable, as well as the professor's several books with such titles as *A History of Natural Philosophy from the Pre-Socratics to the Enlightenment,* published by the University of Wis-consin Press. Miss Hurly echoed Miss Steadman in her enthusiasm for the male academic intellect: "Pro-fessor Harrick has devoted his career to examining how 'false' theories of science have been replaced by 'true' theories through the centuries, to our present-time, mid-twentieth-century America. I don't know the details of course—but Professor Harrick's argument is very persuasive. He is another candidate from Wainscotia for the Nobel Prize."

I asked Miss Hurly if she'd heard of A. J. Axel and she said yes, of course—"One of Wainscotia's great minds!" I dared not ask her if she'd heard of Ira Wolfman, for a quaver in my voice might have given me away.

It made me swallow hard, struck with sadness to think of Miss Hurly and Morris Harrick and to realize that, in NAS-23, each had been long dead; and whether Professor Harrick had won a Nobel Prize, I did not know.

In the museum, often I worked late. I did not like to return to Acrady Cottage where I was obliged to impersonate "Mary Ellen" to my roommates and sister-residents.

Work was a narcotic! Work was my way of sanity, that prevented me from brooding upon my parents, my lost friends, Ira Wolfman—the colorful, tattered kites that Roddy and I had once made together, that were now long destroyed.

Daddy had once advised *One day, one hour at a time, honey. One breath. We can do it.*

(Not to me, Daddy had said these gently urgent words, but to my mother, I think. She'd been crying at the time, in their bedroom with the door shut.)

Resolutely I typed—retyped—labels for the display cases: the Latin names of flowers, fungi, birds and mammals; beautiful names, they seemed to me, because exotic, in a long-dead language. (In NAS-23, Latin was not taught in even the most esteemed schools.) And when I'd had enough of typing on the massive Remington machine, when my fingernails ached with the pressure of striking the keys, I turned to my textbooks, and my notebook, and worked on my assignments. It had not been difficult for me, despite my anxieties, to receive uniformly high grades in all my subjects, including now Intro to Logic; in the narrowness of my Exile-life, which yielded a private, secret depth like that of a chasm in the earth whose depth is not visible from the surface, it was not difficult for me to excel—most of my classmates seemed only moderately engaged with their course work, even scholarship girls at Acrady Cottage. The great, public life of the university was of the surface: football and other sports, "Greek life" (fraternities, sororities whose mansion-sized houses were predominantly ranged along the hilly end of University Avenue), "pledging," "dating." If I worked in the museum on Saturday afternoon I could sometimes hear, in the distance, a roaring of cheers like a frenzied and frothing waterfall from the football stadium at the far side of the campus, which was said to contain more than twenty thousand spectators! In the museum, empty except for me, it was scarcely possible to imagine twenty people, let alone twenty thousand.

Among Wainscotia undergraduates it was considered "square" to study hard, and to seem "serious"; to spend much time on studies was considered a kind of treason, if you were a "Greek." My grades of A and A+ were best kept secret as they were disfiguring to me as acne—(I knew: my roommates had frankly told me). Since the Sigma Nu beer party which I'd fled, and since Hedge, and my roommate Betsy's disappointment in me, I had had no "social life" at all—to my relief. For nowhere are you so lonely as in the midst of a party.

And nowhere do you feel so unloved as when couples are drunkenly pawing at each other, in a crude parody of love.

And when I'd had enough of my schoolwork, and my head and eyes had begun to ache with the effort, and something of the futility of this effort, I prowled the museum, switching on lights in the shadowy recesses—room after room, exhibits on platforms and on the walls, in display cases, what seemed like acres of fluorescent-lit gloom. In winter, when the sun disappeared in a bank of discolored clouds at about 5:00 P.M., it was pitch-dark by 6:00 P.M. as if it were midnight.

Even during the day there were few visitors to the

Museum of Natural History. Some of these were professional guests whom Professor Harrick and a colleague
or two might be showing through the museum, concen-
trating upon special exhibits. Some might be alumni,
or the parents of students. These visitors rarely stayed
long. Their voices too were hushed in the sepulchral
regions of the museum. Between rows of display cases
they moved like wraiths, staring briefly, then moving
on. If they glanced in my direction—shelving books,
or perched behind the giant Remington at a desk
adjacent to Miss Hurly's desk—they appeared startled,
as if one of the stuffed-creature exhibits had stirred to
life.

Wandering the museum after hours! At times I felt
an unexpected sort of happiness, at other times a more
profound sense of futility.

*No matter how much you learn—how high your
"grade-point average"—you are alone here. And no
one cares whether Adriane Strohl lives or dies.*

One of the famed exhibits in the museum was the
Van Buren Glass Flowers, which exerted a kind of
spell upon me. I thought of my mother—I tried to
think of my mother, Madeleine—(yet how strange this
name sounded to me now: "Madeleine")—who would
have admired the extraordinary flowers, ingeniously

wrought in glass of the most subtle hues: the most beautiful were orchids, lilies, exotic tropical blooms of the size of a human head. Yet the flowers were curiously scentless of course. A faint patina of grime lay upon even the most polished specimens, if you looked closely.

The most intriguing of the exotic glass flowers was a "carnivorous" plant from the Amazon rain forest—its elongated flesh-colored petals resembled a crocodile's (opened) jaws, and, in life, were said to be sticky-sweet to attract insects and small mammals. Out of childlike curiosity I lay my fingers on the (opened) petal, to see if the carnivore-plant would shut its jaws on me; but it did not, for it was made of glass, and never moved.

I tried to remember my mother's indoor plants: stunted specimens, which failed to thrive in weak winter sunshine, but which flourished, to a degree, in warm weather, when we set them onto our back steps. But what was their name? A very common name . . . And the blossoms were small, and bright-red. And had no scent.

I missed Mom so much! And Daddy.

And Paige, and Melanie, and . . . what was her name, whose father had been arrested?—Carla . . . ?

The punishment of Exile is loneliness. There is no

state more terrifying than loneliness though you would not think so, when you are not lonely; when you are secure in "your" life.

In these after-hours in the Museum of Natural History it seemed to me that there might be someone who'd stayed behind, until the museum had officially closed; or, more unnerving, a being in the museum whose presence predated my own. My heart began to beat quickly as I moved from room to room— switching on overhead lights, seeing shadows leap in the corner of my eyes. On the high-ceilinged walls were skulls, bones, near-complete skeletons of ancient birds and beasts; in display cases, rocks containing fossils, and more skulls, bones, and small skeletons. And there were stuffed and mounted creatures—such birds as hawks, owls, falcons, shorebirds and song-birds, a glassy-eyed bald eagle; such small mammals as red foxes, raccoons, squirrels, lynxes and bobcats, and on a wall an enormous elk's head with twelve-point antlers and shining glass eyes.

And a beautiful wolf with silver-tipped fur, a wise sharp dog-face, intelligent-seeming glassy eyes. *Canine x, indigenous to Wisconsin.*

Intensely the (dead) creatures seemed to be observing me. Theirs was a profound sorrow, all the more piteous for being mute. I saw that the labels attached to many of the displays were yellowing and supposed that, soon, I would be asked by Miss Hurly to retype them. I smiled at the futility of the museum—this place that felt underground, though it was on the first floor of the building; this place that Time had forgotten. For in the Museum of Natural History it was not even 1959.

A soft film of dust lay over all things. I expected to see, when I walked along the aisles, my footprints on the floor behind me.

I was smiling, in order not to cry. In one of the glass display cases I saw my own wan reflection floating, superimposed upon an exhibit of aged turtle shells, from which the living turtle-bodies had departed. Yet, I thought I saw one of the turtle shells quiver. Something was moving, reflected in the glass . . .

To my shock I saw then that a man was approaching me in the shadowy light, his hand extended. Wolfman! Smiling at me, a forefinger to his lips and the palm of his hand held out to me, upon which he'd written in bright red ink:

FOLLOW ME PLEASE

Shelter

I n silence Wolfman led me deeper into the interior of the museum.

Quickly I followed. I would have followed Ira Wolfman anywhere.

Like a sleepwalker who is but dimly aware of her surroundings but determined to behave as if she were in control of her movements, I followed.

Wolfman had come to *me*! I'd seen in his face a frowning smile, or half-smile—a pained sort of tenderness. *He is risking his life for me,* I thought.

I vowed then, I would love Wolfman with all my strength. I would die for Wolfman.

He knew the Van Buren Museum of Natural History, it seemed. He was not a stranger to its vast subterranean-seeming reaches. And he knew that I worked here—he must have made inquiries about me, to have such specific knowledge of my work hours.

Shyly I smiled at Wolfman. My heart was beating rapidly in my chest like a trapped bird!

Still without a word Wolfman took my hand, and pulled me gently—firmly—forward. His fingers clasped mine with startling familiarity. As in a dream of surpassing wonder and beauty we passed through rooms I had never seen before: entire walls festooned with songbirds perched on replicas of tree limbs, and a great flock of brightly colored warblers; a hall of "wetlands" creatures—rubbery stuffed frogs and toads, turtles of all sizes, snowy egrets perched on a single leg, mute swans, Canada geese, mallard ducks frozen in dark gelid ponds. Clinging to the underside of a tree trunk, a weak-eyed opossum. All these creatures seemed to be watching us, alerted by the life in our bodies.

Wolfman mouthed the words—*Don't speak! Not yet.*

We passed through a display of large mammals of the American West—antelope, deer, buffalo, bison, mountain lions, bears (black, brown); a display that was an enormous whale skeleton, through which we walked furtively, eagerly. And there was an enlarged photograph of the gigantic creature, on a wall facing us. Where was Wolfman leading me? I felt dazed with

happiness, or with dread. In my fantasies of Ira Wolfman I had not made out what we would say to each
other, if we were truly alone together. How we would
declare ourselves to each other, if we dared. I had not
allowed myself to imagine Wolfman actually taking my
hand.

I had not allowed myself to imagine Wolfman holding me, kissing me. My dreams of Wolfman had always
faded at that point.

As if to obscure our trail Wolfman switched on and
off lights as he led me through the museum.

At last we were in a remote corner of the museum,
far from the entrance. Here was a dimly lighted room
crowded with a miscellany of exhibits as if the museum
curator had run out of space and despaired of his mis-
sion, like a distracted Creator, and had stored here
crudely stuffed animals (small deer, lynx and bobcat,
rodents) whose fur was matted and whose glass eyes
were sunken in their sockets; trays of fossil rocks whose
labels had peeled away; unidentified skulls and bones;
and rattlesnakes coiled together on sheets of shale,
looking so uncannily alive with their small beady glass
eyes that I shuddered at the sight of them, and tried to
pull my hand from Wolfman's as he laughed at me—
"They can't hurt you, 'Mary Ellen.' They're under a
spell, too."

At the rear of the room, partly hidden behind a large display case, was a stairway, leading down; at the foot of the stairway was a squat-looking door cut into the wall. Set into the door was a combination of the kind affixed to safes and lockers and this combination Wolfman turned, and turned back, and again turned, with careful fingers, until the lock sprang open, and the door swung just slightly inward. And Wolfman took my hand more firmly now, and pulled me inside.

Wolfman shut the door. "Now, we're safe! No surveillance."

He'd switched on a light. Fluttering fluorescent lights, overhead. There was a smell here of the earth—damp, rich, rotted. We were on a cement landing. More steps led down, to a darkened lower level.

Wolfman tugged at my arm. I felt a moment's panic, that I must follow him—where?

Wolfman preceded me, down the steep cement steps. So that, presumably, if I grew faint, or lost my balance, he could turn and steady me.

We came to another, much lower level. The air here smelled ranker and was fiercely cold.

I rubbed at my eyes. My vision seemed blurred. I saw that we were in the outer room of a basement of some sort, with cement walls, cement floor and (cement?) ceiling; on the floor was a metallic-gray carpet, and on the walls signs containing elaborate instructions NUCLEAR ATTACK EMERGENCY PRECAUTIONS. Close by the entrance was a life-sized dummy equipped with gas mask, thick gray clothing and gloves and heavy boots.

It was impossible not to think that the uniformed dummy was somehow observing us, through his goggle-glasses.

"This is a nuclear bomb shelter, 'Mary Ellen.' You've probably never seen one before. There's another, larger shelter, better-equipped, for more elite members of the university community, in the basement of the administration building, which I know about but have never seen."

In wonderment and in dread I looked around. I could not help but think that, despite our distance from the surface of the earth, Homeland Security was recording us, and that we would be terribly punished.

Wolfman said that there were still bomb shelters in our time—in NAS—but only for Government officials. The average citizen knew nothing about them. But in the 1950s bomb shelters were much more common, featured in mass-market magazines like *Life* and *Time*, and on television; many private citizens built their own shelters in their basements—"Like an extension of the 'family room.' A place in which to be cozy though you would want also to be armed, to keep out neighbors."

Wolfman remarked that the nuclear bombs and missiles had been expected to come from the USSR—Soviet Russia, a "political behemoth" that no longer exists in NAS-23. He asked me whether in present-day NAS Russia was still one of the "terrorist enemies of democracy" and I told him that I thought so, yes, for there were a number of "terrorist enemies"; but Russia was an enemy with whom the North American States made treaties, in opposition to China which was NAS's great and abiding enemy.

Wolfman asked me who was president of NAS-23 but when I pronounced the name, Wolfman didn't recognize it.

Presidents of the Reconstituted North American States were heads of the Patriot Party. The general population knew little about them though they were believed to be multi-billionaires, or the associates of multi-billionaires. Their names were often invented names, fictitious names, attached to individuals or animated human figures replicated endlessly online and on TV; you were conditioned to "like" them by their friendly, smiling facial expressions and by ingeniously addictive musical jingles that accompanied them, as you were urged to "dislike" other figures. To attempt to learn facts about them was in violation of Homeland Security Information and could be considered treasonous.

Wolfman was saying that, for a long time after World War II, Americans had lived in terror of a *nuclear holocaust.* Schoolchildren as young as five or six were drilled in what to do if there was a sudden "nuclear flash"—they were to scramble beneath their desks, bow their heads and cover the backs of their necks with their clasped hands.

"For those fortunate enough there were shelters, stocked with provisions like this one. 'Shelter' was a booming business, for a while."

"But there was never any 'nuclear holocaust'?"

"As it turned out, no."

"But now—here in Zone Nine—they still believe it might happen? Russia might drop a nuclear bomb on the United States?"

"No, Mary Ellen. You don't say 'they still believe'— it's 1959, and it's natural for the citizens of the United States, in 1959, to believe in the possibility of a nuclear holocaust, not an aberration."

I felt a twinge of pain behind my eyes. I'd learned to deal with the perplexity of living in this bygone era *as if it were the present-tense* and not past; but I had not articulated the logic of such a life, and of course I'd never spoken to anyone about it.

Amused by my naïveté, or slightly exasperated by it, Wolfman said: "Yes, the citizens of the U.S., at this time, have a prevailing expectation of nuclear war. They can't comprehend it, really—any more than we can comprehend our own deaths, and the extinction of our identity. We are not capable of imagining ourselves, or our loved ones, *non-existing*. We are not capable of imagining tens of millions of human beings murdered in the twentieth century, in the great 'world wars,' in Soviet Russia and in Communist China. But the populace has been brainwashed to believe in the Communist threat, and to buy into bomb shelters and enormous stockpiles of weapons. Though you haven't had much history education in NAS since the Cultural Revolution of the Public Schools you must know about the Russian satellites of the 1950s—the two 'Sputniks'—and nuclear testing in Russia as in our American Southwest. It's a time of nuclear fetishizing. The Americans of 1959 don't have access to the 'future'—as we do—to know that there never was a nuclear holocaust and no bomb shelters were ever used by anyone. Nor was there a 'Communist takeover' of the U.S. government—or anything remotely approaching it."

"But—that's good news, isn't it? I think it must be."

Wolfman laughed. "You're a sensible girl, 'Mary Ellen.' Of course, you're right. Our parents would not have been born, consequently we wouldn't have been born, in the 'future,' if there'd been a 'holocaust' in this past. So yes, you are absolutely correct."

Strange that what Wolfman meant as "future" was in fact "past" to me—the past from which I'd been expelled. And for Wolfman, who'd been Exiled much longer than I had, this "future" was yet more past.

Seeing my look of confusion Wolfman spoke of post-war American politics: the so-called Cold War, the sinister power of Senator Joseph McCarthy, the army-navy congressional hearings, the "witch-hunting" of Communists by such "patriotic" federal justices as Harold Medina in the late 1940s and the defeat of the intellectual Adlai Stevenson by the popular ex-general Dwight D. Eisenhower. "The history of the United States was always a struggle between 'them' and 'us'— capitalists, and their wealth—and the rest of us. Not surprising, 'us' never had a chance."

Wolfman laughed, and shrugged. In this melancholy underground place, what did anything so abstract as *history* matter? You were aware of breathing, and of the need for oxygen; if something went wrong with the ventilators, you would soon cease to exist.

In such a situation, it was natural for me (I see that now) to gaze upon Wolfman with eyes that welled with both tears and adoration.

Here is my friend! My only friend.

This, like any responsible adult man confronted with the infatuation of a seventeen-year-old, Wolfman hoped to ignore.

"Just be calm, 'Mary Ellen.' This is ordinary life now. *Don't* become emotional—there is too much for us to lose."

With the air of an earnest TV advertiser Wolfman took me on a brief tour of the bomb shelter. He opened storage closet doors to show me the goods inside: floor-to-ceiling shelves with cans of tuna fish and salmon, peas, corn, spaghetti, and "fruit cocktail"; Campbell's soup—tomato, chicken noodle, cream of mushroom; boxes of Cheerios, Wheaties, and Rice Krispies; powdered eggs, powdered milk, boxes of sugar, and salt. A gigantic refrigerator (not turned on, and lacking a light) stocked with Pepsi and mineral water. In another storage room, more gallons of mineral water, gallon-sized containers of liquid soap, bleach. In another storage room oxygen tanks, bandages, stretchers, bedpans, canes, crutches, walkers, several collapsible wheelchairs. Rows of lockers. Lavatories, bathrooms. An unnerving sight of dozens of gray uniforms hanging together on a heavy bar like the husks of great insects. In the event of the nuclear holocaust, survivors were obliged to wear this gear? Including the thick-goggled masks? The prospect was so depressing, I could not bear to think of it.

Wolfman said, "They are like our ancestors, aren't they? They seem so innocent. But fortunately, nothing turned out as they'd feared."

The bomb shelter did not seem to be dust-free. You had to wonder what sort of long-dormant germs, bacteria, dwelt here biding their time. I had an impulse to glance behind me, to see if I'd left footprints on the floor. The air was barely circulating through vents and smelled stale, like soiled clothing.

In an assembly room a single console-model dwarf TV sat against a wall, gray-blank-screened, facing rows of seats. I counted the rows: fifteen. Seats in each row: twelve. More signs on the walls, with numbered instructions and cartoon figures. Here was an air of suspended drama as if a vital scene had been interrupted. On the metallic-gray carpeted floor, as if it had just recently been tossed down, was the crumpled cellophane wrapper of a Milky Way candy bar. Adjoining were two dormitory rooms containing as many as fifty beds each—"One dorm for each sex," Wolfman said. A grim sort of merriment shone in his eyes.

I asked if he had a place in the shelter, in case of an emergency.

"Of course not. I'm an assistant professor, I'm of no consequence at Wainscotia. I just happen to know about the 'nuclear bomb shelter,' as I make it my business to know about many things, and so I tracked it down, and learned the combination. In my former, 'subversive' life in NAS"—Wolfman lowered his voice, with a tilt of his head—"I was an 'outlaw-hacker.' I was pretty damned brilliant for my age if I say so myself—I'd hacked the computers at Homeland Security, Youth Disciplinary, Media Dissemination, Patriot Insurers, my own high school in Manhattan, and a few others. When they finally caught up with me I was twenty years old—but I'd been a star hacker for six years, and would've never gotten caught except a 'friend' informed on me."

Wolfman spoke so openly about his case! After his initial stiffness with me, it seemed scarcely believable.

Wolfman asked what I'd done to become Exiled—"It must be a paranoid time in NAS for them to Exile someone as young as you. Usually it's just incarceration at a youth facility and 'rehab'—'co-opting.'"

Apologetically I told Wolfman that I hadn't done anything nearly so "subversive" as he'd done—"At least not intentionally. I was valedictorian of my high school class and I'd written a speech—a series of questions— that our principal was afraid would get him into trouble with Homeland Security, I guess. No one gave me any warning or asked me to modify the speech—they just arrested me at commencement rehearsal, and took me away." My voice quavered. "I never saw my parents again."

Wolfman regarded me with concerned eyes. Though he meant to keep the mood between us light, matter-of-fact.

"What's your sentence?"

"Four years."

"Four years! That's nothing. Just enough to get a useless college education, and be *teletransported* back."

I didn't want to register *useless college degree*.

"How long is your sentence, Dr. Wolfman?"

"Call me 'Ira,' please. As we're kindred in Exile, so we're on a first-name basis. My sentence is eleven years of which I have just two to go before my case can be adjudicated—God knows what will come of that. I've heard of adjudicators who double the sentence, or worse. It's totally up to a five-man panel, you know."

"It is? I didn't know . . ."

I was feeling sick to hear this. But Wolfman tried to soften the blow by smiling at me.

"All decrees of Homeland Security are provisional. But they can be vacated, too—if your people can pay the requisite 'fine.' Didn't you know that?"

"N-No . . ."

I wondered: Did my parents know? Did my father know, that his MI status might have been revoked?

"But you'll do well, 'Mary Ellen'—you have plenty of time to prepare your case. As for me, I'm not eager to return home. I had enemies there. I was betrayed by people I'd thought were my colleagues. I've tried to make my peace with Zone Nine."

"Don't you miss your family? Your friends?"

"Of course, I did. For a long time I did. Most EIs suffer from severe depression for the first year of Exile, and are at risk for suicide. But I've been an 'orphan' so long, and my parents 'deceased,' I've come to believe my Exile-identity, almost. It's hard for me to think seriously of being 'reconstituted'—I'd be at risk of falling into my previous pattern—'L and S'—("Liberalism and Subversion")—and getting arrested again, and 'vaporized.' No one goes into Exile twice."

Rapidly I'd calculated: if Wolfman had just two more years to his sentence, I would be left behind by him. Already I was feeling a mild panic at this loss.

"I know that you've been taking your transition hard, 'Mary Ellen'—I've felt sorry for you but there wasn't much that I could do. Encouraging you to meet with me in my office, and to cry over your fate, would not be helpful. I've tried to keep our relations professional, and I will continue to do so. Tell yourself: Zone Nine isn't so terrible a place, set beside NAS. It may take you about eighteen months to become adjusted, as it did me. During that time I felt so totally estranged from everyone, it was like they were dead, and didn't realize it; or I was dead, and didn't realize it. I can't shake a feeling of pity for them—though I've come to like some of them. I even admire Axel—the die-hard behaviorist. I earned my B.A. from Wainscotia, for whatever that's worth, and my Ph.D. in experimental psychology; the department was so impressed with me that they hired me immediately as an assistant professor, due to the influence of A. J. Axel. In Zone Nine I have a kind of career I couldn't have in NAS since my personality is naturally 'subversive'—that's to say, skeptical—and 'questioning of authority.' It was astonishing to me that I hadn't been Deleted instead of just Exiled—I think they must have felt that my hacker skills were too valuable to destroy."

"Are there others like us here?"

"Scattered through Zone Nine, yes. Since I've come here I've encountered individuals, mostly male, who'd seemed to me fellow EIs—obviously. My first year, I looked for them everywhere. But I was wary of approaching anyone, or identifying myself. And the others were terrified, and avoided me. You're different of course—distinctive! You have the courage of youth, as few of us do."

Courage of youth. That did not seem flattering.

"Is there anyone you know like us—Exiles?"

"Well, possibly. I have suspicions. But I've kept my distance, as I've said. For of course you can't tell if someone is a spy, even in Zone Nine. I assume there are spies here, as well as agents of our Government. How they communicate with one another, how they travel from one zone to another—if they do—I don't know. Recall, cyberspace is 'eternal'—'timeless'—if you know how you can traverse it in any direction. My parents were scientists who'd been drafted to work for the Government—so I know some things about NAS cybertechnology—though my information has got to be dated. I do know that Wainscotia State University is the default university for people like me, and you, who have intellectual pretensions and have been 'subversive.' Wainscotia is the teeming petri dish of mediocrity."

Wolfman went on to speak with contempt of Wainscotia's "preeminent" men: Amos Stein and his team of physicists and mathematicians who were working on a "proof" of the steady-state universe, in order to rebuff those astrophysicists who believed that the universe was infinite, and infinitely expanding; Myron Coughland, an intellectual chauvinist who argued that the history of philosophy from the pre-Socratics to the present day culminated in the trivial babblings of American "positive-thinkers"; Morris Harrick, with his comically chauvinistic history of the "progress" of science, culminating in the present "Christian, Caucasian" era; another historian, C. G. Emmet, who believed also in the "progress" of humankind, culminating in twentieth-century northern European and American civilization, without any acknowledgment—at all—of the Holocaust—"As if it had never been." Wolfman spoke disgustedly.

And A. J. Axel himself, Wolfman's mentor, so steeped in Skinnerian behaviorism he'd stopped thinking as an experimental scientist a decade ago, and had no clue that a "cognitive psychology" revolution was close at hand—"Within a few years, B. F. Skinner will be finished. His 'great achievement' will be history, a fossil. I hope to leap clear of the wreckage if I can."

Wolfman spoke recklessly, defiantly. I was astounded by his words. For months I'd believed all that Miss Steadman, Miss Hurly, and others in the University community reiterated with such enthusiasm, that Wainscotia was a center of excellence—that we were all so very fortunate to be here. Now Wolfman was laughing.

"Why are you looking so surprised? Did you think that Professor Axel *was* a genius? Every place and every time has its resident 'geniuses.' A naïve fool who'd fallen for Walter Freeman's gospel of the lobotomy—at least Axel is extricating himself from that debacle after he'd witnessed a few deaths. His zeal now is 'social engineering'—shocking men and boys who are attracted to other men and boys until they're reduced to quivering masses of nerves, unable to be attracted to anyone, or anything, and likely to commit suicide. Which Axel won't include in his data since it falls outside the perimeter of his experimentation."

Wolfman laughed, seeing the expression on my face.

"But—but isn't Wainscotia—"

"No. Wainscotia *is not*. To punish 'free thinkers' for subversion they sentence us to 'the Good Place'—Wainscotia. One of those idyllic American campuses in the Heartland where no research or creative work comes to anything. No matter how much effort is poured into it, how much 'talent' and 'perseverance.' Perfectly intelligent scientists originally from decent East Coast universities here take disastrous turns, wind up in dead-ends—and won't realize it until they're embalmed and can't leave. No one is 'original' here—no one is 'significant.' A promising young astrophysicist from Cal Tech gave up his Ph.D. project in 'string theory' to pursue 'extra-terrestrial life'—that's it for him, until he retires. Scientists, mathematicians,

scholars, artists, writers and poets—even chemists—
nothing they discover in Wainscotia will outlive them.
Nothing they accomplish will have the slightest value to
anyone. Their heirs will hide away their self-published
autobiographies and melt down their gilt 'lifetime
achievement awards.' Their ideas are derivative, or re-
dundant, or just plain mistaken, silly. In the meantime
they live exalted lives at Wainscotia, as inside a bell jar,
like pampered bacteria. They win awards and government grants administered by their friends. They're
featured on the front page of the student newspaper
and the local newspaper. They may even make it into
Time, once. They're invited to give Sunday sermons.
Some are *worshipped* by their post-docs, as by the local
ladies."

This was stunning. Shocking. I listened in silence to
Wolfman's words like buoyant flames. It was clear that
Wolfman meant to be funny, and yet—Wolfman was
angry too, and sad.

It was true, I'd thought that Professor Axel's behaviorist psychology was limited in its scope and technique,
but I'd supposed that this was a limitation of my own;
what I'd learned of Freudian psychology hadn't seemed
more convincing, and had the added disadvantage of
being undemonstrable in a laboratory.

But—poor Morris Harrick of the Museum! I felt

particularly sorry for this elderly gentleman who seemed, like a species of underground mole, to have spent his entire professional life in a burrow, to no purpose.

Zone 9 would be my world for the next three and a half years. Its air of collective mediocrity would be the air I had to breathe, to survive.

I felt as if the ground were tilting beneath my feet.

Wolfman's cruel laughter turned into a fit of coughing. His skin looked clammy. I wondered if he was well.

He sat heavily in one of the chairs facing the blank-screened TV. The merriment had faded from his eyes. He regarded me as one might regard a child bright for her age yet handicapped in some way.

I would wonder why Wolfman had come to me at this time. Near the end of the first semester—when soon, within weeks, I would no longer be his student.

I would wonder if he'd followed me to the museum. If he'd made inquiries about "Mary Ellen Enright" of the Class of 1963, College of Liberal Arts.

I loved Wolfman so much, I needed to believe that Wolfman might love me.

After his initial ebullience in the bomb shelter Wolfman was quieter now, and looking rueful. I saw his fingers fumble for a pack of cigarettes in his shirt pocket—but fortunately he thought better of lighting up a cigarette in this airless space.

I thought how strange it was, Ira Wolfman *smoked*. As if he'd been born in Zone 9, and not *teletransported* to it.

The shelter filled me with a sense of dread. I could not believe that we were so safe in it as Wolfman seemed to believe. For why wouldn't Surveillance have followed us here?—I could not think other than that our Government of NAS-23 was capable of penetrating any barrier.

The terrible thought came to me—*Can you trust him? Wolfman?*

Wolfman said quietly, "Don't be afraid, 'Mary Ellen.' You can trust me, I am your friend in Zone Nine."

I told Wolfman yes, I trusted him.

And I love you.

But you know that.

Wolfman asked me my name, and I told him.

Wolfman asked me where I was from, and I told him.

Wolfman asked me to tell him what was in my heart.

Wolfman opened his arms to me, and I came to him.

And all that passed between us that night went unrecorded in the shelter beneath the Van Buren Museum of Natural Science.

The Sacrifice

I t was a famous behaviorist experiment of 1920 conducted by John Watson.

The eleven-month infant, Little Albert, had not been frightened of any animals until a gentle white rat was placed in his lap and a sudden loud noise of two steel bars struck together behind his head, several times in succession. Soon then, Little Albert began to cry at the very sight of the rat, as of a dog, or even a fur coat, and to exhibit symptoms of terror preceding the clanging of the steel bars.

We were shown a film in the lecture hall. Old, grainy, jumpy but unmistakable—the infant was convulsed with terror as the steel bars were struck behind his head, and soon he learned to hate and fear the gentle white rat he'd previously seemed to like.

One day I would ask Wolfman—Why hadn't the experimenter de-conditioned the infant, after the experiments? Hadn't anyone thought of this?

Wolfman said he didn't think so. Didn't think that Watson or anyone else had thought of "de-conditioning" at the time.

I asked Wolfman if Little Albert had grown up to be frightened of animals and fur coats and Wolfman said, No. The poor kid hadn't grown up at all, he'd died at age six.

Adoration

We don't have to see each other to be near each other. Remember, I am your friend.

Waking in the dark, in the Wainscotia winter. A half-mile away the chapel bell thinly tolled the hour of 6:00 A.M.

My final morning of exams! It was January 1960.

Hurriedly I dressed in the dark as my roommates slept. It had been my exam-week schedule to wake early and work downstairs in the study room, then run through the snow to the dining hall for breakfast, and then to my first exam which might be scheduled as early as 8:00 A.M. Today was my Psychology 101 exam, at 9:00 A.M. in Greene Hall.

I was nervous and excited. So badly I wanted to *excel.*

I wanted Ira Wolfman to be impressed by me. I wanted him to be proud of me, even if in secret.

Many times I'd studied the semester's material: notes assiduously taken at Professor Axel's lectures, and the textbook from which the lecture topics were taken, which A. J. Axel had helped edit. In my agitated sleep, I skimmed columns of (unreadable) print. I was underlining, taking notes. I woke with a headache, eager to be examined. I wondered if the microchip in my brain would affect my memory generally, or only just "censored" memories.

Wolfman had told me that there was no microchip inserted in my brain! He was certain.

They want EIs to think this. The effect is that we "censor" ourselves, through suggestion.

(I had no idea what to believe, now. Though I wanted to believe that Ira Wolfman was correct.)

My grades, as I went into the final exam for Psych 101, were A's and A+'s. I had virtually memorized my lecture and textbook notes. Yet I feared a sudden reversal of fortune, that would disappoint and disillusion Ira Wolfman and he would no longer want to be my friend.

Wolfman had informed his students that most of the questions on the final exam would be multiple choice, to be graded mechanically. There would be a few brief written answers, and a single essay of approximately 750 words. Wolfman had told us dryly that no new, original thoughts were expected on the exam, or welcomed:—"Each question has an obvious answer, and that's the answer that's correct. The other answers will be marked 'wrong.'"

Dr. Wolfman's attitude toward the course he was helping to teach had become ever more ambiguous during the semester. Often he seemed to be speaking ironically, as if reciting words in which he didn't believe. He seemed to be losing faith in behaviorism, which was the foundation of the Wainscotia psychology department and of the institute which A. J. Axel would be heading, to "cure" aberrant/perverse behavior. I wondered—did his colleagues notice? Did the other students notice? Or was I the only one?

Or was I imagining, in my obsession with Ira Wolfman?

From our State-monitored public high school I knew how to answer multiple-choice questions. At least 80 percent of our education was tested in this way; our teachers had taught us to take exams, essentially. Originality, subtlety, and skepticism were not valued.

The more you knew of the material, the more complexity you saw in it, and so the more difficult it often was to provide a simple, crude answer. Yet, if you were a canny exam-taker, you understood that only one answer could be "correct"—this was the answer you'd been drilled in over the semester. It was understood that Professor Axel's assistants drew up exams that followed his lectures and his textbook scrupulously; often, questions were really just restatements from either, which might be memorized. Only in essays could you hope to be original—but in essays you could also sabotage your own chances.

Wolfman would be grading my exam, since I was in his quiz section. He'd coolly informed me that he graded all student work "blind"—he wouldn't know whose work he was grading until he'd completed all the exams. And he never changed an exam grade—"I get it right the first time."

Since the museum I'd seen Ira Wolfman only a few, fleeting times outside class. He would not telephone me—of course. He'd warned me not to try to call him; or to write to him, or leave notes for him.

He'd said *When the semester is over. When you're not my student any longer.*

That night in the museum we'd remained together until a quarter to twelve, which was my curfew at Acrady.

Curfew! Only undergraduate girls at Wainscotia had curfews, not boys. It was an unexamined principle of male privilege, that no one seemed to have noticed; the precise hours of curfew, which varied from 11:00 P.M. weekdays to midnight on Fridays, 1:00 A.M. on Saturdays, and 10:00 P.M. on Sundays, had been devised by the dean of women.

That night, Wolfman had held me, and comforted me, and encouraged me to talk—to tell him everything, anything.

So long had I had no one to whom I could speak! Words had spilled from me, like tears. And tears spilled from me as well.

I had not been close to any boy, still less any man, in my life. The only man who'd ever hugged me was my dad.

There were many girls at Pennsboro High who were like me, in our discomfort with boys. My mother had said that this hadn't always been the case, when she'd been in high school she'd had friends who were boys, and boy-friends whom she'd "dated"; but times had been different then, teenagers hadn't been encouraged to spy upon each other, and inform upon each other, quite so much as they had been in the past twenty years.

And the boys at our school hadn't been sympathetic, mostly—like my brother Roderick they'd been opportunistic, untrustworthy, mean-spirited, mocking.

Across a narrow abyss we'd seemed to be regarding each other—female, male. There were no "friendships" but rather "sex-contacts" that were crude and curt and likely to be ridiculed online in ugly words or photos posted by boys.

Ira Wolfman was the first man I'd *loved*. The first man with whom I was *in love*. It would not discourage me that Wolfman didn't reciprocate my feeling for him—so grateful was I that Wolfman simply *existed*.

That night he hadn't kissed me except on the forehead, and lightly on the cheek, as you might kiss a fretting child. He'd laughed saying he was *way too old* for me. He wasn't *the kind of guy who takes advantage*.

I'd wanted to beg Wolfman—*Please! Take advantage.*

In The Instructions it was clearly stated: an EI is forbidden to *procreate*. But I had no thought of such a development—*pregnancy*. No more than any other Wainscotia "coed" did I imagine that such a quandary could happen to me; and I could take solace in the fact that Wolfman was indeed older than I was, a responsible adult.

I did believe that Wolfman was my friend. I did believe—(maybe)—that Wolfman might love me, in time.

I wasn't so desperate now. I wasn't so lonely now.

If Wolfman was in my life, I would not ever be lonely again. I thought.

Yet still I couldn't keep from seeking out Wolfman, in public places. No one could ever suspect us, in public places!

In the week following the museum, I attended a lecture given by a visiting professor of psychology from Purdue, which Ira Wolfman also attended, and at which he'd asked questions. Not a very interesting lecture—(on a behavioral topic involving a complicated schedule of "reinforcement" in primates)—but Wolfman's questions were lively and provocative; and I thought *But you must not call attention to yourself!*—for older professors were present, one of them white-haired A. J. Axel, and they might not approve of the young psychologist's manner.

In the lecture hall I'd watched Wolfman covertly. And Wolfman was aware of my presence, I thought. But at the end of the lecture Wolfman remained at the front of the room, talking with colleagues, and I left without speaking to him.

Just being in his presence suffused me with a sense of well-being, happiness. I thought—*That you exist in this world, with me. That is enough for me, for now.*

In psychology it is known: a mentally ill person can

have "insight" into her illness, yet the illness remains. As a physically ill person can understand the circumstances of her illness, yet the illness remains.

In love with Wolfman, how pathetic is that? When Wolfman does not love you.

The Searchers

It was a mistake. Would be a mistake. Maybe.

Attending a Friday evening Film Society screening of a "classic" western starring John Wayne called *Red River*. In the bomb shelter Wolfman had happened to mention that while he disliked the TV of Zone 9 he generally liked the movies; and so I'd gone to the Film Society showing with the hope of seeing him.

I'd arrived late. Not knowing where the Film Society was, going to another (darkened, locked) classroom building. Steep steps in a hill. And now making my slow way into the darkened room in—at last!—the right building, in a first-floor alcove. Where chairs were set up. At first, I didn't see Wolfman in the audience and hesitated, thinking I wouldn't remain—then,

I saw him sitting alone, in a side-aisle seat near the front of the room.

(Had he seen me? I wasn't sure.)

(I did not sit near Wolfman. I felt that this restraint would commend me to him.)

Since I'd begun studying what was called "twentieth-century psychology"—since I'd researched the history of behaviorism, predating B. F. Skinner—it had begun to seem to me that most human situations were analogous to psychological experiments. The usual experimental subject was a pigeon or a rat but some-times human subjects were used. You saw, or in some way experienced, a "stimulus"—the way you reacted was the "response." It was the case that, the more de-tailed and "objective" the description of the subject's behavior, the less the experimenter was likely to know what was happening; for one could not infer an inner life, a subjective mode of being, from mere observation. Inevitably, living things were perceived (from the out-side) as resembling clockwork mechanism. You wanted to protest—*But I am me! I am unique and ungraspable.*

But now I was here at the Film Society, where my (unreciprocated, futile, sublime) love for Ira Wolfman had drawn me. Was that not predictable? Had not (probably) Ira Wolfman predicted it? In a new and unexpected variant of a "Skinner box" everywhere I went, in Zone 9, I brought this (invisible) box with me, for I was at its epicenter.

Before Skinner, but not unlike Skinner, there were leading scientists who claimed that animals were essentially machines whose behavior could be explained in simple terms, and manipulated by conditioning; yet, there were scientists, if fewer in number, who argued for a kind of *vitalism*—a "non-material" essence that suffused living things. (These were likely to be scientists discredited by their colleagues, as in the case of a German named Hans Driesch.) In my life, in the obsessive nature of my thoughts, and in the circumstances of my Exile state, I saw myself as an experimental subject of some kind, for (of course) I was being observed, and "recorded"; but at the same time, in the emotion that Ira Wolfman aroused in me, and in my yearning for him, I saw myself as unique, secret, unpredictable.

My yearning for Wolfman was leading me to places I would not otherwise have gone. As if, slowly, another being was evolving who was both *Mary Ellen Enright* and *Adriane Strohl.* For the behaviorists also believed that the self is created out of the environment, and out of accidents in the environment, rather than out of the rigidity of genetic determinism. *We are what we are made to be—we must only not resist.*

Often I caught sight of myself in reflective surfaces, and was struck—stricken—by the person I'd become, in Zone 9. For an eighteen-year-old girl—(my eighteenth birthday had recently come and gone unremarked: I could not bring myself to tell Wolfman), I was *not young*. My skin was ashy, my eyes were stark and staring, my manner was vigilant, hyper-alert. I'd become one of those lab rats that has been frustrated or frightened or shocked (by electricity) so many times, it has lost its essential, original *ratness* and is something else now, almost a new species: a creature waiting to be defined by the next, possibly lethal stimulus.

Yet, my love for Wolfman couldn't have been inferred or deduced from my appearance. (I was sure!) This was my secret happiness.

How unexpected, the movie!—the "western."

At first I couldn't determine if *The Searchers* was intended as a sort of comedy, in its exaggerations, or meant to be serious—"heroic." It was riveting and even enthralling—as a cartoon would be to a credulous child. The Technicolor was luridly bright, the actors awkward in their dialogue, the music accompanying every scene, from the credits onward, distracting as a clattering of drums. John Wayne was not an actor I'd ever seen before—conspicuously he seemed to be playing "John Wayne." The camera was fixed upon him, often in close-up, at the center of every scene, and scenes were both melodramatic and slow-moving; you knew that something was about to happen by the "suspenseful" music, but it did not happen quickly. No one on-screen looked anything like an actual person in an actual situation—it was obvious that these were professional actors in costumes reciting lines of dialogue they'd more or less memorized.

Indians were the enemy here. Menacing near-naked savages who behaved cruelly in scenes of deafening violence followed by scenes in which Indians were shot off galloping horses, to fall heavily into sagebrush. Scenes in which Indians were treated "comically" were almost worse. And—so much killing of buffalo, by the John Wayne "hero"!

Yet, at the end of the film, many in the theater applauded. Even Wolfman!

After the lights came up viewers stood about discussing the film, which they seemed to take seriously. All, except me, were adults. Most appeared to be faculty members. There was much praise for John Wayne's "performance"; there was praise for the "direction" and the "western landscape." There was a pretentious sort of talk of the "myth of the American frontier." Almost, I'd have thought that these people were joking, as Wolfman often joked, but evidently not.

Myth. American frontier. Not a frontier to those who'd been living there.

Patiently I waited for Wolfman to turn to me, or at least to glance in my direction. Patiently I waited for the people with whom he was speaking to drift away and go home. I was feeling a kind of righteous indignation for I had not liked the bombastic film and I didn't think that anyone else should like it, either.

Wolfman was friendly with these people, but they did not seem to be psychology colleagues. There was a couple, who appeared to be married; and there were two women who'd come alone to the film, but had sat together, near Wolfman. I felt dismay, that one of the women, whom Wolfman seemed to know well, was lingering in Wolfman's presence, clearly waiting for him to leave, so that she could walk out of the student union with him. There was some fuss about putting on jackets, and fur-lined hats. The woman's hair was dark, and parted in the center of her head, where her hair had begun to turn silver. Her eyes were large, heavy-lidded, staring— like my own. She was not a beautiful woman and she may have been older than Ira Wolfman but her face was sharp-boned and striking and you could see that she was edgy, and intelligent. I could taste jealousy like hot acid in my mouth. For a dizzying moment I thought— *She is myself only older. They are Exiles together.*

But this was not likely. This could not be.

Their laughter was grating, like knives and forks clattering together. I did not realize that what I felt was sexual jealousy, which strikes like a virulent illness those to whom it is previously unknown.

They were even smoking cigarettes together! I hated them.

Still I waited unobtrusively, I thought, near the back of the hall, studying posters advertising upcoming Film Society movies including several "classics of the silent era."

Nothing is so depressing as films-to-come that, if you see them, you are destined to see alone.

Seeing me alone, a lone undergraduate at the Film Society, several people spoke to me. Except that I was very quiet, and avoided looking any stranger in the eye, for fear of seeing a glitter of recognition, I might have been "befriended" at the Film Society—this would have attracted Wolfman's attention!

Trying to overhear what Wolfman was saying. I did not like the high-pitched laughter of the woman with the center-parted hair. (I'd seen her glance in my direction. But I had not glanced at her.) At last, the little group broke up. The woman had no choice but to depart with her friends.

It would have seemed to the casual eye that Wolfman

had been ignoring me until now, not rudely, but incidentally, as if it had to be chance merely that a faculty
member and one of his undergraduate students were in
the same room together; now, he acknowledged me
with a frowning sort of smile.

"Hello, Miss Enright!"

My eyes were heavy-lidded, as if I'd been crying.
But I had not been crying. Until seeing Wolfman with
these strangers, I'd been feeling alert, excited, hopeful.

Wolfman understood, seeing my stricken expression.
But Wolfman would not indulge me in any public place.

He meant to be nice. He meant to be kind. His
questions to me were the questions a university instructor might make to one of his students, whose name
he probably didn't recall. Politely he asked me how I'd
liked the movie?—and was surprised when I told him
what I thought, for I hadn't spoken at all sharply in the
shelter, beneath the museum. I'd been meek and melting then but now there was a sort of adolescent vehe-
mence in my critique of the film, and an impatience
that others should pretend to admire the ridiculous
"western."

Wolfman laughed—"Whoa! I guess you aren't a fan
of John Wayne."

His manner, both startled and amused, reminded
me of my father.

I said, I thought the movie was insulting. It was so *simple*, and so *crude*. If I'd been a Native American, I would be furious. If I'd been a woman—

But of course, I was a woman.

Wolfman regarded me with a quizzical sort of admiration. You could see he was a man who liked being surprised. In a lowered voice, though no one was likely to overhear us, he said, "You'll get used to intellectual 'insult,' my dear. If you see enough TV and movies in the Happy Place."

Not wanting to leave my ranting subject I was saying how the women's faces were so *artificial*. And the way the Indians were shot off their horses, screaming as they fell. And the awful "musical score" that ruined every scene . . .

"No one behaved in the slightest way convincing. No one even *looked* convincing."

Wolfman said, "Movies aren't about the way people look, 'Mary Ellen.' Movies are about our perceptions of them."

What this meant, I didn't understand. But I thought that I would ponder it, instead of asking Wolfman to explain.

"You could do one of your behavioral experiments, following a western. Ask people questions with multiple answers, and you'd see that their bias against Indians has increased, and their general antagonism. Seeing so many people shot off horses, the viewers would want to shoot, too."

Like Wolfman's brightest student I spoke.

Wolfman laughed as if my idea was too fanciful: How could you establish that "bias" had increased? For all you knew, bias might have decreased. And how could you establish what had caused an effect, the movie alone, or other factors? Yet, Wolfman conceded that such an experiment could be revealing—except attitudes are not "behavior" and can't be measured.

Excitedly I said, "You could administer two experiments, one a few weeks before the movie, and one immediately after the movie. And why isn't a thought 'behavior'? It takes place in the brain—you could probably see it. Some sort of X-ray."

My head was feeling blurry. I was blundering into the "censored" area, I think—remembering something that, in January 1960, did not yet exist in experimental psychological research, and could not be articulated.

"Thoughts can't be X-rayed, Mary Ellen. Not yet."

"Well—*not yet.*"

We were speaking quickly, quietly. I would almost have thought that I'd clutched at Wolfman's hand, to keep him from running after his friends, and away from me.

For I was remembering—my brain had been scanned. A sequence of images had been made of my brain, to determine if I was lying or not.

(Hadn't this happened? In the Youth Disciplinary Division, Homeland Security?)

Wolfman was frowning, working his mouth in a way to signal me—*No more! Stop.*

An alarmed look had come into his face. Wolfman's brashness was calculated, and mine was—only just brash.

Quickly Wolfman walked away, without waiting for me to come with him.

I was left alone in the little movie theater, deserted except for the Film Society officers who were shutting things down. It seemed to me that quizzically—pointedly—they were observing me, but I did not meet their gaze, and quickly left.

A few minutes later I saw, outside, on the snowy walk in front of the building, the woman with the stark staring eyes, still with her friends, and now Ira Wolfman had caught up with them. In a loose group they walked off toward Moore Street for a drink in one of the pubs.

I did not follow. I wouldn't have given Wolfman the satisfaction.

The Test

Hurriedly dressing in the dark. I did not want to disturb my roommates. My thoughts were preoccupied with Wolfman, which was not a good thing—my thoughts should have been preoccupied with the upcoming psychology exam.

It was difficult to eat, so early. It was difficult to force down food. But if I did not eat breakfast, by 9:30 A.M. I would be famished. My eyesight would grow blurred. My mental capacity would be affected.

I brought my notebook with me. I would study in the dining hall, as I ate breakfast.

In the brightly lit dining hall there were very few students at 7:05 A.M. These were dark-skinned "foreign" students who sat together at a table near one of the windows, usually amid a sea of Caucasians except, at this early hour, the dining hall was near-deserted.

ST5 or ST6. A rare sight at Wainscotia.

The foreign students were not undergraduates but graduate students in such subjects as physics, chemistry, engineering. They were exclusively male. Their eyes, lighting onto me, registered something tentative and marginal in me, that was akin to their own sense of estrangement. Once or twice, the young men had beckoned to me to come sit with them; but I'd pretended not to have seen.

In their own countries, it was said, male and female did not so easily intermingle. Not before marriage. In beckoning to me the young "foreign" men excited themselves, testing the limits of their taboo. I felt dismay and dread, to be so considered, in their eyes, as an *object* of their (male) perception.

Especially this morning as I passed along the cafeteria line, I felt their eyes upon me. They did not seem so friendly. I fumbled placing on my tray a small glass of orange juice, a ten-cent waxed container of milk, a five-ounce box of cereal, two pieces of white-bread toast . . .

The smell of breakfast-food made my mouth water. I never realized how hungry I was until I smelled food.

Adriane! Is it—Adriane!

Adriane come sit with us.

(I didn't hear this.)

(Did I hear this?)

(No. I did not hear this.)

Pushing the tray along, and a roaring in my ears. The cafeteria worker who punched my meal ticket, a heavyset black woman with kindly creases in her face, asked if I was all right?—or maybe did I want to sit down, for a minute?

I must have seemed confused. I didn't seem to know how to answer her.

The woman took the tray from me, so that I wouldn't drop it. She set it on the nearest table, which was empty.

This all right, honey? You be fine here.

The roaring in my ears was near-deafening. I could not bear to look at the table of "foreign" students who were looking at me, and who seemed to recognize me.

They, too, were Exiles in Wainscotia. That had to be the explanation.

I drank a small mouthful of the orange juice, which tasted as if laced with turpentine. I could not manage to open the waxed milk-container. I ate some of the cereal, dry out of the box. The pieces of toast I cleverly wrapped in paper napkins to take with me, for the morning's ordeal.

I'd been in the dining hall less than ten minutes. When I left a half-dozen students were entering, stamping snow off their boots. These, too, were dark-skinned—"foreign." They were exclusively male. I saw their malicious eyes, savage-eyes, like the eyes of the doomed Indians in the western, whose fate it was to be shot off their horses. They smiled at me, and said something to me, words I couldn't quite hear, which I chose to believe were friendly.

In their wake I heard *Adriane? Adriane?*

Slightly mocking, ululating—*Ad-riane?*

So desperately I fled, I slipped on the icy pavement, and fell hard, the breath knocked out of me; but in the same instant I managed to scramble to my feet, and ran back to Acrady Cottage.

If I'd had a telephone number for Ira Wolfman I would have called him. I'd have cried into the receiver *There are other Exiles here! They know me.*

But then, a few minutes later, in a less hysterical state I thought that perhaps this wasn't the case: the dark-skinned young men were not actual students but virtual images, operated by an agent in NAS-23 as military and domestic drones were operated, at great distance, to confuse and terrify me; but primarily to tempt me into acknowledging them, and identifying myself to them, in violation of The Instructions.

That is, it had been a test. The first such test (so far as I knew) since I'd arrived in Zone 9.

If I'd spoken with them, if I'd acknowledged myself as *Adriane Strohl*, this would have constituted grounds for "vaporization"—on the spot.

The Exam

Discuss, in 750–1,000 words, the principles, techniques, and significance of Behaviorism in 20th-century psychology, and its possible and probable social applications.

The exam was several pages long, stapled together.

More than two hundred somber-faced Psych 101 students, in rows of desks in the university gym.

Proctors prowled the large echoing space, to discourage cheating.

(Yet, cheating in such large lecture courses was known to be "rampant" at Wainscotia. Almost, there was a tradition of such cheating at Wainscotia, the more brazen the more celebrated, especially by fraternity men, alongside a tradition of good citizenship, honor, integrity, and school pride.)

(At Pennsboro High no one cheated. Surveillance cameras and monitors were everywhere. And no one wanted to get a really high grade, in any case.)

Quickly I skimmed the exam. My heartbeat was pleasantly quickened.

I thought—*Around me, the Skinner box materializes.*

My initial impression of the exam was that there was nothing here that I didn't know intimately. For I had studied, studied, and studied like a rat in a maze who keeps running in hope of a reward even after the reward has been removed from the maze.

I considered the essay question which was both disappointing and provocative. I thought—*I can write something original, and "analytical." Wolfman would wish this.*

If I answered the questions with the obvious answers, like a creature in a Skinnerian experiment, I would receive a grade of perhaps 100 percent—no one taking the exam on this day was likely to receive a higher grade. But if I experimented with the essay question, for instance, a tracing of Darwinian evolutionary thought with regard to B. F. Skinner, and something of the historical background of behaviorism, before Skinner, I could say something unexpected, and interesting.

Wolfman will recognize my writing. Wolfman will be impressed.

He'd cautioned me not to write more than I needed to write. Not to range beyond the narrow scope of the course. But I was sure he'd only meant to protect me.

I took approximately twenty minutes to answer the fifty multiple-choice questions. Following A. J. Axel's eccentric manner of testing, the multiple-choice questions were not conventional. In each, you were asked to choose the single "correct" statement—or the single "incorrect" statement—of four statements. In this way, the tester was testing not only the student's knowledge of the subject but also the student's mental agility. You could know the "correct" answer but not feel confident about choosing it because of the other, competing statements. Perhaps this was unfair?—it was distinctly Skinnerian.

Around me, my classmates were shifting in their desks, sighing, running their fingers through their hair. These were laboratory rats being run through a maze!

Yet, there was nothing in the exam that had not been set forth clearly, and repeatedly, in Professor Axel's lectures. If the students had been receptive, passive vessels for information, they'd been programmed to give the correct answers now. We were the pigeons and rats of Skinner's experiments, behaving in ways to assure rewards and not punishments.

Something in me rebelled against this limitation—
the tyranny of merely correct answers!

In my logic course I had wanted to ask our professor if it was possible that x could be both x and non-x
simultaneously—but I'd known that my question would
have been greeted with a look of startled concern, as
one might greet the ravings of a lunatic.

In life, it is (invariably) the case that x is both x and
non-x simultaneously. But in formal logic, no.

*Your sentence is to surrender to Zone 9. You must
not resist.*

It was Wolfman's voice, in warning.

There was Wolfman in another part of the gym.
Restless on his feet. Fortunately he wasn't assigned to
my quadrant of the gym.

Wolfman knew, I could write a perfect essay. But
Wolfman deserved better, if he was going to read/grade
my exam. He would want to think highly of me. If only
in secret, he would want to feel *pride*.

Since the incident in the dining hall I'd been feeling
excitement, apprehension. Like one who has narrowly
escaped with her life, I felt both relief and restlessness.

I would write an "original" essay of 1,001 words! I
smiled to think this.

I would write an essay that would begin with several questions: *What is "free will"? What is "The Law*

of Effect"? What is entelechy? *What is "mind"? What is "the problem of imitation"?—Is there a "natural selection" of thought?* and then I would answer the questions, or rather, I would weave together provisional answers in a complex statement. I would refer to the history of behaviorism only in passing. I would not waste time stating obvious facts. I would be ambiguous, purposefully unclear. I would be highly critical of B. F. Skinner whom I would compare with the German researcher Driesch whose concept of animal *vitalism* allowed for something like a "soul" in both animals and human beings. I would write also of John Watson, Skinner's precursor, who'd made important discoveries in childhood conditioning, and whose boast of having the power to "create" any sort of human being out of rough, raw materials was thrilling, as Watson's behaviorism seemed to repudiate any sort of fatalistic/genetic determinism. And I would write about Darwin—of course. Charles Darwin was one of Wolfman's scientist-heroes.

Then—midway in the essay—a brilliant idea came to me: *I would write in the voice of a maze-rat!*

I would deal with the riddle of subjectivity from the point of view of the (hapless, powerless) subject. Whether "interior" states are in fact measurable as exterior states. How to measure the seemingly immeasurable. Can a shadow be dismissed as non-existent, because it has no weight? Yet, a shadow has visual properties. A shadow can be *perceived.* Is there something inside the brain that receives, organizes, and interprets sensory perceptions? Is this something the "self"—is this "self" the "soul"?

I hadn't time to return to the beginning of my essay, to make the rat-voice consistent. I would hope that Wolfman would smile, and be impressed.

So deeply immersed in my maze-rat essay, like a rat in the innermost depths of a maze, I was shocked when proctors announced that there were just five minutes remaining before blue books had to be turned in—already, it was 10:25 A.M. But I wasn't finished!

Heedlessly, thrillingly, like one plunging down a steep hill, and not yet at the foot of the hill, I'd covered a dozen pages in the blue book, I'd written more than 1,001 words, I was sure; I'd intended to go back and edit what I'd written, and I'd meant to insert several important footnotes . . . Though the gym was not over-heated, I'd begun sweating inside my clothes. I glanced around for Wolfman but didn't see him—he must have been at the rear of the gym, behind me and out of sight.

Three more minutes!

To my dismay I saw that my "original"—"brilliant"—essay hadn't turned out as I'd hoped. It was too ambitious—too diffuse. It was rather a précis for a fifty-page paper—a critique of behaviorism. In the rat-voice I'd digressed onto a secondary issue, the "social consequences" of behaviorism, and realized too late that I had lost precious time. I had neglected to set down the principles of behaviorism—these were so elementary, and so often repeated! I could not see the point of setting down what was obvious. My head was aching from tension, and from a lack of sleep. My thoughts were becoming jumbled like laundry in a dryer. I could not escape the accusing eyes of the "foreign" students who knew me as one of them, unless the "foreign" students were agents of the State. (Or were they but "virtual" images? I had not approached them to see if, horribly, I might have been able to pass my hand through one of them as the others looked on, snickering.) One lengthy paragraph, on page six of the blue book, a paraphrase of several passages from Skinner, had been x'd out by error, in my hasty editing; I saw now that the paragraph was required for my argument, and could not think how to eradicate the effect of the X. I'd memorized the passage from Skinner, or anyway most of the passage, which I'd read independently of our textbook, in a primary work, Skinner's *Science and Human Behavior* (1953):

What is meant by the "self" in self-control or self-knowledge?

The self is most commonly used as a hypothetical cause of action. So long as external variables go unnoticed or are ignored, their function is assigned to an originating agent within the organism. If we cannot show what is responsible for a man's behavior, we say that he himself is responsible for it. . . . The practice resolves our anxiety with respect to unexplained phenomena and is perpetuated because it does so.

Whatever the self may be, it is apparently not identical with the physical organism. . . . A self is simply a device for representing a functionally unified system of responses.

In quoting and paraphrasing Skinner, somehow I'd come around to seeming to agree with him—I could not now remember what I'd objected to, initially. I was struck also by Skinner's remarks on the "absence" of self-knowledge—this, too, from the primary work, and not our textbook: *One of the most striking facts about self-knowledge is that it may be lacking.*

There was something terrifying here. And yet utterly clarifying. If I could not know myself, I could not know anything—if the lens is smudged, the vision will be smudged.

My pen fell to the floor. My blue book was filled with smudges, sentences crossed out, misspellings. But now, there was no more time—the last of the blue books were being gathered by proctors, most of the desks in the drafty gym had been vacated, a frowning proctor was approaching me with his hand extended—"Miss? Exam's over."

Like Wolfman the proctor was a quiz section instructor. Obviously, he didn't know "Mary Ellen Enright"—Wolfman had not mentioned to him that he had a brilliant undergraduate this semester . . .

With a polite smile I surrendered the blue book. My skin felt bathed in sweat. I was deeply ashamed. Yet, I was suffused with hope. *Wolfman will be impressed. He will see that I could have written an A+ paper, but tried for something more. He will—forgive me.*

When I stood from my desk my legs were weak. I looked around for Wolfman—he was halfway across the gym, stacking blue books into a pile. He and another proctor were laughing together. The exam-ordeal was nothing to the proctors as observing rats running a maze, or pigeons pecking desperately at a key that refuses to move, or a cat reacting in terror when it is shocked, is nothing to experimenters.

Throughout the two-hour exam Wolfman had ignored me. Or perhaps Wolfman had been oblivious of me. At about the halfway point there'd been a mild commotion in another part of the gym, where a student or students had been caught cheating, or (possibly) had become suddenly ill; while I'd been hunched over my essay I'd heard lowered, intense voices, and I'd heard the sounds of someone being led from the room, but I had not glanced around. I wondered if Wolfman had been the proctor involved.

I took some time to put on my fleece-lined jacket, which was heavy, and tugged at my arms. It was very cold outside: nine degrees Fahrenheit.

Strange how, in Zone 9, there was true winter. In our sector of NAS-23 there had not been "winter"—low temperatures, snow—in decades, though my parents spoke nostalgically of "winter" as of other phenomena now bygone, mere memories.

Then, I left the gym. I was one of the last students to leave the gym. A shining light fell upon me as I stepped outside.

Everywhere were banks of snow. Blinding-white.

Wainscotia Falls, Wisconsin, was a place of snowy hills, tall trees topped with snow. It was a place of beauty, I thought. Yet—it was not *my place*.

I did not want to die here. So far from anyone who knew me or loved me. Or felt responsible for me.

In the fresh frigid air my breath steamed. I realized that I was very tired though it was only mid-morning—the entire day stretched before me, unfathomable. I thought—*If I fail, I will lose my scholarship. I will be vaporized.*

Stumbling and short of breath I ran in the direction of the central campus. I did not glance back to see if Wolfman might be following me nor did I hear Wolfman, or anyone, call after me—

Adriane! Ad-riane!

The Failing Grade

Wolfman said, "I told you."

"Told me—what?"

"Not to be 'original.' Not to be 'analytical.' Just give the answer—the minimum."

Stubbornly I protested, "But the exam questions were all so obvious. I could have written the answers in my sleep."

Wolfman laughed. I felt a hot flush rise into my face.

I said, "I thought Professor Axel might appreciate a response that wasn't like every other response. I thought, if you showed the essay to him . . ."

"Are you serious? Axel hasn't glanced at an undergraduate exam in twenty years. Even an A+, which you didn't get, Axel wouldn't trouble to read. Graduate students don't interest him, let alone undergraduates."

I was stung by Wolfman's casual remark. *Which you didn't get.*

Still stubbornly I said, blinking back tears of disappointment, "I wasn't thinking of a grade, Ira. I didn't write the exam for a grade. I didn't learn the course for a grade. I didn't do all the outside reading I did, for a grade. But I'd thought—"

Wolfman squeezed my icy fingers, which had the effect of stopping my mouth.

"It's over now, 'Mary Ellen.' You didn't fail, except by your own exalted sense of yourself. And I am not your instructor 'Dr. Wolfman' any longer."

Wolfman My Love:
Selected Memories

"'Adriane.'"

Only when we were alone did Wolfman call me by this name. He would be the only person in Zone 9 to call me by this name.

And when we were in a public place, or a quasi-public place, he called me "Mary Ellen" or, more often, "Miss Enright." It did not matter that no one was near us, as in the university arboretum where we walked sometimes, not holding hands, not touching, but close together as companions.

We hadn't returned to the bomb shelter. We'd begun going to Wolfman's apartment, after dark. Where we rarely stayed long.

As Wolfman said, now we weren't instructor and undergraduate, it was not *wrongful* for us to see each other, as it would have been otherwise.

"Still, you're too young. Or, I'm too old."

Slyly I thought—*Yes. But I can wait, to catch up with you.*

Once, and then a second time, I'd made my way through the Museum of Natural History, to look for the steep steps descending at the rear of the museum, and the entrance to the bomb shelter. I recalled the combination lock that Wolfman had turned carefully in his fingers, but of course—I could never have recalled the combination itself, I hadn't seen so closely.

It was strange, I hadn't been able to find the entrance to the bomb shelter.

Each time, I'd lost my courage and returned to the lighted area at the front of the museum. I'd heard Miss Hurly call my name, or a sound of voices in the library, visitors expecting to find someone on duty at the checkout desk, and hurried breathless back to my post.

In a vexed voice Miss Hurly said, "Mary Ellen, where were you? I called and called you—I went to look for you in the museum—but couldn't find you. And now—here you are."

"But Miss Hurly, I was here all along . . ."

The woman did not believe me, that was clear. Once, Professor Harrick was waiting for me also with a stack of documents to be (re)typed.

In a mild panic I thought—*But where have I been, if I haven't been here?*

"That's ridiculous. That never happened."

Wolfman laughed at me, when I'd begun to tell him about the "foreign" students in the dining hall, who'd seemed to recognize me as an Exile, on the morning of the psych exam.

"You were hallucinating out of exhaustion and worry. Just forget it."

"But, if I see them again . . ."

"You won't see them again, Adriane. I promise."

And then: walking with Wolfman on Quad Street, south of the campus.

In this public place we were not—quite—a couple. Rather, we resembled individuals who'd happened to meet by chance and were walking together in the same direction, by chance.

A tall man of about thirty, bareheaded, with thick dark hair, dark eyebrows, a face that glowered with thought. A girl not yet twenty, in a heavy fleece-lined jacket that hid her hair and part of her face, and seemed a size or two too large for her. A girl intensely aware of the man beside her.

This was late Saturday morning, in February 1960. Following a night of snowfall. And the sidewalks, and the streets, hastily shoveled and plowed, glaring white.

We had not been together the previous night. (Where Wolfman might have been, I had no idea. Whom he might have brought back to his apartment, I didn't want to speculate.)

Let's meet. I want to see you. How have you been?—so Wolfman had contacted me.

Since the psych exam when I'd failed to follow Wolfman's advice and Wolfman had punished me with a bare blunt C on the exam, and a B in the course—"That should have been an A. But isn't."

I'd felt rebuffed. But I'd thought—*What does a grade matter? I am fortunate to be alive.*

And I thought—*No grade can matter in Exile.*

Since the psych exam there'd been a precarious sort of tenderness in Wolfman, toward me. Mingled with exasperation, and concern. I didn't want to think that this was the kind of feeling an individual might have for a younger sister or brother.

In this public place, with so much to say that could not be said safely in any public place. I wanted to take hold of Wolfman's arm, or grab his (gloved) hand, but didn't dare.

Wanting to ask him if, the night before, he'd been with any woman—the woman with the stark staring eyes, for instance, who so clearly liked him. I'd found out that her name was Cornelia—"Nelia"—she was an older graduate student in social psychology. *But no. You must not intrude. His private life is his own. He is not your lover.*

It was then that I saw, as we were crossing the street, several dark-skinned young men approaching us. These were graduate students, obviously "foreign"— their eyes moved onto me, and onto Ira Wolfman, and back onto me, with expressions of intense *interest*— almost, I'd have thought *recognition.*

In that instant I was stricken with fear. As we passed the young men I could hear them speaking in undertones to one another in their unintelligible speech. *They are talking of us—are they? What are they saying?*

In a daze I managed to cross the street but on the curb, I came to a dead stop. Like a laboratory creature that has been conditioned by a menacing visual stimulus to "freeze"—can't comprehend why he has been overcome by paralysis—I shut my eyes and stood very still until Wolfman prodded me.

Wolfman asked what was wrong?—and I told him,

in a barely audible voice, "Those were the students—just now."

"What students?"

"The 'foreign' students. Who'd seen me—I think they'd recognized me—in the dining hall last week . . ."

Wolfman glanced behind us. "Who? Where?"

Were they gone? Had they never existed? I could not bring myself to look around.

"How would you know who they were? You didn't memorize their faces, did you? 'Foreign' students all look alike, in Wainscotia, Wisconsin."

Quickly I walked along Quad Street. Nearly colliding with pedestrians. Slipping-sliding on the slick sidewalk, so that Wolfman had to take hold of my arm, to steady me.

"I saw them, Ira. I did. They saw *us*."

Wolfman laughed in his way of dismissal, that was also a way of comfort.

"Maybe they were psych students. Graduate students who'd been auditing Axel's class. Maybe they know *me*—nothing to do with you at all."

We'd left the Moore Street commercial neighborhood, that was hardly more than two or three blocks. We were on the university campus now, making our way steadily uphill in the direction of the main library. Around us was a snowy expanse blazing with noontide light. Seeing that I was very quiet Wolfman took hold of my wrist that was bare between my jacket sleeve and my glove—a gesture of unexpected intimacy, in this public place.

"Didn't I tell you, Adriane—there is nothing to fear from them? There is no *them*."

I believed that Ira Wolfman loved me then. In some way, that was perhaps not a sexual way, or a way of possession, he loved me.

A beautiful place. I wanted to think, a safe place.

This was the university arboretum, north of the campus.

In the NAS-23 that both Ira Wolfman and I knew there were no longer "public" lands—desirable city and state parkland, and 90 percent of the old, national parks like Yellowstone, Grand Canyon, Yosemite had been sold to private interests, mining, fracking, logging, and vacation places now for the very wealthy. Trespassing on these lands was now punishable by death. (The most egregious felonies in NAS were in the category VPR [Violation of Property Rights] second only to Treason and Questioning of Authority.) Beautiful privately owned shore lands along the Atlantic and Pacific coasts were protected by ten-foot electrified fences and gates manned by armed security guards. The only "parks" remaining for public use were vacant lots filled with rubble, wetlands and landfills, uncultivated land contaminated by chemicals and waste. (The Burnt Fly Bog Superfund in New Jersey, ten miles from Pennsboro, was claimed to be "safe" for picnicking and water sports but it was rare to see any visitors there above ST4.) And so it was a thrilling surprise to me to discover the Wainscotia arboretum.

Wolfman, too, loved the arboretum. It was the place that had "restored his sanity" when he'd first arrived in Wainscotia, a dazed and demoralized twenty-year-old who had been, at the time of his arrest and *teletransportation*, a brilliant undergraduate at NAS-Cambridge (formerly Harvard) majoring in computer science, math, and cognitive psychology.

Wolfman had been a runner, too. But in Zone 9, in the early 1950s, the only individuals who "ran" were athletes in training. And the only "running shoes" were ordinary sneakers.

The Wainscotia Arboretum adjoined the Wainscotia Agricultural College but extended for hundreds of acres into forestland abutting Wainscotia Bay, that emptied into vast Lake Michigan to the east—which I'd never seen except in photographs and on a map. (The lakeshore fell outside the ten-mile radius of my

official confinement, as, to the west, the much smaller
Lake Hallow lay outside my confinement.) By February 1960 I had not ventured more than two or three
miles from the epicenter of my residence in Zone 9,
which was Acrady Cottage.

Wolfman spoke disparagingly of his "epicenter"—
which was Greene Hall on the university campus.

"If I want to, I'll leave—maybe. Just walk away. Or
better yet, bicycle."

When Wolfman spoke in this way I felt both thrilled
by his bravado and uneasy. He said:

"It has been observed, in laboratories, that animals
in cages are sometimes fearful of leaving their cages,
even when their doors are left open. Even when their
doors have been removed."

"But—this isn't us, is it? I don't understand."

Was Wolfman saying such things to test *me*? Did he
want to determine how reckless I was, or how diffident?
In the desperation of loneliness I'd many times fan-
tasized running away from Wainscotia, and violating
The Instructions—but I'd never come close to such a
dangerous act.

I didn't doubt that I was under surveillance in Zone 9.
My figure was projected onto a screen, somewhere. If
I left the ten-mile radius I might be "vaporized"—
instantaneously.

For hadn't I witnessed the vaporization of the high school boy Z., in a DDS attack? Hadn't I seen the expression of incredulity on Z.'s young face, in the instant before his head exploded like a nova?

I'd begun to tell Wolfman about seeing the execution on a TV monitor in the Youth Disciplinary Division of Homeland Security, but Wolfman cut me off short—"If it was a TV monitor, you were probably seeing just a reenactment. You have no way of knowing if the execution was authentic."

"It was authentic! It was actual, and horrible. There were four of us being interrogated—high school valedictorians who'd been given 'Patriot Democracy Scholarships.' We were told to confess to being conspirators, and if we didn't, one of us would be 'disciplined' . . ."

"There is absolutely no way for an ordinary citizen to distinguish a 'virtual' staging from an 'actual' event. Especially via TV. Believe me!—I know."

Why was Wolfman not more sympathetic? I knew that the boy, whose name had begun with Z, had been executed—it was no reenactment, but actual death. I *knew*.

Domestic Drone Strike: a matter of less than sixty seconds to liquefy the subject, with a laser ray emitted by a flying object no larger than a robin, that self-implodes at the strike-target and is itself vaporized.

I was trembling with indignation, and anxiety. The boy's death was a sight I would not ever forget for, unlike other recent memories, it had been imprinted vividly into my brain.

"Maybe you've never seen a DDS, Ira. I have."

This was a sad little boast. Wolfman seemed about to reply to it, then did not, hiking briskly ahead of me.

On this bright sunny-snowy day we were hiking in the arboretum. Our breaths steamed for it was well below freezing. We took care not to walk too closely together and we did not ever grip hands—of course. Often, Wolfman walked ahead of me, like an expert hiker showing the way to a less expert hiker. We did not usually talk much for Wolfman preferred silence in the arboretum. He'd told me, in an undertone, hearing other hikers chattering to one another, how he'd like to *vaporize* these rude people who ruined the silence and beauty of the arboretum for others.

This was shocking to me. Just the term—*vaporize.*

How could Ira Wolfman of all people say such a thing, even in jest?

When he was alone Wolfman hiked for miles. His legs were ropey with muscle. When we were together usually we hiked for no more than two miles, along a looping trail through snowy hills. Many of the trees in the arboretum were identified with little plaques so

a hike in the arboretum was educational, like prowl-
ing through the Museum of Natural History; though
after a snowfall the plaques identifying the trees were
likely to be obscured. Often after a snowfall the arboretum wasn't immediately plowed and so, hiking
there, as Wolfman insisted, we had to make our way
in knee-high boots along the trails that were difficult
even to discern when covered with snow. It was my
fear—(Wolfman laughed at this fear)—that we might
go off-course, and unintentionally violate The Instructions, that forbade EIs to go more than ten miles from
their epicenters; Wolfman thought it was ridiculous to
imagine we could hike so far unintentionally, and even
so, if we did, Wolfman doubted that there would be
consequences.

It was Wolfman's belief that outdoor settings were
"safer" than indoors, generally; the vast reaches of
the arboretum were safer than the university campus;
though no place was as safe from surveillance as the
nuclear bomb shelter beneath Van Buren Museum,
where it was certain NAS surveillance couldn't reach.

Initially I'd had no reason to doubt Wolfman. When
he'd led me down into the bomb shelter I'd been so
astonished, so intimidated, I had not been capable of
thinking clearly. But in subsequent weeks I'd come to
wonder how Wolfman knew what he claimed to know

about surveillance systems in faraway NAS-23, beamed at Wainscotia, Wisconsin.

In a bemused undertone Wolfman told me: "Their security isn't perfect—NAS. We're not continuously on their radar. They want EIs to think that they know everything about us, but they can't possibly. For one thing, and this is basic, Wainscotia isn't *wired.* There's no cyberspace here. There's no grid. It's like 'atoms and the void'—preceding creation. They may have agents here, but they can't have many. Back home, in our time, it's taken for granted that everything is 'monitored'—every cell phone or computer transaction, anything electronic. We take for granted that we're being recorded—like lab animals in cages, who've been born into captivity. But Zone Nine is very different. That's why they call it the 'Happy Place.'"

But—who called Zone 9 the Happy Place? I didn't understand.

"And the connection between 'future' and 'past' is tenuous. It isn't 'Big Brother is watching you'—not at all. It's my theory that the aperture could shut down— the connection could snap like a rubber band—they could lose us, and never see us again."

This was not altogether comforting to me. If I understood Wolfman correctly.

"You mean—we would never return home? We would be permanently exiled here?"

Wolfman laughed. "Yes, it's pretty suffocating here—our 'hotbed of mediocrity.' But the alternative is not so obviously superior, is it?"

I wanted to protest—I missed my parents. I loved my parents and wanted desperately to see them again—I hadn't been allowed even to say good-bye . . .

Wolfman hadn't left behind anyone he'd loved much, evidently. Or, if he had, his Exile had been so long, his feelings had atrophied.

"Something could very easily happen in NAS, to render the Government powerless. Ordinary citizens are unaware that there are contentions within NAS—the president has his faction within the Patriot Party but there are other factions, too. There are secret dissenters, rivals. There are military uprisings that are quelled—or maybe not. In this case, it would be a 'cyberspace' uprising—whoever has control of the computers has control of NAS. The so-called leaders of NAS are invisible to us but hardly to one another. Their 'power' depends upon electric power. It's the most elemental source of power, generating a vast computer-system. It's all generated by wind now but it isn't foolproof and one day, the entire structure could just go *down*."

Such rapture in Wolfman's voice, I knew that he had fantasies of returning to NAS in triumph. The bright brash rebel-Exile who returns, overcomes his enemies, takes away their power and takes their place.

I wondered what Wolfman's role had been in NAS-23. Had he been more involved in the Government than he'd told me? Clearly he was of a caste higher than my parents'—my father was an intelligent man but lacked the confidence of Ira Wolfman, even in Exile.

Half-pleading I said, "I wish you wouldn't say those things, Ira. I—I want to go back . . ."

"Yes, they control you in exactly that way, Adriane. All 'Exiles' think they yearn for home—until they return to it."

"That's a—a terrible thing to say, Ira . . ."

"Why? Isn't it true?"

"I love my parents, I m-miss them . . ."

On the verge of tears. Throat shut up tight.

Didn't want to think that this might be true, to a degree. Painful, how much of what Wolfman said was true. To a degree.

Often as a high school student I'd been moody, sad, angry, even despondent—so *trapped* by the perimeters of my life, and my parents' lives. I'd felt sorry for my parents and (maybe) impatient with them, as a child might be impatient with her parents, unable to comprehend the complexities of their lives.

To return to a variant of that life, knowing what I knew now of the power of the State, would be difficult.

Yet, I was feeling elated suddenly. Wolfman had called me "Adriane."

I heard love in his voice, when he called me this forbidden name. I heard tenderness, respect, regard, concern—friendship and protectiveness. Of course I also heard amusement, condescension.

I heard *intimacy*. This was the most precious gift to one in Exile.

Now that I was no longer his undergraduate student Wolfman did treat me slightly differently, as if I were more adult. In the spring of 1960 I was enrolled in five new courses but I was not continuing with Psychology 102, not just yet.

Wolfman, too, thought it was a good idea that I wasn't continuing the course this semester. If I'd had a different quiz instructor Wolfman would have been overly curious about my work for this person, and how he was grading me; and if I'd been assigned to Wolfman a second time, our relationship would have been a strain to both of us.

(I did admire Wolfman for having read my final exam "blindly" and for having graded me as honestly as he had. I'd been hurt—of course—for we always want to be assured that we are special; but Wolfman had certainly done the right thing. He had not compromised his academic standards for even a fellow EI. He had not made me feel beholden to him.)

I said: "You call me 'Adriane'—you know my true name. But you have never told me your true name."

"That's right."

"But—why not?"

"My name is what you call me, Adriane. Anything you call me—that's my name. My birth name is of no significance."

"But—why can't I know it? You know mine."

"I've grown to fit 'Ira Wolfman.' I think I might prefer it, as a name to attach to my publications. And in any case it's close enough to my original name."

"Which is closer—'Ira'? Or 'Wolfman'?"

"Both."

"Is 'Wolfman' a—Jewish name?"

Wolfman laughed at this. Telling me that yes it was, but no, not, rather an "Anglo approximation" of a Russian-Jewish name back in the early twentieth century.

Despite the deep snow (which no other hikers had yet penetrated) Wolfman had been increasing his pace by degrees. It was a habit of his—I didn't want to think that it was a stratagem—walking in front of me on a trail so that my breath was taken up with the effort of following him and not with the effort of speaking with him.

Several times I staggered in the snow. My heartbeat began to hurt. I was beginning to be overwarm inside the shabby fleece-lined jacket.

Wolfman don't leave me! Wolfman please protect me.

High overhead the sky was a bright blue like china and when we passed beneath trees, dark-winged birds fluttered in the highest branches, calling to us in hoarse cries, like crows, or starlings, with indignant yellow eyes.

And sometimes, we met at the Rampike Street Laundromat.

Warm-yeasty smells of the Laundromat. Soft collapsing sounds of laundry tossing in the dryers. In this era before cell phones the place was often quiet even when relatively crowded for the clientele was mainly graduate students, who brought their work with them. (Most undergraduates had access to washers and dryers in their residences. Acrady Cottage had these, in the dank basement, but I preferred the more impersonal Laundromat where I might meet Ira Wolfman.)

This was a place of refuge, it seemed. There was a

soothing and dreamlike air here. You would not ever be "vaporized" in the Rampike Street Laundromat, such a thought was preposterous.

Initially we'd met by accident at the Laundromat. But ever after that I'd contrived for us to meet.

I'd offered to iron Wolfman's cotton shirts damp from the Laundromat. This was not an era before wash-and-wear fabrics but such fabrics were considered cheap, and were in fact cheap. Cotton and linen were more formal, and more desirable. Wolfman had a half-dozen long-sleeved cotton dress shirts which he wore when he lectured. When he wore a tie he loosened it soon after lecturing and, as soon as he was off campus, pulled it off saying he felt choked—"Literally."

It was a novelty—*ironing!* I'd seen advertisements on the Acrady TV. "Housewives" happily ironing their husbands' shirts.

In Wolfman's sparely furnished three-room apartment on Myrtle Street there was, kept folded upright in a closet, an ironing board with a badly scorched covering, and a shiny iron so heavy it nearly fell from my hand the first time I lifted it. (The ironing board came with the furnished apartment.) These were artifacts of an old, vanished America of which I'd had but a glimmering awareness for I'd never seen my mother "ironing"—we'd lived in a post-cotton era, of quick-drying and wrinkle-less fabrics.

I wondered what my mother would have thought of her daughter wielding a heavy iron like a pioneer woman! Yet—I would have liked to assure her—there was some small comfort in the task.

If you love the task. If the shirts belong to some-one you love. If you are not forced to "iron," but have chosen to "iron."

In NAS-23 there were households in higher-caste neighborhoods in which servants were employed. In some households, a team of servants. These were usu-ally of the IS (Indentured Servants) caste which meant desperate individuals who, having no money, and being very likely in debt, entered into contractual relation-ships with employers for a prescribed number of years; many, indeed most, but not all of the IS were ST5 or lower: dark-skinned. You would not call these *slaves*, which was an offensive term, not even *indentured servants*, but simply "servants."

To this Wolfman observed *Hey! I didn't make you my friend to make you my servant. I'm not colonizing you, Adriane.*

Still Wolfman appreciated the ironed shirts. Other-wise he'd have had to take his shirts to a laundry, which was expensive and a nuisance. (It seemed that Wolfman, for all his skill as an experimental psychologist, wasn't capable of ironing his own shirts. Why was this? A masculine deficit?) And yes, Wolfman appreciated my cleaning dishes he'd left to soak for days in the sink of his "kitchenette." And to scour the sink itself, and put away things in cupboards and drawers.

Colonize. This was an ambiguous term.

For the *colonized* might be complicit in such an arrangement. In Skinner's rat mazes the rats soon learned that treats awaited them when they ran the gauntlet correctly. And so, why not run? Why prefer being locked in a cage?

And we prepared meals together, Wolfman and me. And ate meals together.

I waited for Wolfman to kiss me more forcibly, to suck at my lips so that my breath was drawn from me. I waited for him to run his hands over my body which was eel-like and yearning, that would have wrapped itself around him if he had. I waited.

Yet we lay on Wolfman's bed, in the semi-dark. Quietly talking, or not talking.

So that I thought—*This is the happiest I can be. I want this never to end.*

Listening to Wolfman's favored music, on what he called *long-playing records:* symphonies of Mozart,

Beethoven, Brahms, Mahler. In his own time, growing up in New York City of the Reconstituted North American States, he'd had virtually no contact with classical music but only the electronically driven post-rap "heavy metal" music of his generation which was generic and anonymous.

It was a surprise to him, Wolfman said, to discover music that was labyrinthine like thinking and feeling commingled. Music that didn't need to be deafening to penetrate the soul.

(Did Wolfman, a scientist, really use the term "soul"? I think he did—unconsciously. For often Wolfman spoke in extravagant ways when feeling, and not just thinking, was involved.)

Wolfman had been kindly, asking me to speak about my life. Less easily, he spoke of his own.

There were secrets in Wolfman's life, I had to suppose. He was older than I was by a decade, at least—of course, more secrets would have accrued.

One evening he told me about his parents. His voice trembled with childlike wonder and another, less definable emotion—a kind of elation verging upon terror.

He had not seen much of his "famous" parents while growing up, he said. But he'd admired them—very much—for they'd been distinguished research scientists at the (former) Columbia University Medical Institute, epidemiologists whose specialties were bacterial diseases of the tropics. Unfortunately, at about the time Wolfman had begun middle school, his parents' highly publicized findings brought them to the attention of the Defense Strategies Department; soon then they were drafted into the MRP (Military Research Program) where their (secret, classified) assignment was the cultivating of strands of virulent bacteria to be "weaponized." Their work of several years was with a particular species of bacteria that could exist only within a narrow environment, to be targeted by the military in case of a declaration of war with one of NAS's many enemies. ("As you know, 'Declaration of War' is *ex post facto* since the War in the Middle East," Wolfman said dryly. "It's so much wiser to declare the war after it has begun, not before.")

At first Wolfman's parents, particularly his mother, had been upset by the nature of their new research; then by degrees they were drawn into the competition and excitement of the work-team at MRP, which employed the most prestigious research scientists in the country. "My parents received all sorts of special perks including a rent-free condominium overlooking the Hudson River, a car and a driver, joint election to the National Academy of Sciences, and virtually unlimited funding for their research; also, for me, their only child, admission to the most elite prep schools though I'd never been a 'good citizen' as a student, and had actual demerit marks on my record. As it was, I went to three private schools before I finally managed to graduate. I'd told you, Adriane, that I'd been a computer hacker in middle school. I also created video games, several of which were bought by Nightmare Works, Inc., when I was twelve, and became modest best sellers, and several of which were considered so politically dangerous, and so obscene, they were banned. I was the Mystery Teen who'd penetrated security at Congress in December, NAS-11, and sent a flotilla of toy 'drones' into the legislators' midst as they were debating one or another lobbyists' bill—you probably wouldn't remember, you were too young at the time. But it was everywhere in the media. It was a real scandal—if a teenaged kid could breach congressional security with toy domestic drones what about our enemies with their 'sophisticated weaponry'?—everywhere online and on TV. "

Wolfman laughed. He was drinking beer from a can, set atop a copy of a journal called *Brain* on his bedside table. I was feeling dismay at what he'd told me about his parents but said nothing to Wolfman.

"The legislators panicked of course—stampeded and trampled one another in their desperation to get out. The few females in the room, legislators and aides, were stomped and injured. Fortunately, no one was killed. I'd planned to perfection the onslaught of the toy drones—but hadn't given much thought to what would follow. That's a kid's brain, typically—no matter how bright, the kid is immature. Immediately, I stopped hacking for months, not wanting to get caught. My parents knew nothing about my 'experiments'—they were wholly innocent. I wouldn't have been tracked by FCS—Forensic Cyberspace Security—except a 'friend' informed on me. By this time I was a freshman at NAS-Cambridge—formerly Harvard. My parents tried to intervene for me but failed. Unlike you, I was incarcerated in a Youth Facility for a while—the Government was hoping to co-opt me in one of their 'defense security' programs but I refused." Wolfman swallowed hard, and fell silent.

Lying beside Wolfman, just lightly touching him, the side of my upper body, the side of my legs, I held my breath wondering what he was not saying.

I asked Wolfman about his parents: Had he been close to them? Had they confided in him? What had he said to them, the last time he'd seen them? (For in my case the last time I'd seen my parents I had had no idea that it would be the last time. I was sick with regret that I'd probably been my usual moody self-absorbed self, and could not even clearly remember what we'd said to each other. Oh, terrible!) Did he know if they'd been arrested too, in connection with his arrest? Did he know what—if anything—had happened to them after he'd been arrested?

Wolfman didn't answer immediately. Wolfman gave the impression of one who is searching his mind, trying to recall, like a man with a wide rake dragging the rake along the ground.

"I—I think—they are all right. I think so."

Then, "Well—my mother suffered some sort of breakdown, and had to be hospitalized in a NAS facility in Bethesda, Maryland. This was after my arrest. While I was incarcerated."

I asked Wolfman if he'd seen his mother, since his arrest? If she was still hospitalized?

"I—I'm sure my mother isn't hospitalized after so long. I've never heard—never been informed—exactly what happened to her, or even if—if she's still alive."

I asked Wolfman if the interrogators had tried to make him confess to having been "influenced" by his parents?—"That's what they tried with me."

"No."

Wolfman's answer came too quickly. I could feel heat lifting from his skin as he lay beside me, only part-consciously aware of me, staring at the ceiling.

"I—I do miss my parents. I guess. Just now, I could 'see' them—almost—as I hadn't seen them in years." Wolfman began trembling. I was shocked, but I held him tightly. It had not been the case in my life, that I'd had the opportunity to comfort others.

I thought—*I can love him more than he knows. I am strong enough to love for him, too.*

Wolfman said, "I was 'drafted' too—but managed to be phased out. Not at DSD but CSD—Computational Strategies Division—a younger generation, with some extreme personalities. Of course, they'd all been co-opted. No one so vindictive as those who've been co-opted by the enemy. For much of their energy is fueled by *shame.*"

I wondered what Wolfman meant by this? But I didn't feel comfortable about asking him.

"What happened was—it was a stupid mistake on my part. Inadvertently I'd texted a friend, using a code we'd devised, which aroused suspicion . . ."

Wolfman was saddened. Wolfman couldn't continue.

Wolfman pressed his face against my neck and we lay together in silence comforting each other in our separateness, our ignorance.

"I love you."

I spoke softly, tentatively. So quietly, Wolfman could pretend not to hear.

SANE

The voices were pleading yet bold: "Come join us! March with us."

And: "Save your life! The lives of your loved ones! Save the life of the Earth! March with us."

A chorus: "Come join us! March with us. Come join us! March with us. *S-A-N-E*—now!"

But I held back. I was very frightened.

I remembered—my father had been arrested at a public demonstration when he'd been in his mid-twenties. He'd paid for the remainder of his life for that single impulsive act of curiosity and sympathy.

And my uncle Toby—he'd paid with his life.

A large rowdy crowd had gathered in front of the university chapel, spilling onto the snowy campus green. Was this a spontaneous sports rally? A parade?

The mood of the crowd didn't appear to be cheerful or festive but rather angry, jeering. Were they heckling marchers? But why were they heckling marchers? In Wainscotia everyone was so *friendly.*

Dirt-tinged snow lay in heaps beside the walks and drives. It was an overcast afternoon in March 1960. On my way to class I'd been hearing voices—shouts—a sound of agitation and derision that was upsetting in this place, for it was unusual. Only on Saturday afternoons in the football stadium, in football season, did such excited calls and cries waft across the campus, or on weekend nights on the Hill, where fraternity and sorority houses glared with festive lights.

My instinct was to turn the other way. I could take a back-way to Masson Hall, to my literature class, and avoid the commotion.

Yet somehow I found myself pressing forward. Curiosity drew me, and a sense that, if something was happening on campus, I would want to know what it was, to discuss it with Wolfman. Through each day I accumulated incidents, episodes, paradoxes and riddles to present to Wolfman for his reaction. For I wanted to entertain and intrigue Wolfman, badly I wanted to be essential to the man's life.

Go home! God-damn Commies go back home to Russia!

I saw that the loose, rowdy crowd had surrounded a small group of marchers who'd been making their way from the chapel to the administration building across the quad. Just as I'd arrived the marchers had had to halt midway. There were about thirty of them, ringed in by as many as two hundred individuals of whom most appeared to be vociferous male undergraduates. The marchers were carrying picket signs, swords in vivid red letters—

SANE

NATIONAL COMMITTEE FOR A

SANE NUCLEAR POLICY

SANE

NUCLEAR TESTING—

STOP STOCKPILING WAR

Demonstrators for peace! They were protesting U.S. nuclear experimentation in Nevada and in the South Pacific—protesting war. I had heard of this newly formed national organization, in fact Wolfman had spoken of it with reserved admiration, but I'd never met anyone who belonged to it. I had never seen a "peace march" before.

The hostile jeers of the crowd, raised fists and angry

faces—these were shocking to me. *Commies! Traitors! Go back to Russia, you don't like it here.*

How contorted with hatred, the usual bland-white midwestern faces, and how shiny their eyes with rage!—you could not comprehend the power of so small a gathering of protesters, the effect of their hand-made picket signs, to rouse such emotion.

Campus security guards were holding back the hecklers and simultaneously urging the SANE marchers to leave the area. Security vans had arrived to carry the marchers away in safety. Yet, the SANE protesters resisted. Bravely and stubbornly, they resisted. They were strangers to me though it would be revealed, in the student newspaper, that several protesters were on the Wainscotia faculty, and several were graduate students; most of the protesters were from Milwaukee and Chicago. They ranged in age from mid-twenties to mid-sixties or older. Many white-haired, and a scattering of bearded men. The elders appeared to be the leaders. A revelation to me—at least one-third of the protesters were female.

Eagerly I looked but saw no one I knew—at first, I'd thought that Ira Wolfman might be among them. (He wasn't. I felt relief yet also disappointment.)

The crowd wasn't dispersing, and the marchers remained where they were, prevented from marching across the quad but brandishing their handmade signs aloft. Their chanting was drowned out by the shouts of the crowd. When they passed out pamphlets most of the pamphlets were taken rudely from them, torn and tossed down.

I thought—*How can they take such risks? How are they so brave?*

No one would be shot down or "vaporized" in Zone 9. Yet surely there were federal agents, F.B.I. informers, in Wainscotia. I'd learned from Wolfman of the Cold War, the anti-Communist hysteria, Senator Joseph McCarthy's campaign of slander, innuendo, and persecution. To be anti-war, anti-weapons, anti-nuclear was to risk being persecuted as a Communist in 1960 though there was, legally, *freedom of speech* and *freedom of assembly* in the United States at this time.

Subsequently, sometime in the troubled years post-9/11, these freedoms were curtailed, or banished outright. It had happened easily, Dad had said—at the time, few had seemed to notice.

Many of the hecklers were fraternity boys. A scattering of agitated girls. To my dismay I saw my roommate Hilda among them. And others from Acrady Cottage. Their faces were baffled, stern, indignant. They were "scholarship girls"—how did they perceive the SANE marchers as threats? Several young men in ROTC uniforms were shouting at the marchers, approaching them in a threatening manner.

Badly I wanted to support the SANE marchers. I felt sympathy for them, and shame that the Wainscotia students were so hostile, and so ignorant. I thought that the marchers must be nervous or anxious, in this chaotic place, yet they appeared calm, and they were certainly courageous.

A voice bellowed through a bullhorn—*This is University Security! We are asking you to evacuate the quadrangle! Evacuate the quadrangle immediately! Everybody—no exceptions!*

The noisy crowd was beginning to back away if not disperse. The marchers were smiling in relief. Some, in giddy relief. Several young women sighted me, and must have seen the sympathy in my face for they began chanting, "Come join us! March with us! Save your life! March with us!"—appealing to those of us who hadn't shaken fists at them or turned away in disgust.

Yet I held back. I had not the courage, or the recklessness . . .

"March with *us*! Save your *life*!"

As the marchers began moving away, tramping through the dirtied snow, I followed after them. No one could hear me, I think, but I was calling to them, trying to tell them that I was sympathetic with their ideas for war was "evil"; I told them that they were very brave and that I respected them—"Where I come from, people can't protest the way you are doing."

(Oh, what was I saying? Fortunately in the din and confusion no one heard me.)

One of the male marchers approached me. Was this someone I was supposed to know, from one of my classes? A burly youngish man built like a wrestler with coarse flyaway hair, a scruffy beard, urgent eyes. Evidently he was one of the SANE leaders—I'd seen him being confronted by the head of the campus security police. Unexpectedly he smiled at me—"Hey! Hello! You and I know each other—yes?"

"We do?"

"What's your name?"

"My name is"—I faltered, for the name seemed so obviously fraudulent—"'Mary Ellen Enright.'"

"'Mary Ellen'—whatever. Come with us! Here's a sign."

"But I can't. I have a class . . ."

"Hell with your class, 'Mary Ellen'! Come with us! Save the Earth."

"I—I don't think there will be a nuclear war . . ."

Weakly I stammered this. What was I thinking of!

The burly young man stared at me bemused.

"'Don't think there will be a nuclear war'—what the hell, you *don't think* there will be a nuclear war? How in hell can you say such a thing? You're a prophet? You can see into the future? Nuclear weapons have already been used—atomic bombs dropped on Hiroshima and for no God-damned reason anyone can explain, Nagasaki. Why not again? Why not many times? The president is a U.S. war general, the U.S. Congress are rabid anti-Communists, there is plenty of profit to be made from the Cold War, so why not a nuclear war? How can you make such an irresponsible remark, 'Mary Ellen'?"

I was mortified, the burly young man stared at me with such disdain.

I stammered an apology. I said that, even if there wasn't a war, it was important to educate people against nuclear war. It was important to support SANE.

"Yes! Right! Come with us! March with us!"— the young man grabbed my hand and pulled me after him; I was too surprised to resist, and he was too strong in any case. He gave me a picket sign which I brandished as the others did. I was very excited by this time, suffused with emotion. *These are my friends. My family.*

I asked the young man what his name was and he said what sounded like *James, Jamie.*

Now came a resurging of hostility. A swarm of yelling frat boys storming the quad from a new direction. *Commie traitors! Bastards! Get the hell out of Wainscotia!* The picket sign was wrenched from my fingers. Someone collided with me, hard. I found myself on the ground, in the snow. I saw only legs and feet—I heard only shouts and screams. Then, I saw the SANE regrouped marchers being escorted off the quad by security police. One of the white-haired leaders was bleeding from a cut in his forehead. The burly young man who'd given me the picket sign was running as a football player might run, aiming his right shoulder at—whoever it was, I couldn't see.

The crowd was breaking up another time. Sirens were deafening. Emergency vehicles were driven onto the quad. Hecklers were being pushed back. Marchers were being escorted into vans, unresisting now. Picket signs lay strewn in the snow, many of them broken. Pamphlets lay scattered and torn. The SANE demonstration of March 11, 1960, at Wainscotia State University, Wisconsin, the first such demonstration at the university in its history, had ended in a sort of stalemate after a tumultuous forty minutes.

Back at Acrady Cottage girls looked at me in surprise as I limped inside.

"Mary Ellen!—what on earth happened to you? Did those awful 'SANE' people knock you down?"

Wishing I could tell my parents about the demonstration—the "march for peace."

No one was arrested.

No one was beaten or (badly) bloodied.

Had the march been a failure, or a (qualified) success?

That there'd been a demonstration for peace at all seemed to me a wonderful thing.

My shoulder ached where someone must have run against me to knock me down, the way guys knock one another down in football. My right knee ached from the fall. And there were scratches on both my hands. But I was elated, and anxious—as if a border had been crossed, that could not be recrossed.

I'd limped away from the scene. I was thirty minutes late for my class. Yet I would go to class, I would not miss a single class for I was determined to be an A student here in the Happy Place, Zone 9.

The rest of that day my eyes repeatedly glanced up, narrowed. Steeling myself for the quick-darting appearance of *domestic drones* en route to vaporize us all—though the year was 1960, and the setting was idyllic Wainscotia, Wisconsin.

NUCLEAR PROTESTERS ROUTED FROM CAMPUS—next day's banner headline in the student newspaper. Photographs of outraged Wainscotia frat boys shoving back protesters. (The burly young man built like a wrestler might have appeared in one of the photographs, seen from behind: I looked.)

In the local newspaper, the *Wainscotia Falls Journal-American*, the banner headline was less friendly:

COMMIE PICKETERS ROUTED
FROM WSU CAMPUS
"Outside Agitators" Blamed

That evening, Wolfman telephoned me.

For the first time, Wolfman telephoned me at Acrady Cottage.

Did the girl who picked up the phone in the parlor understand what an extraordinary event this was, that Mary Ellen Enright had received a telephone call?

Any telephone call. From anyone.

Most remarkably, from her psychology instructor.

Benumbed I came to the phone. I had no idea who would call me and could only think that I was being informed of something unhappy.

I had long given up the foolish fantasy of my parents calling me.

Dad's voice—*Hiya, kid. How're you?*

Mom saying—*Oh, Adriane. Oh . . .* Bursting into tears.

"'Mary Ellen'? Hello."

No need for Ira Wolfman to introduce himself. Of course.

"Ira . . ."

"What did you do, this afternoon? What the hell did you do?"

"You mean?—the SANE protest . . ."

"How could you do such a reckless thing? Participate in a mob scene? Call attention to yourself in an act of 'civil disobedience'? The SANE people didn't have permission to march on campus—they were defying orders. Their request had been turned down. They're very lucky they weren't all arrested, taken away in vans. Their heads broken." Wolfman paused, breathing audibly. I knew better than to try to interrupt. Relenting he said, "It's good of them to come here. It's foolhardy but—noble. I admire them but—look, you can't possibly get involved. I can't possibly get involved. There will be no nuclear holocaust—not as they are imagining it. No Russian-provoked conflagration. So, that's that. They don't need us." Again Wolfman paused.

Then: "You know there are spies here. You know that 'Mary Ellen Enright' is under surveillance. Everyone who participated in that demonstration will be noted in FBI files. And probably in university files."

"But, Ira—it isn't against the l-law here . . ."

"It isn't against the law—legally. But since when does the FBI or the federal government give a damn about 'legally'? Seeming to side with communism is perceived as treasonous."

"These people aren't 'Communists'—they are protesting nuclear weapons . . ."

"I know what they're 'protesting'—for Christ's sake. And I know that *you are not Adriane Strohl here*, if you want to survive."

Wolfman sounded disgusted with me. I could not believe how harsh his voice was.

Stammering I told Wolfman that I hadn't thought of all those things—I hadn't had time. One of the protesters had handed me a sign. In fact I'd expected to see him among the SANE protesters . . .

Now Wolfman became vehement.

"Are you crazy? Join the marchers? Of course not! I'm up for adjudication in two years, I'd never risk resentencing."

"But it's the right thing to do, isn't it?"

"The 'right thing to do' is to survive, Mary Ellen. You know that."

"I—I'm not sorry, Ira. The SANE people are very nice. I really liked them. They were courageous, and everything they said made sense about nuclear 'stockpiling'—the 'Cold War'—the 'tragic lesson of Hiroshima' . . ."

"I told you: the *nuclear holocaust* never happened. You know that, so fuck this crap. Just—fuck this."

Now Wolfman had truly shocked me. And hung up.

The Lonely Girl I

Ira, forgive me! Please don't cut yourself off from me. You know, I love you so much. I can't bear to live in this place without you . . .

These words I wrote in blue ballpoint pen on a sheet of notebook paper.

Pleading and without dignity. Words spilling like blood from a slashed wrist.

Dear Ira, I am sorry for having behaved "recklessly"—as you'd charged.

Please forgive me for behaving foolishly. You are right, I should have thought more carefully of the consequences . . . that is, the consequences that might have been.

(I'd begun to worry: What might the consequences be? *Would* there be consequences for "Mary Ellen Enright"—sometime in the future?)

I don't think it is fair to break off our friendship over this matter—I will never behave so foolishly again.

Please don't punish me! I think that I am "punished" enough . . .

Though I don't really think that I did anything other than what was the right thing to do, by showing my sympathy with the marchers—I hope you will forgive me.

These words I wrote in days subsequent to the SANE march. Trying to compose a letter for Wolfman—an actual letter to be addressed to *I. Wolfman*, 433 Myrtle Street, Wainscotia Falls, Wainscotia.

Impossible! I could not.

Could not send such childish pleas, Wolfman would be repelled. Wolfman would laugh at me.

Had I lost my only friend in Wainscotia? Like a sleepwalker I continued with my "life"—attended classes, wrote papers and took exams—worked fifteen hours a week in the Museum of Natural History. Would not have wished to confide in anyone how Wolfman's harsh words had hurt even if there'd been someone in whom I might confide.

One evening, Miss Steadman invited me to dinner

in her sitting room, with another girl—another girl
without friends. What did we think about the SANE
protesters?—Miss Steadman asked; the other girl had
much to say ("My father knows all about Communists—
he's a Korean War veteran") but Mary Ellen Enright
only just listened, politely.

So lonely, several times I had meals in the dining
hall with my roommates. Since Betsy had (mysteri-
ously) withdrawn from school we had a new roommate
named Millicent who'd had a single room in Acrady
since the start of the fall term, and had grown to hate
being alone; and so Miss Steadman had allowed her to
move upstairs into our room.

Yet, Millie was still lonely. Sulky, easily vexed, and
lonely. Millie was a plain, somber, stern-faced girl from
a Wisconsin dairy farm, a scholarship holder like the
rest of us; she'd hoped to major in something called
agriculture education but her fall semester grades had
been mostly C's, which put her scholarship at risk.
Often when I returned to our room there was Millie
sitting at her desk, blankly staring at an opened textbook. Sometimes she sat slouched on the edge of her
bed, eyes welling with tears.

Millie was enrolled in Psychology 102 which, she
complained, was too hard, and boring. Her quiz section instructor was Dr. Wolfman—"He doesn't like

me. He looks right through me. He's a hard grader—I think he's unfair. He's *sarcastic*. He's *mean*."

When I didn't respond Millie said, hissing, "People say—he's a *Jew*. From New York City."

When I still didn't respond with anything more than a vague sympathetic *Uh-hmm* Millie said, with a harsh little laugh, "—What Daddy calls Jew York City. *That's* where."

Never would I ask Millie about "Dr. Wolfman" for I would not betray my interest in Wolfman, and I did not want to encourage Millie to talk to me.

Yes, it was cruel of me. Yes, I am sorry.

For I might have been the one to tell the new, so very unhappy roommate the somber wisdom I'd acquired at Wainscotia/Zone 9: *You can live a life even if it is not the life you would have chosen. You can live breath by breath. You can live.*

The Lonely Girl II

Returned to the Film Society. Not that I expected to see Ira Wolfman there but that in my loneliness I had to be *somewhere*.

This time, a "classic" Alfred Hitchcock film, *Rear Window*.

And this time too, though it was billed as a suspense film, the film moved with excruciating slowness. The actors were so obviously *acting*. The film was so obviously a *film*. Serenely blond Grace Kelly was very beautiful and not so made-up as actresses in the John Wayne western, and James Stewart was sympathetic and winning, but it was impossible to take them seriously as anything other than glamorous movie stars going through the paces of an improbable story, again to heavy-handed background music that made me so restless, I had to press my fingers against my ears.

Midway in *Rear Window*, I had to slip away. My head had begun to ache, I felt so—*exiled*.

How was it possible, the other viewers were totally absorbed in this movie! I could concede that it was superior to the western, and not so garishly colored, but each scene ran for a predictable length, always too long—my mind skittered ahead of the dialogue, and it made me restless and resentful to wait for the dialogue to catch up. Bewildering to me, how in the flickering light of the screen the viewers' faces were rapt as children's faces . . . I felt trapped, as in a child's cartoon-world. I felt as I did those several times when I'd tried gamely to watch television at Acrady Cottage, not sitting on the sofa with the other girls but standing close by, tentatively; wanting to be drawn into the stilted comic sketches, or the melodramatic scenes.

Wolfman had had a name for it—*intellectual insult*. Yet he'd been entertained by the John Wayne western and would have liked the Hitchcock suspense film even more, as it was more cleverly plotted.

There is terror in such revelations. *You can't be deceived. You can't "suspend disbelief." You are trapped inside your own head.*

Later that week I went to a poetry reading in the

university chapel given by the distinguished Wainscotia poet Hiram Brody on the occasion of his seventieth birthday and the publication of *The Collected Poems of H. R. Brody.* At first, because poetry is a more subtle art than Hollywood movies, I was intrigued by the poet's words, and by the musical cadences of his poems, which rhymed in the way of Robert Frost's, whom we'd been studying in my American literature class; there were echoes too of Archibald MacLeish, another revered American poet whom we'd been studying. At the front of the large audience H. R. Brody performed brilliantly, you would have thought for the first time though in fact (it seemed) he had committed much of his poetry to memory and recited it, rarely glancing down at the page. For his age he was youthful, silky-white-haired, with a white beard that looked as if it had been lovingly brushed and combed; his manner was sly, self-effacing and elfin. The audience loved his poems and applauded after each as I did as well, though I began to realize, after about fifteen minutes, that the poems were essentially the same poem, of familiar "rural" subjects, presented with a sort of self-righteous coercion, and invariably rhyming—like a music box that strikes only the same notes, repeatedly. You could tell when the poet was concluding a poem by the expression in his face, and by the cast of his voice.

There were echoes of Robert Frost, I had to think others heard—though possibly not—for the applause continued with uncritical ardor, like a narcotic that must dull the poet's senses.

Overhead the snow-boughs sweep the sky.
Our promises to keep are bye-and-bye.

And:

Nature never will betray
A heart that cherishes each living day.

At the end of the hour-long reading the poet's eyes shone with tears. Several times H. R. Brody bowed low, his silky-white hair falling into his face so that it had to be brushed away. The crowded university chapel was deafening in applause. The audience sprang to its feet with uplifted hands, excitedly applauding.

I felt so sad! I'd tried to be swept away with these others, but had failed.

Clapping until the palms of my hands smarted. And thinking—*If I am being watched they will see how I belong here.*

Soon then I attended a lecture given by a historian of science from Michigan State University, introduced by

Professor Myron Coughland; the thesis of the lecture seemed to be that *Homo sapiens* is comprised of distinct races and these races are genetically determined in all things, including I.Q. According to "historical data," certain races (Caucasian, Asian) are superior to other races (African, Australian aborigines).

I tried to listen but for the distracting words of Ira Wolfman muttering in my ear—*Nothing they do will have the slightest value to anyone. No one is "original" here—no one is "significant."*

Wolfman wasn't at the lecture. Wolfman would have held the lecturer in contempt, perhaps.

Gamely I tried to take notes. All serious students take notes. For it seemed to me an important gesture, *to try to learn something—anything.*

So lonely for Wolfman!

Even for Wolfman's disapproval, contempt.

In my restlessness drifting through the Fine Arts Building, peering into the high-ceilinged studios whose doors to the hall were all flung open—studios of painting, figure drawing, sculpting. There was a sharp smell of paint here, and turpentine. There was an air in this building of risk-taking, and bravado.

I was envious of the art students, who didn't have to concern themselves with "ideas" or "data"—who weren't doing work that could be shown to be "mis-taken." I resolved that, the following year, if I was still in Exile, and still at Wainscotia, I would take a course in art.

Yet, the paintings which the students were working on, and the canvases displayed on the walls, were not very promising. Most of the paintings were meant to be "realistic"—awkward attempts at landscapes, sun-sets, old barns, covered bridges; awkward attempts at sketching the human figure, or the human face. It did not seem to occur to the artists that these subjects had been done before—many times before. A few of the more daring paintings were "abstract"—bold swirls and streaks of color in the style of European expres-sionists of the early twentieth century, or maybe it was the large paint-splattered canvases of the late Jackson Pollock whose radically experimental work had been featured in *Life* magazine.

It seemed to be true, as Wolfman had said: there were no new ideas here in Wainscotia. No originality, no—surprise. Everything they undertook had been done already, and done more beautifully by others. Or it was wrongheaded.

Yet everyone worked energetically, enthusiastically. Everyone was convinced that whatever work they were doing was important; if you'd inquired they'd have surely said with modest bravado—*My work will out-live me . . .*

The last studio in the Fine Arts Building into which I peered was a sculpting studio. Here some ten or twelve students were working earnestly in model-ing clay, trying to capture the likeness of a model that was in fact a life-sized female mannequin in emulation of a Greek statue, draped in a white sheet. The man-nequin had a perfect, symmetrical face with sightless eyes, its arms were broken off at the elbows, and its legs were missing. A quick glance into the sculpting studio told me that the students, mostly male, were not very gifted as sculptors; their dwarf-sized "Greek statues" were subtly misshapen, each with something flawed though it would have been difficult to say what it was. Yet, their instructor appeared to be intensely involved with their work, and spoke passionately to them—not uncritically, but not unkindly—for you could see that he *cared.*

"Good work, Mark! Good work, Jonny! Very im-pressive."

In the doorway I stood hesitantly, hoping not to be seen. But no one was interested in me, for the mood of the studio was electric; the instructor spoke rapidly and knowledgeably, making occasional corrections in his students' clay figures. I wondered what the man had found to say over the years about these diligent amateur efforts—his voice was both critical and comforting. For he did care. You need not be exceedingly talented to feel welcome *here.*

Again, Wolfman's pronouncement murmured cruelly in my ear—*Hotbed of mediocrity!*

And then I was astonished to see that the instructor was the broad-shouldered youngish man who'd been one of the SANE leaders, who'd pressed the picket sign into my hand. In a sweeping attack of fraternity brothers I'd lost sight of him.

So the SANE marcher was a member of the art department at Wainscotia! Evidently he hadn't been fired by the administration. (Maybe arts faculty were regarded differently from other faculty?) It was touching to see what respect the students felt for their instructor.

Indeed, James, or Jamie, was an appealing figure, if somewhat ridiculous (as Wolfman might have thought) in bib-overalls soiled with clay, and a tattered T-shirt, and crude sandals worn with gray wool socks; his hair was coarse and gnarly, straggling onto his shoulders, and his beard was scruffy, not at all "sculpted" like H. R. Brody's beard.

Quickly I looked away, before he could turn to see me.

April

"Hello, Adriane."

Adriane! In this place where, not so many feet away, in an adjoining office, Miss Hurly was speaking on the telephone.

Wolfman had returned, unpredictably. After three weeks of estrangement he turned up in the Museum of Natural History at closing time.

So often I'd imagined glancing up to see Wolfman, when he did appear it was with the unsettling authority of a vision, or a hallucination.

He was smiling at me. He extended a hand, to take my hand.

"Ira! Hello."

Outside, it was April: rain-lashed, chilly as winter.

———

Never would Wolfman speak of SANE, nor would I speak of SANE to him. I came to think that he'd been embarrassed not to have joined the marchers, and this had made him unreasonably angry with me.

I thought—*Maybe someday. We will both belong, and we will both march for peace.*

"Terminated"

Now, I was not sure that I could trust Wolfman.
I loved Wolfman more than ever.

Something had gone wrong in Wolfman's life. Or perhaps in Wolfman's career, for Ira Wolfman scarcely seemed to have a life.

He was preoccupied, moody. He frowned a good deal, until the furrows in his forehead didn't fade. Then, his laughter was quick, loud, and inappropriate. As Millie had said, he was *sarcastic*.

Compulsively he lit a cigarette and took several quick puffs then left the cigarette burning in one of the ashtrays scattered through his apartment.

I waved away smoke. I tried not to cough. I thought—

Has he forgotten all that we know about smoking, and cancer? Has he forgotten who he is?

When I was in the kitchen preparing a meal or cleaning after a meal I was likely to hear Wolfman, in an undertone, speaking on the phone in his bedroom. And if the phone rang, he asked me please to wait in another room while he answered it.

That woman, Cornelia. "Nelia."

I had to think that she was as desperate for Wolfman as I was. And that she knew much less about Wolfman than I knew.

More frequently now, I was the one to hold Wolfman in my arms. As he lay on his back, on his bed, smoking, staring at the ceiling, wracked with thoughts like sharp-serrated waves that worked their way through his flesh.

Given to saying recklessly, he might just *walk away*.

(From Wainscotia? But where would Wolfman walk *to*?)

Given to saying he had new, radical ideas for experiments, of which A. J. Axel would not approve.

For much of the time, A. J. Axel was an (invisible) presence in Wolfman's life. In the sparely furnished apartment, at Wolfman's table, there were three chairs of which one was (invisibly) occupied by the white-haired professor.

As if pleading his case Wolfman said, to me: "I'm not making a break with behaviorism. I want just to stretch the concept. I want to postulate a 'mind.' I want to manipulate and expose a 'mind.' This is a post-Holocaust era, you know, Adriane, though no one at Wainscotia is likely to talk about it—the Nazi death-camps, the 'Final Solution' of the Jews, experimentation with human beings. Eichmann—the seemingly ordinary man who was 'only following orders.' None of this is taught in the history department there, still less is it spoken of. America is founded upon amnesia—denial. Conscience cannot keep up with acts. I want to investigate the mind of the 'ordinary' man—and woman. I will devise a series of experiments that replicate, in miniature, the Nazi experiment—for Nazism was a social experiment of a kind unique in history. Skinner has led the way— now, others will continue. There is a 'cognitive'—and 'moral'—revolution soon to erupt. I envision experiments that are, to the uninitiated, theatrical events. Experimenters would wear uniforms of authority, like Nazis. But more clever than Nazis, we would wear white uniforms that suggest medical or clinical authority— professorial authority. We would involve our experimental subjects in decisions of a moral nature. Not the equivalent of rats running mazes, or pigeons pecking for seeds, but the equivalent of a 'good German' comply-

ing with the Nazi agenda. In the experiment there will
be a 'captain,' and there will be a 'private.' The figure
of authority, which will be the psychology professor,
will instruct the 'captain' in the necessity of punishing the 'private' who is slow to learn, or doesn't obey
orders quickly enough. The 'captain' will administer to
the 'private' a sequence of escalating punishments, as
the figure of authority bids him. The figure of authority says he will accept 'all responsibility.' The intention
of the experiments will be to investigate to what length
a seemingly ordinary, 'moral' human being will go, if
he's told what to do by a figure of authority. I envision
punishments that escalate, ending in 'death' . . . of
course, it's just an experiment: no one is punished, no
one dies. But the subject will be revealed to himself,
irrevocably. When I publish these results, American
psychology will be changed forever."

Wolfman spoke excitedly, as I had rarely heard him.

How complicated, Wolfman's proposed experiment!
I had to wonder uneasily if in fact it was an experiment
that Wolfman was remembering, out of his past; an
experiment, or a series of experiments, devised by another psychologist; if the filtering device in Wolfman's
brain had failed to block this forbidden knowledge . . .
The Instructions forbade all EIs to "remember" any-

thing that had not (yet) occurred in their places of exile. Wolfman was putting himself at risk with such ideas.

Yet, his experiment was not so very different, in essence, from the experiment I'd suggested to him after the Film Society evening. For it was the pursuit of the elusive "consciousness" that underlay behavior, whose shadow behaviorists shunned.

I did not know what to tell Wolfman. Since the SANE episode he'd become edgy and impatient; feeling the need, it seemed, to explain himself, defend himself in a way he'd never done before. Almost, another Wolfman was emerging, insecure, argumentative.

In a faltering voice I told Wolfman that the experiments sounded "very exciting"—"important"—but would be controversial. There was the "moral question"—for instance.

"What 'moral question'? Jesus!" Wolfman laughed derisively.

Diligently I continued: Was it fair, was it ethical, to so deceive the subject—the "captain"? After the experiment was over, this person would feel very bad about himself, and bitter at being used . . .

"Also, from what I know of behavioral psychology, which admittedly is a small fraction of what you know, Ira—Professor Axel will certainly not approve."

There. I had said it. The obvious: Wolfman's mentor would not approve.

"But I will be measuring behavior, Adriane," Wolfman said irritably. "That is—exactly—precisely—what I will be doing. Do you not comprehend?"

"But—"

"*Do* you not comprehend? How important this work will be? In the history of psychology? 'Obedience to authority'—a uniformed patriarch. Please help me, Adriane. Don't discourage me. You could be my lab assistant, as well as my friend and companion. My *kinsman*. I could teach you all that I know, we could work together, a series of brilliant psychological experiments . . . Like John Watson and his graduate student, whom he eventually married."

For a moment I could not speak. The heat of elation lifted from Wolfman's skin. His face was slick with perspiration. I could hear only the words—*eventually married*.

"But, Ira—is this experimental work that has already been done, that you are remembering? The Instructions forbid us to—"

"No. It is not work that has 'already been done.' It is, it will be, *original work.*"

Wolfman was vehement. I could not challenge him.

"Where would we do this work? Here at Wainscotia?"

"No. Not here. Don't be obtuse. We would need to be independent researchers. We can make our way to California, or Oregon. I have contacts there. I mean, as 'Ira Wolfman.' Of *that other*, no one but you knows. We would have to leave here. My time here is finished, in any case. In the department."

"But we can't leave. We're Exiles. We each have sentences, we can't travel more than ten miles from . . ."

Wolfman shrugged impatiently. Wolfman threw off my hand, where I'd been stroking his twitchy arm.

"Fuck 'Exile'! Fuck 'NAS'! It's here and now I'm concerned with. All that—phantasmagoria"—Wolfman waved his arm dismissively—"the hell with it. I think it has all evaporated—it's *gone down*. The fact is, Axel isn't happy with me any longer. He knows beforehand that I'm the son who will betray him. He's shrewd—you can't run rats through mazes for most of your life and not know how they will run in the future. And pigeons, exactly how they will peck. Accordingly, Axel has 'axed' me—as he has axed other protégés—I've been denied tenure. The departmental meeting was last week. They won't even be sending my name to the president's committee. Axel invited me to dinner at his home, to inform me. And for the last time to dinner, I'm sure—'It was a tragic mistake on their part, Ira. I tried to intervene on your behalf, but I was outnumbered.'"

I tried to comprehend this. Wolfman, the most promising of assistant professors in the department, the young man who'd been selected by A. J. Axel to substitute for him in his lecture course, and to work closely with him in his laboratory, had been fired from the Wainscotia psychology department?

"Not *fired, terminated.* Supposedly there's a distinction. I'm not being promoted, and I'm not getting tenure, because they perceive me as rebellious, which happens to be true. Axel has arranged for me to have two more years, however. (Just coincidentally, the terms of my so-called sentence.) But we can leave earlier, Adriane. At the end of this term."

All this was stunning news to me. Though I could understand Wolfman's harsh-bitten words, I could not comprehend their meaning.

Tried to explain to Wolfman, I didn't think it was possible for us to leave Wainscotia. He had to know that it was forbidden to leave the "epicenter"—"It must be the same sentence, for you as for me."

Wolfman flung off my arm, and sat up. He didn't want to be held now. He didn't want female comfort, or solicitude.

He swung his legs off the bed. We had not—yet—become lovers, and now I understood that we never would be. At least, not in this place. Not in Wolfman's apartment on Myrtle Street.

"If we violate The Instructions . . ."

Wolfman laughed harshly. He was lighting another cigarette, his fourth or fifth of the evening. He flung the wooden match in the direction of an ashtray, and it fell to the floor.

"You believed that crap? 'Exile'? 'Teletransportation'? 'Zone Nine'? None of this is real, Adriane. It's a construct."

"A 'construct'? What do you mean?"

Weakly I sat on the edge of Wolfman's bed as Wolfman paced about the room, sucking in smoke, coughing. Rain continued to lash at the windows of the room, so thickly that a streetlight just across the street was virtually invisible except for a nova-like halo of light at its top.

"As I've told you, I don't think that NAS is monitoring EIs as they'd once done. It might be that the Government is under attack—there could be a new president, in fact—a new administration. Or a new war. You've been out of contact for at least eight months." Wolfman laughed. "Maybe NAS has lost a war? Maybe one of the 'terrorist' enemies has conquered North America? Maybe there has been a 'reform' overthrow, and the old regime is gone. We wouldn't know—maybe, we will never know. And what has it to do with *us*?"

Seeing the look of confusion in my face Wolfman said, extravagantly, "Look: it's possible to see that this is all 'virtual'—Zone Nine. The 'Happy Place.' I'm your friend Ira but I'm also a researcher at CSD—Computational Strategies."

Now Wolfman spoke more calmly, matter-of-factly.

He might have been explaining something to his students that was both an astonishing revelation (to the naïve) and the most obvious common sense (to one like himself).

"You believed it! All Exiles do! Such credulity is based upon your—our—sense of guilt and inadequacy. Zone Nine is 'virtual'—it isn't real. As a CSD researcher I did VVS work—'Visceral Virtual Settings'—my most ingenious project has been a replica of a state university in a small town in Wisconsin, 1959 to 1960—Wainscotia U. It doesn't exist on any map, except the CSD map. I think it's pretty damned impressive—built absolutely to scale, in space and in time. Did you discover any glitch? Any anachronisms? You did not—because the person who created Zone Nine is a genius in his highly competitive field—(you should see the skills of the kids coming up, as young as thirteen—killer sharks!)—and because you didn't expect to see them. In fact,

Adriane, you're still in custody in Youth Disciplinary.
You've never left the state of New Jersey. You've been
there—I mean, here—for approximately eight months,
in a comatose/hypnotized state. They're feeding you
through a tube, and emptying you out through a cath-
eter and no, your parents never did get notified. *They*
feel guilty, thinking it's something they did to have a
child taken from them."

I was staring at Wolfman. Speechless.

Not just struck dumb but struck blank. Brain-blank.

Wolfman, smiling at me slyly. Defiantly. Thinking maybe he'd gone too far?—but no, Wolfman never
went too far.

"Hey. Listen. I'm a staffer at YD, part-time. They
lend me out from CSD. The challenge was to create a
virtual reality appropriate for EIs in which to incar-
cerate you, via the microchip. The microchip *is real*.
But nothing else is. You've been dreaming that you
were 'teletransported' to a past time, absurdly—how
could a past time *exist*? Time travel is a preposterous
notion, my dear girl. How could you, so skeptical about
B. F. Skinner, fail to understand that simple concept?
There is no *past*. There is no *there*. For instance—if
we were to 'travel back' in time thirty seconds, how
could this be? Would we 'travel back through' our
own bodies? And what would we encounter? Our

own bodies, at an earlier age? If we traveled back an hour, eleven hours, a month, a year—our own bodies? Would we see these bodies, or would we inhabit them? Which would be 'us'? You've fallen for all of this phantasmagoria, because our virtual creations are so exquisite. I've been particularly praised—my code name is 'the Wolf.' I'm especially pleased with the Van Buren Museum of Natural History and the 'nuclear bomb shelter' below it. Quite a joint achievement! And the pompous professors of Wainscotia—Axel, Morris, Coughland, Harrick, Stein. I know them intimately, since they are my creations. You didn't get to meet them all yet. It did take me a while to create Zone Nine. But I'm patient, as I am skilled at my craft. *That* was why I was drafted into 'special forces' within CSD." Wolfman smiled at me, much pleased with himself. "And, absurd as it sounds, I truly feel protective of you, 'Mary Ellen'—almost, at times, I've come to feel that I've created *you*."

I was stunned by Wolfman's remarks. I could not think how to respond.

I felt like a soft, winged thing, a moth that has been batted out of the air. Not hard enough to break its wings, but hard enough to knock it stunned to earth, and the wings slow-moving, wounded and mute in wonderment.

In a teasing voice Wolfman said "You will never know, 'Mary Ellen,' will you?"

"I—I don't understand . . ."

"But I've told you: Zone Nine is a virtual construct. Not one thing here except you, and me, is *real*."

"Ira, are you serious?"

Wolfman spread his fingers like a magician intent upon showing that he has no hidden tricks.

"Do you think that I'm 'serious'? Or—what is the opposite of 'serious'?"

I stared at Wolfman who smiled at me with maddening insouciance. As if to prompt me, he said: "As a dreamer doesn't know she is dreaming, so you can't know your circumstances."

"But—you know, don't you? Please . . ."

Wolfman lay his hand on my shoulder to comfort me. In his face was an expression of both kindliness and exasperation.

"Yes, I'm joking, Adriane. Of course. I was just running a maze—that is, exploring a possibility. If I were a cybertech staffer at CSD, instead of a teletransported EI, what I've told you might be plausible. Or plausible in some way. But the painful fact is, I'm at a loss to control my life in Zone Nine, just like you." Wolfman laughed, baring his teeth in a grimace. "Maybe I did create Zone Nine but my supervisor appropriated the program and trapped me inside it! Like my parents who'd invented a biological weapon who might then have been infected by it as a part of the research . . . possibly by their own supervisor, to get rid of them once they were no longer useful. We're trapped in our own experiments. Please don't look so dismayed, Adriane—I'm telling the truth now. The bare, plain, irremediable truth. If Zone Nine were my invention I'd have arranged for my own freedom—and now, for yours. But I'm trapped here, in the epicenter—just like you."

Wolfman held out his arms, to comfort me. Sobbing I pressed myself against him.

I could not trust him. His words had been devastating to me, even those I could not truly comprehend.

Yet, I had no one else.

Elopement

Wolfman insisted that we leave Wainscotia at the end of the term.

"No one can stop us. No one will even notice. We'll 'elope'—and begin a new life."

Elope. So long I'd waited for Wolfman to seriously love me. Or, at least to say that he loved me.

He had not uttered the word, yet. But if he wanted me to leave Wainscotia with him, and to begin a "new life" with him, it must be understood between us that he did love me, so far as Wolfman could love another person.

Wolfman's plans were vague but thrilling. We would live together under assumed names, somewhere in the West. In April 1960 the United States was not yet the (Reconstituted) North American States in which all citizens were under continuous surveillance. Much of it, in the western states, was unpopulated, virtually uncharted. It had not yet been *wired.* There was no *grid.*

"Our enemies thought to exile us in this 'prehistoric' place," Wolfman said, "but in fact, the absence of technology will be our salvation. There are vast empty zones where human consciousness doesn't intrude. We can get work of some kind when we need money. I can use my hands as well as my wits. I have friends in Berkeley who will take us in. We can prepare new documents—birth certificates, ID's. No one will know who we are, or once were."

Wolfman spoke with such conviction, I could not doubt him.

It was the end of the spring term. "Mary Ellen Enright" had completed her first year at Wainscotia, with a near-perfect grade-point average.

Impulsively Miss Steadman hugged me when she'd received the news from the dean's office. "All of us in Acrady Cottage are so proud of you, Mary Ellen!"

I was embarrassed by Miss Steadman's words. And I felt a vague shame, for my high grades had been a consequence of desperation and loneliness, and few other students could have been so motivated. My very misery had given me an unfair advantage.

Overnight, Acrady Cottage had emptied. My room-mates had departed with hugs, kisses, promises to see me in the fall—though there were no plans for us to room together again.

In the summer term I would continue to live on campus, but in another residence. I would work at the university library five days a week. During the university's summer session, which was an accelerated six-week period that began in late June, I would take a course in mathematics, which was a weak subject for me. (So Wolfman had advised me, months ago.) A life of routine lay before me like an unmarked calendar. I felt the comfort of such emptiness—no emotion, no anxiety. If Wolfman departed Wainscotia as he'd been threatening to do.

Without Wolfman, I would live my life from day to day, until my sentence was completed. Could I endure this life?

In despair I said to Wolfman, "How can I come with you, when it's forbidden?"

And when you've never said you love me.

"I've told you, Adriane. No one is watching us."

"But—how can you be sure?"

"Trust me."

Badly I wanted to trust Wolfman. His teasing words about Zone 9 as a virtual construct in which I'd been placed unknowingly had had a profound effect upon me—I woke in the night, frightened that Wolfman had been telling the truth, and that he was an agent of NAS; at other times, I was certain that he'd been joking.

I said to Wolfman, "What is the meaning of our lives? Does psychology tell us?" and Wolfman said, "Psychology is a mirror into which we look, and see our own faces. No science can tell us *why*."

Though Wolfman had spoken disparagingly of the psychology department at Wainscotia, I understood that he'd been deeply wounded by his failure to be granted tenure, and promoted. And I understood that the reason was probably the reason he'd told me—his ideas were unacceptable to the older faculty members, particularly A. J. Axel.

Wolfman had the idea of packing a selection of our belongings and mailing them c/o General Delivery, Berkeley, California. A half-dozen cardboard boxes filled with clothes, books, personal items, neatly taped and stamped for third-class mail.

"But—how will we leave?"

"We'll leave unobtrusively. We'll hike in the arboretum—and we'll never return."

So Wolfman convinced me. Ever more, Wolfman was affectionate with me, and appealing to me as he'd rarely been in the past. His disgust with me over the matter of SANE seemed to have been totally forgotten.

So it happened, I brought my things—a small selection of my mostly unwanted things—to Wolfman's apartment, where we packed them into boxes as he'd planned. Wolfman was a perfectionist in taping boxes shut, making sure they were secure and snug. Then, we took them to the post office to mail to Berkeley, California.

Did I ever think, as we hauled the boxes to the post office, that I would open them? Remove my folded clothes, my books?

Did I ever think that Ira Wolfman and I would journey to California together, to begin a *new life*?

In the days before our planned departure, I was very excited—frightened, elated. I felt both reckless and resigned.

And Wolfman, too, seemed both reckless and resigned.

For every time I expressed doubt of what we planned to do, Wolfman cut me off: "Adriane! Have faith in me."

I was very frightened at the prospect of violating The Instructions. But I was more frightened of losing Wolfman and finding myself again alone in Exile.

I thought—*I have lost my parents, but I have Wolfman.*

Wolfman's plans were becoming more specific. The latest news was that we would definitely have jobs in a research institute at UC Berkeley, where Wolfman had friends. These friends would provide legal documents for us, as well.

"They think it's romantic, that we're 'eloping,'" Wolfman said happily. "And they have no idea who we are—of course."

On May 19, at 8:00 A.M., Wolfman waited for me just inside the arboretum. We wore hiking clothes and boots. On Wolfman's head, a baseball cap. "It's important that we look like anyone else," Wolfman said. "The more ordinary, the better."

We were both wearing backpacks. Wolfman stipulated that we were to carry several bottles of water apiece as well as food for several meals, a change of clothing, warm socks. Wolfman would supply a Swiss army knife.

Wolfman had charted our route. We started out on our usual trail but, instead of taking a loop that would return us to campus after two miles, we took another fork, that led us farther from campus, in a region of pinewoods that stretched for miles to its northern boundary at a state highway in the adjacent township of St. Cloud.

Wolfman had calculated: we would take a Greyhound bus from St. Cloud to Minneapolis; from Minneapolis, we would take another Greyhound bus to Denver, Colorado; and so to San Francisco, California, and Berkeley. Wolfman knew the departure times of these buses, and Wolfman had money for our tickets.

Briskly Wolfman was hiking into the arboretum. I had to half-run to keep pace with him.

It was early enough in the morning that no one else was around.

It was a partially cloudy day in spring, not warm, but clear, still. My heart was beating in that quick erratic way it had learned to beat, when the arresting officers had come for *Strohl, Adriane* and Mr. Mackay had so eagerly handed me over to them.

This was not a good memory. Blindly I clutched at Wolfman's sleeve. "Will I ever see my parents again, Ira? How will I return to see my parents?"

"Please don't cry."

I hadn't known that I was crying.

Why, when I was so happy?

The Bat

We set our faces forward. We did not look back.

Soon we were out of sight of the university campus and ever more faintly came the chapel bell like something heard undersea.

The trail ascended. The trail was soft with pine needles yet there were outcroppings of rock that mimicked steps, you had to be careful not to turn your ankle as you climbed.

The trail was steep enough yet would have been steeper, near-vertical, were it not for numerous switchbacks.

These switchbacks cast us back upon ourselves, it almost seemed. Our progress was slow for the trail was shaped like a great snake with a rippling body. If Wolfman plunged ahead, the switchbacked trail cast him not so very distant from me, approaching and then passing me, as I followed trying not to stagger beneath the weight of my backpack.

Wolfman had said—*A backpack can mean the difference between death and survival. A backpack can save your life.*

High overhead in the trees, quarrelsome birds.

The trail became fainter. The trail was lost in the pine forest.

Yet, Wolfman pressed forward. And I followed.

Miles of forest. Climbing what must have been the side of a mountain. And then, beginning a sharp descent that was as difficult as the ascent.

Small avalanches were loosed by our feet.

We were panting, from the ascent. We were wary of the descent for descents are always dangerous.

The sun had shifted in the sky. The sun had been blinding, our eyes filled with tears.

We were very happy! Soon, we would be free of Wainscotia.

Yet, after six hours of hiking Wolfman cried out in surprise and disappointment—"My God!"

At first, I didn't understand.

Then, I saw.

Though we'd been walking for six hours, following the trail that Wolfman had carefully chosen for us, to lead us to St. Cloud, it seemed that the trail had looped back upon itself, and had brought us again to the entrance of the arboretum, close by the university campus. The tolling sound we'd been hearing was the chapel bell.

Wolfman said, "This isn't possible . . ."

I could not believe that we'd returned to the campus, yet it appeared to be so—the trail had betrayed us, leading us in a large looping circle. We had climbed up the side of a mountain and we had descended the side of a mountain. We had believed that we were miles from Wainscotia and yet—we had covered less than a quarter mile.

Somehow, the trail with its many tortuous switchbacks had turned us around, though on the maps it led out of the arboretum, unmistakably.

Wolfman was staring at the map, trying to determine where he'd made a mistake. But I could see that Wolfman hadn't made a mistake, except in his conviction that we could leave Wainscotia.

"We're trapped, Ira. We can't leave. I knew this."

"Go back, then! Go back alone. I'm not coming back with you."

Wolfman's voice shook with fury.

Wolfman pushed away my hand. He'd turned and was half-running, panting, back along the trail.

A roaring rose in my ears. I wanted to follow him, to stop him. But I could not move any farther, I was so very tired.

Six hours and more I had been hiking in this accursed place. Six hours and more, and the trail had brought us back to our beginning.

I called after Wolfman, who ignored me. Wolfman, my love!

Overhead, birds were fluttering in the trees. Was it dusk, so soon? A nervous chattering of birds, a flurry of wings.

In pine branches overhead a small bird, possibly a bat, was circling strangely, as if rabid. Then, as I stared, the thing—black, swift, unerring—swooped down to rush at Wolfman, struck him on the side of the head and entered his head, suddenly aflame, engulfing him in flames, within seconds turning the man to vapor only a few feet from me.

There had been time for only a brief high-pitched cry of horror and loss—I think it must have been mine.

For in that instant Wolfman fell, Wolfman died, Wolfman vanished from Zone 9.

III

Wainscotia Falls

HIKER STRUCK BY LIGHTNING, WAINSCOTIA ARBORETUM

18-YEAR-OLD WAINSCOTIA STUDENT HOSPITALIZED

Found Unconscious on Trail by Hiker, Dog

Wainscotia Falls Journal-American, May 20, 1960

Saved

A warm soft muzzle against my face that had gone stiff with cold.

For in shock the blood had drained from my brain.

My breathing had ceased. Like a living creature that has been pinched cruelly in two, and its life snuffed out.

Where I'd fallen heavily on the trail. Outcropping of shale sharp against my stunned face which bled from abrasions I could not see and could scarcely feel.

Could not move not even to cast my eyes into the place where Wolfman had died.

What had been Wolfman, destroyed.

Shock like icy water into which I'd been flung. The shock of an arrested heartbeat. Eyes blinded by light.

Then came a sudden warmth against my face. The panting-hot breath, a dog's quick damp astonishingly soft tongue.

There came a cry—Rufus! Where are you?

A hiker on the trail. Running up behind us where we'd fallen.

Then—Hello? Are you hurt? What has happened . . .

Through the haze riddled with pain came a dog to lick my face to revive me. Eagerly, anxiously. Emitting sharp-distressed cries so close to human, I wept to hear and to know that I had been saved.

The Miracle

For a long time then I was sick.

It might have been weeks. Months.

For there were intervals of "wakefulness"—followed by periods of "forgetfulness."

For there was not what could be called a *steady recovery.* There was not a *steady progress.*

More like switchbacks on a trail. With painful slowness you make your way forward—only to find yourself switched-back, facing the direction you'd come from.

In such a way time turns back upon itself. You believe that you are making progress, but it is an illusion.

Yet, this is *progress* of a kind.

At first I wasn't sure where I was. These (austere, white-walled) rooms to which I was taken (gurney, wheelchair) were different places serving different functions, purposes. Different medical workers, in different uniforms. Often I would open my eyes—(my aching eyes with their blurred vision)—to find myself in a place that was new to me.

Possibly, this was a hospital. Or a rehabilitation clinic.

Some place in which there are degrees of "hospitalization" relating to degrees of physical injury, psychological deficit.

Do you know your name?

Do you know where you are?

Do you know the date?

Do you know who is president of the United States?

Like a small child who is eager to talk but doesn't yet have the power of speech I was eager to give the correct answers to these questions but I did not feel confident that I knew the correct answers. I understood that it was wiser to give no answer than to give an incorrect answer, that might be held against me.

For I was remembering an elaborate examination I'd once taken—when I'd been a student—(I think this was recent, since I've been told that I am a student at the present time, at Wainscotia State University in Wainscotia Falls, Wisconsin)—in which it hadn't been enough to know the correct answers to questions, you had to know which "correct" answer was the "most correct" choice of multiple choices.

*Your name is "Mary Ellen Enright"—do you re-
member your name?*

And do you know where you are, Mary Ellen?

Do you know why?

Sometimes I woke, and the voice(s) continued.

As if there'd been no interruption, the voice(s) continued.

Do you know what happened to you, Mary Ellen?

*The doctors believe you were STRUCK BY LIGHT-
NING.*

And, you survived!

*It's very amazing, Mary Ellen! It's considered a
"miracle."*

*Your picture has been in the newspapers, Mary
Ellen! At least, in Wisconsin papers and on local,
Wisconsin TV.*

*You will be a sophomore at Wainscotia State in the
fall. Do you remember your freshman year?*

*Do you remember—you are an honor student? You
are the recipient of a University Scholarship?*

*You are recovering, Mary Ellen. Dr. Fenner—your
neurologist—says the prognosis is GOOD.*

All of your doctors say the prognosis is GOOD.

*You were found on a trail in the arboretum—a hiker
found you—in fact his dog found you.*

You were unconscious. You did not seem to have a pulse nor did you appear to be breathing.

The hiker's dog led him to you. By his quick actions he saved your life.

Mary Ellen, you are a very lucky young woman.

You were in an acute state of shock but—you are recovering.

Your blood pressure had plummeted. Your left eardrum was perforated.

You are recovering steadily—you are ALIVE!

A MIRACLE—people have said.

STRUCK BY LIGHTNING in the arboretum where you might not have been found for hours and already it was believed to be approximately ninety minutes you'd been unconscious, before you were found.

Hiking alone in the arboretum. In the more distant parts of the arboretum, it can be dangerous.

It is always recommended that no one hike alone. Even an experienced hiker should not hike alone.

Fortunately, you were discovered. In time.

Your lips were blue. You appeared to have ceased breathing. You appeared to have no pulse.

Fortunately, the hiker knew CPR.

Mouth-to-mouth resuscitation. He'd been trained in first aid as a Boy Scout.

STRUCK BY LIGHTNING and survived—that's very rare.

That's a "first" for Wainscotia Falls!—we are proud of you.

If you had family, Mary Ellen—they would be so very grateful that you are *ALIVE*.

Mary Ellen—why are you crying?

Are you in pain, Mary Ellen? Where is the pain?

You can point, Mary Ellen, if that's easier.

Your heart? Your heart hurts?

Or do you mean—your heart is broken?

Grief

*C*an you explain but I could not.
Why you are crying as if your heart has been broken.

So much to be grateful for! I knew.

For slowly I was regaining the use of my legs. And the coordination of muscles that in normal people is taken for granted.

If for instance you decide to stand, your legs will not meekly buckle and cast you to the ground.

If you decide to lift a glass in your hand, your fingers will not release the glass to fall clattering onto the floor.

If you open your mouth to speak, you will not begin shivering, shuddering, weeping inconsolably instead.

Weeping as if I'd lost something—or someone—and could not remember what, or who.

Nor could I remember who the person had been—*Mary Ellen Enright*—(the name on the hospital bracelet on my left wrist)—though I stared into a mirror at the unfamiliar face, shaping the unfamiliar name with numbed lips.

Mary Ellen Enright. A riddle that, no matter how long I puzzled over it, I could not solve.

For I knew—(but how could I *know?*)—that it was a false name.

As I knew—(but how could I *know?*)—that I had not been alone on the trail when the lightning struck.

As if I'd been flung down from a great height onto the needle-strewn trail. And the breath had been knocked from me. And when I shut my eyes there came rushing at me a mysterious object the size of a bat—in panic I ducked, cried out in terror, covered my head with my arms, tried to scream but could not.

No no no no no.

They believed: the patient was reliving the lightning-strike. The powerful charge of electricity that threw her to the ground, and the deafening thunder that followed, that perforated her eardrum.

They believed: the patient was an orphan, had been an orphan since early childhood, and had lost her adoptive parents as well, in an automobile accident. These traumatic losses the patient was mourning in her weakened and semi-delirious state.

Often I was very happy! With each improvement in my "condition"—I tried to rejoice that I was *very lucky.*

Yet in the midst of, for instance, physical therapy— (which included swimming)—the terrible tears came, and would not soon cease.

Like a convulsion of the body, such grief.

Like a great snake rippling inside me, that cannot be contained or controlled and whose outlet is tears.

Why did I cry so helplessly, and bitterly—I did not know.

(It was not pain. Or it was not solely pain. The many pains in my legs, my backbone and my neck, my head, my eyes—these I could bear without crying, for they were only *physical symptoms.*)

Slowly my ability to *think* was returning. My ability to *concentrate*, and to *remember.*

The neurologist explained to me that my "short-term" memory had been affected by the trauma of the lightning strike. There had been, he believed, some (temporary) brain damage, judging by my symptoms.

Memories stored (temporarily) in the hippocampus before being stored (permanently) in the cerebral cortex had been lost, and could not be retrieved.

It was a normal reaction to a traumatic brain injury, Dr. Fenner said. I had not lost my grasp of language—how to speak, read and write—and certain skills—like walking, climbing stairs, swimming—but it was evident that I'd forgotten much in my recent life.

As if someone with a giant sponge had vigorously washed, scrubbed, wiped a part of my brain clean.

I asked Dr. Fenner if there had been a CAT scan of my brain? Or—what was the term—"MRI"?

Dr. Fenner smiled quizzically, cupping his hand to his ear.

"What was that, dear? Something about a—cat?"

"A CAT scan. Or an MRI."

"But—what are you saying, dear? 'MIA'?"

Dr. Fenner was an older gentleman, kind and solicitous to his patients but with a very limited patience for foolish questions; I had noticed that the nurses were careful in his presence, behaving more like servants than trained staff workers. He wore a stiff-starched white shirt and a necktie beneath his physician's white coat, that bulged over his small high belly. Involuntarily I'd shrunk from his touch, as from the nurses' touches, which were with bare hands, where I would have expected thin rubber gloves, when I'd first become conscious of my surroundings; but by this time, after several weeks in the hospital, and now in a rehabilitation wing adjacent to the hospital, I'd become accustomed to the hospital staff working with bare hands. I told myself—*But they are probably washing their hands all the time. When they leave a patient's room.*

Dr. Fenner's necktie fascinated me also. For it was just perceptibly mottled with stains—(food stains?)—and when Dr. Fenner bent over me, it swung at my face.

"'MIA'—'Missing in Action,' I think?—why are you asking about that, Mary Ellen?"—Dr. Fenner was utterly bewildered.

Rapidly I tried to think. But my thoughts came slow and halting, like my walking—sometimes with a spurt of strength, sometimes a flurry of weakness.

"I—I don't know. I guess I don't know what I mean, Dr. Fenner."

It was so: I had no idea what I'd meant. The terms *CAT scan, MRI* were bewildering to me too, like the arcane Latin terms I'd typed in the dim-lit university building whose name I couldn't quite recall—a museum of natural history with which I had an association both vague and exhilarating, like a tumultuous dream that has faded except for its emotional residue.

"Well! You've had a brain trauma, my dear. But you'll recover—I've seen miraculous recoveries in the past."

So often the word *miracle* was voiced in my presence, I was beginning to believe—*miracle!*

(Yet I wondered what percent of the neurologist's patients recovered. And what percent of the neurologist's patients were untreatable.)

Again, when Dr. Fenner left, I burst into tears.

Out of nowhere a terrible sadness swept over me, and I began to cry helplessly, like an abandoned infant.

One of the nurses asked what on earth was wrong?—Dr. Fenner had been *so positive*.

Visitors

F ew visitors came to see me. And each was a surprise to me, as if stepping out of a pitch-black part of my brain.

The first identified herself as *Ardis Steadman,* who'd been the resident adviser of Acrady Cottage, my freshman residence.

Did I remember Miss Steadman? Did I remember my roommates? Did I remember Acrady Cottage—"Such a spirited group of freshman girls this year! And you, Mary Ellen, pulled our grade-point average 'way up.' We were all very grateful for *you.*"

I told Miss Steadman that yes, I did remember her—of course.

We'd gone to a music recital together, I thought. Or—we'd watched TV together in the sitting room of the residence.

As Miss Steadman spoke, reminiscing of events I could not recall, and had no interest in recalling, I began to feel the sensation of terrible loss wash over me, and began to cry.

"Oh, Mary Ellen! What's wrong? Have I said something—?"

I tried to think *why*.

"It's like—I've lost something. But I don't know what it is."

"But when did you lose it, Mary Ellen?"

"I—I don't know . . . Maybe in the arboretum."

"From what I've read and heard, there was nothing on the trail that you'd left behind, evidently. You were hiking alone, and you were wearing a backpack—that was all."

"I remember the arboretum—from before. I'd gone there before. But the last time—" Quick sharp pains struck my eyes, from inside. My vision, that had been improving, became misty now, so that I could barely see Miss Steadman's concerned face. "—the last time, I don't remember."

Miss Steadman clasped my hand. "That may be a blessing, dear. No one would want to remember being struck by lightning!"

And there came, with some embarrassment, Miss Hurly—she'd been astonished to read about me in the

papers, and to hear about me on the radio, and to realize that the girl-struck-by-lightning was *Mary Ellen
Enright.*

"Such a shock! Dr. Harrick sends his regards and
very best wishes for your recovery. He said—when I'd
told him about you, and showed him the news stories—
that he had once come close to being struck by lightning
himself, boating on Lake Michigan as a teenager—
when a sudden storm came up. It was quite a suspenseful tale Dr. Harrick told, really quite emotional—how
terribly close Dr. Harrick had come to being killed, at
such a young age; and only think, all the great work he
has done in science would have been lost . . . He did
remember you, Mary Ellen, though at first he'd mixed
you up with our other girl Lorraine who'd been working on Mondays and Wednesdays."

And there came a woman whom I didn't know,
whom I had never seen before, who introduced herself
as *Cornelia Graeber*—"Please excuse me, Miss Enright, but I saw your picture in the newspaper, and I—I
felt that I knew you, somehow—and I wonder if you
know me? In some way? I'm sometimes called 'Nelia.'"
This individual was edgy, nervous; as she spoke to me,
she picked at her fingernails, and tugged at her hair;
she seemed quite anxious in my presence, as well as
bewildered—she had no idea why she'd been drawn to

see me, but the idea had obsessed her, and at last she'd come. She was about thirty years old. She reminded me of myself—somehow. Her eyes were disconcertingly intense, fixed upon me in a way that suggested that yes, she knew me; but she wasn't sure why. She explained that she was a Ph.D. candidate in psychology, working with A. J. Axel. She'd looked up my course work, out of curiosity, and discovered that I'd taken Axel's popular lecture course Psychology 101 the previous fall, and that I'd had an instructor named *Ira Wolfman* as my quiz section instructor—"Do you remember him? 'Ira Wolfman'? He left Wainscotia abruptly, at the end of the term. He didn't say good-bye to any of us. Not even A. J. Axel. It was very—upsetting. Of course, Ira may have had reasons—professional reasons. But to leave without saying good-bye to any of his friends and colleagues—that wasn't like him . . ."

The sharp shooting pains behind my eyes were making me blink rapidly. Tears flooded my eyes. I could not hear the woman's words clearly for a roaring in my ears like a freight train. Badly I wanted to tell the woman to go away—I didn't know her, I didn't know what she was talking about, the names of most of my professors had vanished from my memory, and could be retrieved only with great difficulty. And it wasn't clear why this stranger was addressing *me*.

Drawn by the sound of my sobbing, one of the nurses intervened. Quickly the woman apologized, and departed.

The fit of convulsive sobbing was so extreme, I could not catch my breath and began to hyperventilate. I had to be rushed to the ER and given oxygen and an IV medication to bring down my suddenly accelerated heartbeat, that was racing at 260 beats a minute.

Then, there came Jamie Stiles to see me.

"Hello? Mary Ellen—"

At first, I didn't remember him. In ungainly stained bib-overalls and no shirt beneath, with bristling dark whiskers, and sandals on his large gnarly feet, he was a startling and intimidating sight.

Telling me, with awkward humor, that "Rufus" wanted to see me also but hadn't been allowed inside the hospital—his leash was tied to a bicycle rack outside.

For it had been Jamie Stiles's dog Rufus that had discovered me fallen on the trail, and rushed barking to me.

It had been Jamie Stiles who'd been hiking on the trail—(not the trail that I'd been on but one close by)—and who'd applied mouth-to-mouth resuscitation to make me breathe again.

Jamie Stiles, who'd been one of the SANE protesters. Who taught sculpting part-time in the fine arts department at Wainscotia State.

Jamie had remembered me, he said. Seeing my picture in the newspaper he'd remembered me from the SANE march.

By this time he'd stepped inside the room. For a big man he was shy. Nurses were glancing at him curiously as they passed by in the hall. A flush rose in his face. I saw now that in his right hand he clutched a bouquet of flowers which looked as if they'd been picked in haste in a field.

There was some fuss about getting a vase for the flowers. When I lifted the flowers to smell them, the scent that lifted from their petals was very faint, yet sweet. Confusedly I thought—*Is this a long time ago, or now? Or has it not happened yet?*

In fear of shutting my eyes. For there was the possibility that, if I did, something small and dark would rush at me and cause me to scream and when I dared to open my eyes again, I would be alone; or worse yet, one of the nurses would be bending over my body.

As Jamie Stiles spoke haltingly to me I thought that yes, I would have remembered this man—I wanted to remember him. For his face was familiar, in a way that a face is familiar which you have been seeing all your life.

Jamie Stiles was deep-chested, with a thick neck, muscular arms and shoulders, jaws covered in bristling dark whiskers that looked as if they would be wiry to the touch; yet his eyes were kindly and concerned, and puzzled. For he'd seemed to know me, he said. When he'd seen me on campus at the time of the protest he'd felt this strongly—"No reason, I guess. The phenomenon is called *déjà vu*."

(*Déjà vu.* The term was familiar to me. Though in the psychology textbook in which I'd encountered it the phenomenon was discounted as usually mistaken, delusional.)

Jamie Stiles was soft-spoken at my hospital bedside but I recalled from his behavior at the protest march that he was a man of strong feelings, impulsive, courageous.

He'd spoken scornfully to me, I recalled. Oh but why?

But then, he'd spoken tenderly to me. He'd forgiven me for my ignorance.

Despite the size of his hands, and his stubby clay-stained fingers, there was gentleness in Jamie's hand-clasp. In his voice, sympathy and hope.

I felt tears threaten me. Though I tried very hard to keep them back tears spilled onto my face like acid and I began to cry as Jamie looked on in distress.

Unlike the hospital staff Jamie Stiles did not ask why I was crying. He did not remark that I was *very lucky* to be alive.

He said very little on this or subsequent visits. For Jamie Stiles is not a verbal person.

He did not say *What have you lost, why are you grieving. Why, when you should be grateful to be alive!*

He did not say *In another story, you were electrified to a crisp. A smear and a smudge and a smelly hole in the snow, that's all of you.*

So that I knew, and there was great comfort in the knowing—*He will be the one.*

"Uncle"

His name was Cosgrove, David R. He introduced himself to me as *an old-fashioned family doctor.*

He didn't know Dr. Fenner, or any of the physicians at the hospital. His practice wasn't in Wainscotia Falls but twenty miles away in St. Cloud. He'd been "intrigued" by my picture in the newspaper. He'd come to visit me just to say hello and to ask a question or two.

"Like Benjamin Franklin, I have an abiding interest in electricity. It's a hobby. The history of 'reanimation'—for instance."

Reanimation? I tried to think what this might mean.

Dr. Cosgrove was a lean wiry man of some mysterious age—fifties?—sixties? Slightly ill at ease, though boyish, and very friendly; thistle-colored hair had nearly vanished from his head, and his eyes were couched in shadowy puckered skin. He had a long thin nose with a tiny bump in the bone and he was smiling hard at me as if to impart some secondary meaning to his words, totally lost on me. In his left cheek was a tic or a twitch, which was distracting. He was carrying a brown leather bag much creased from years of wear.

"Unless you'd rather not talk about it? The 'lightning strike'?"

Vaguely I shook my head, no. Meaning—yes.

Meaning—yes, I could talk about it. Though I didn't remember anything helpful at all.

Dr. Cosgrove continued to smile at me in that curious way. A strange sensation came over me—*I know this man! I have seen this man before.*

Dr. Cosgrove chattered about lightning, electric current, those instances of individuals who'd been "struck" and yet lived, until one of the nurses who'd been in the room left; then, he ceased speaking abruptly.

He went to the door, and shut it carefully.

Doors to hospital rooms are rarely shut, still more rarely are they shut so carefully, so that the lock clicks.

"Very good to see you, 'Mary Ellen,' dear! I've been told that you will be discharged in a few days, you've made a miraculous convalescence."

Dr. Cosgrove continued to smile, even as he removed an object from the brown bag. It looked like a wand, or a small phone—a small, flat phone?—a shape that was familiar to me, that fit in the palm of the man's hand, but which I could not have identified.

Ah, a cell phone! I had not seen a cell phone in— how many months? Years?

But no, the object was not a cell phone after all.

Dr. Cosgrove was frowning, turning a dial between his thumb and forefinger, that caused the small flat object to stir, to emit a low buzzing sound like a hive of wasps.

Seeing the perplexity in my face he said quickly, "Just a little 'baffle'—of my invention."

"'Baffle'?"

"A kind of 'white noise,' in case anyone is listening to us. Advertently, or in—"

Dr. Cosgrove adjusted the buzzing-level of the object in his hand. Now it sounded like honeybees at a little distance, a friendly sound. But all this was utterly mysterious to me.

I wondered—why would anyone be interested in our conversation? I could not imagine who these people could possibly be—no one on the hospital staff, certainly.

Satisfied that the small flat object was operating as he wished Dr. Cosgrove pulled a chair close beside my chair—(for I'd been sitting up and reading beside my bed; I'd become very tired of lying flat and helpless in bed)—and smiled at me with an air of complicity.

An eccentric individual, I thought—but a gentleman.

Dr. Cosgrove asked if indeed I did remember any-thing about being struck by lightning; and when I shook my head no he said, frowning, "But think again, 'Mary Ellen.' Try to remember."

I had tried, many times. This request had been put to me frequently. Most recently by a *Wainscotia Falls Journal-American* reporter who'd been assigned a feature article with the sensational title THE GIRL WHO CAME BACK FROM THE BEYOND. The disappointed reporter had had to interview several doctors, nurses, and a professor of physics from the university, since I hadn't been able to supply him with much information.

"Did it feel as if you'd been 'transported' from—somewhere? I mean, when you woke up."

"I—I don't know. What do you mean 'transported'?"

"Or, a more accurate term might be 'teletransported.'"

Teletransported. What did this mean!

(I wished that my new friend Jamie Stiles were here. It had become a habit to tell Jamie most of what hap-pened during my days in rehab, as Jamie told me what happened during his days, when he came to visit me in the evening; but this exchange with Dr. Cosgrove was so peculiar, like something in a dream, I despaired that I would be able to convey it successfully.)

In a yet more cautious voice Dr. Cosgrove asked if the name "Eric Strohl" meant anything to me

Eric Strohl. I wasn't sure.

"'Eric Strohl.' 'Madeleine Strohl.'" The doctor spoke slowly, and quietly, just loud enough for me to hear him over the buzzing sound of the flat little object in his hand, even as he held his hand over his mouth as if to shield his lips.

Eric Strohl. Madeleine Strohl. I began to tremble. I had no idea why.

"Does the name 'Adriane Strohl' mean anything to you?"

My heart was beating rapidly. I was frightened that I would begin to hyperventilate again. The pain in my eyes throbbed.

Dr. Cosgrove reached out to take hold of my wrist. Gently, he pressed his forefinger against my pulse.

"Calm, now! Remain calm."

"I—I don't—"

"Calm, my dear! Just breathe normally. You may want to count your breaths."

I counted my breaths, to ten. By ten, I was not so agitated. Dr. Cosgrove released my wrist.

"'Adriane Strohl.' I'm just curious—if you have ever heard this name before."

"I—I think—" I was straining, trying to remember. I felt as if I were about to stumble over a curb, as in a dream. "I don't *know*. What is it again—'Adrian'—"

"'Adriane.'"

Very deliberately Dr. Cosgrove pronounced this name. It did not mean anything to me—did it?

Dr. Cosgrove and I stared at each other as if across an abyss. Not a wide abyss, but very deep. I felt that familiar weakness in me, as if my bones were turning to water.

From some long-ago time I remembered being told, unless I'd read these words—*The striking thing about self-knowledge is that it may be lacking.*

When I'd awakened from my comatose state in the Wainscotia hospital I'd felt this weakness through my entire body—no way to describe it except as terrifying, appalling.

That sense that the body is a precarious entity comprised of numberless atoms, that might disintegrate at any moment.

And beyond the body, the world itself—the very Universe—poised at the brink of detonation.

Leaning close to murmur in my ear Dr. Cosgrove said, "It may be, dear, that I used to know—your parents . . . In fact, I have reason to believe that I am related to your father. And so, to you."

This was astonishing! For a long moment I stared at the bald-headed doctor with the earnest eyes, and had no idea how to reply. "I don't mean to surprise or shock you, dear. I realize—you've been told that you were 'adopted.'"

"I—I don't really remember my parents, I'm afraid. The parents who adopted me, and the parents who . . ."

Dr. Cosgrove regarded me thoughtfully. He reached out to take my hand in his, my hand in both his hands. I thought—*He knows me.* The absurd thought came to me—*Maybe he was the doctor who delivered me.*

"Your father Eric was—is—my older brother. I have reason to believe. For you look very like him—unmistakably. I saw the resemblance in the newspaper photograph—I was sure." He paused, wiping at his eyes. "But we've been separated, your father and me. We have not seen each other in nearly twenty years."

Have not? This man was speaking as if my father were alive at this time.

I was very confused. Pulses pounded in my head, exacerbated by the drugs that coursed through my veins, seeping into my blood.

"You're my uncle? But—where did you—where did my parents—live? How is this possible?"

It did seem to me now that Dr. Cosgrove looked familiar. The uncanny dark glisten of his eyes, the tiny bump on his nose . . .

"I think that it is possible, 'Adriane.' You won't remember—probably—because you were very young when I'd last seen you. About two years old, I believe."

"Oh—where was this?"

"In another part of the country."

"But—which state?"

"In New Jersey, I believe."

But I have never lived in New Jersey—have I?

"Have you ever heard of Pennsboro? New Jersey?"

"N-No . . . I don't think so." I could not think at all.

"Maybe—y-yes . . ."

I was shivering badly. Wiping tears from my eyes. Dr. Cosgrove apologized for upsetting me.

He held my chilly hand in his and stroked it, for some time.

"Adults have not treated you well, my dear girl. I would not exacerbate your confusion and grief. But let me ask—do you know the name 'Tobias'?—'Toby'?— 'Uncle Toby'?"

I did not know how to reply. If this man was my uncle, I wanted to say *yes*.

"I—I'm not sure. 'Uncle Toby.'"

"That was my name once—'Tobias.' Before I was sent to Wisconsin to complete my medical degree at U Wisconsin–Madison; then I settled north of Wainscotia Falls, and haven't left St. Cloud since. I'm married— have been married for a long time. I married a dear, kind, beautiful girl from here—Zone Nine. I have children—that is, you have cousins . . . But we may not see each other again, I think. It's too risky for us both." Dr. Cosgrove blinked tears from his eyes, though he was smiling. "I've been concerned about coming to see you—I wasn't sure if it was a good idea. But of course, I wanted to see *you*—my dear niece Adriane. I wanted to ask about your father—your family. How they are, how things are in that other—dimension. But you can't answer me, I think. You can't 'remember.'"

"I—I can almost—remember something . . ."

When Dr. Cosgrove gazed at me with his dark-brown glistening eyes, and as he smiled at me in so kindly a way, almost I did remember—something. But at once it evaporated like a dream in bright daylight.

"You seem to be doing well, 'Adriane'—that is, 'Mary Ellen.' At least physically, now that you're re-covering. Young people are so much more resilient than older people—you're still young, though you've traversed decades."

"But—how old are *you*? When were you my uncle?"

"Ah, dear—it hasn't happened yet! And when it happens, when I am a young man, in my twenties, and you are newly born, some years from now—we won't remember a thing. Amnesia is all that saves us from the abyss."

Seeing that I was looking confused Dr. Cosgrove said quickly, "All we can do is persevere in our own time. No one has to deal with more than one day at a time. That's the blessing of our temporal universe—time is spread out horizontally, you might say; it doesn't all happen at once, as at the instant of the 'big bang.' Some of us are political beings, and some of us are not. But it can't be the case that any of us—in 1960, in the United States—or elsewhere, at another time—can be wholly *well*."

I didn't understand this. I knew nothing about politics—(though I knew, now, who was president of the United States: Dwight D. Eisenhower, an actual person, a former general, and not a genial smiling emoji). I knew that the United States had recently been "at war" with a faraway foreign country called Korea and I knew that World War II was a "fresh memory" to many.

"The new decade will bring us true 'newness'—even revolution. But it will be revolution mixed with tragedy, and not a little farce. And beyond that—!" Dr. Cosgrove laughed, with a shudder. "But we must not look ahead, you know. That is the essential lesson we Exiles learn. We must look to save ourselves."

I told Dr. Cosgrove that I wanted to know more about my parents—please! And how it was that— somehow—Dr. Cosgrove had known me, as a small child; and he'd had another name at the time: Uncle Toby . . .

A sensation almost of delirium overcame me. What would it mean to me, what happiness, to have an *Uncle Toby* in my life!

"No. We must live *here*, Adriane. I've learned that, after having made painful blunders. The 'future' exists only in the way that the other side of the earth exists, whether we can see it or not. Or," Dr. Cosgrove said, indicating the sky outside the window of my third-floor room, "those clouds in the eastern sky that look so sculpted—they exist in our immediate future be-cause they are being blown in this direction, from Lake Michigan. In some time—it might be an hour, or several hours—the clouds will be overhead, the sun-shine will be obscured. But now, we can see the clouds approaching, we can see into the distance and so, in a sense, we can see into the future. Most things are too distant for us to see, however, and we have to surrender the effort. 'One breath at a time'—your father used to say, wisely; though I was too young to listen to him at the time."

With a snap Dr. Cosgrove turned off the small flat object that had been buzzing and slipped it into his breast pocket.

"Dear Adriane—good-bye! Maybe we will meet again, if you wish—you know my name, and you know that I live in St. Cloud, just over the mountain."

Smiling Dr. Cosgrove squeezed my hand tenderly in parting. Badly I wanted to say *Good-bye, Uncle Toby!*—but the words could not come.

Heron Creek Farm

"Rufus! Time for our walk."

Rufus is a six-year-old mixed-breed dog, part boxer, part retriever, part border collie. His fur is sand-colored and coarse. He weighs about thirty-five pounds—eager, clumsy, hot-panting. His ears are alert and his eyes are alive with happiness when his name is called. If he rushes at you, tail thumping, he's heavy enough to cause you to stagger.

He swathes your face with his damp soft eager tongue.

You do not want to think what that tongue has touched. You do not want to think of a dog's myriad loves of which you, as yearning as any dog, but determined to disguise that fact, are but one.

Rufus and I walk together in the fields behind the farmhouse. There is a bond between us, I want to think: this is the creature who saved my life.

An animal is a kind of machine, the behaviorists teach. Yet Rufus is hardly a machine. Rufus's soul shines in his eyes, when he is in the presence of someone he loves.

Rufus's great joy is fetching a stick. Especially from out of the pond in which Jamie stocked trout a few years ago, and where a colony of noisy frogs live.

When I hug Rufus, and when Rufus licks my face, I feel tears stinging my eyes for this reason—*I am so happy.*

Someday, I may hike over-the-mountain to seek out Dr. Cosgrove in the place with the beautiful name—St. Cloud. But I have not, yet—my new life is too demanding.

There was no need for Jamie Stiles to ask me. Somehow it seemed to have been decided between us that when I was discharged from the rehabilitation clinic I would come to live with him in the farmhouse on Heron Creek Road.

You know—you have a home with me.

You know I love you.

The first sight I had of Jamie's house I fell in love with it—a sprawling clapboard farmhouse someone had painted the startling hue of goldenrod, with dark blue shutters. Other farmhouses scattered along the rural Heron Creek Road were a uniform weatherworn white.

The farmhouse is set back from the road. The (dirt, rutted) lane must be a quarter of a mile long. In the front yard are a 1949 Ford pickup truck with a smashed windshield and no tires, the remains of an ancient International Harvester tractor, an eviscerated 1947 Buick convertible, a child's sled with badly rusted runners: these are not remnants of discarded, formerly functional objects but an elaborately constructed scrap-metal sculpture titled, by Jamie Stiles, *Hazards of Time Travel.*

On the front porch, in addition to rattan sofa, chairs, and a Schwinn bicycle leaning against the wall, a display of—quilts? But these are not ordinary quilts for they have been fashioned of Plexiglas, heavy brocade, and aluminum, in stark metallic hues—*Quilt Legend Diorama* 1958.

Behind the house, a large hay barn that has been painted brick-red. On the peak of the roof is a weather vane bearing the heraldic figure of a stag. On the front of the barn is a large copper sunburst-face, like the face of a (benign) ancient deity. Beside the barn is a crumbling stone silo, and close by are several smaller outbuildings.

And behind these, the pond Jamie has stocked with trout.

In the red barn is Jamie Stiles's sculpture studio. Several feature articles for Wisconsin newspapers have been published about the sculpture of Jamie Stiles, as well as interviews on TV arts programs, and these always include coverage of the studio which resembles, at first glance, something between a mortuary and a junkyard—the myriad, very *physical* materials of a sculptor's trade. In the smaller outbuildings are studios used by artist-friends of Jamie's, some of whom have had the rent-free studios for years while others are "just visiting."

As he has inherited and accumulated people in his relatively young life—(Jamie Stiles is thirty-one)—so Jamie has inherited and accumulated farm animals. These include a chestnut-red mare named Hedy, retired from harness racing at the punishing track at Traverse City, Michigan; Leila and Lee, two goat-companions who graze with Hedy; a dozen dingy-coated sheep— (for sheep are nothing like storybook pictures of them, I've discovered: they are not naturally *white*); a half-dozen cats of various sizes, ages, and colors of whom some are affectionate house-cats and others, more feral, live in the barns; and Rufus our ever-vigilant guard dog. Also, a flock of chickens—white-feathered, Rhode Island reds, Plymouth Rock barred—to provide eggs for the large household. (Chicken-tending, egg-gathering, are tasks that quickly fell to me, with help from my young step-niece Chloe and step-nephew Tyler.) On the pond behind the barn, often squawking and contentious, are Canadian geese, domestic (white) geese, and a shifting company of wild ducks.

Sometimes, a pair of swans arrives at the pond from Heron Creek a short distance away. Vivid-white and usually silent amid the smaller waterfowl the swans are beautiful like figures in a dream, that seem to represent something for which there are no adequate words.

The oldest part of the farmhouse was built in 1881, by a long-ago relative of Jamie Stiles's; it had come into Jamie's grandparents' possession, and they'd left it to him a dozen years ago, along with forty acres of mostly uncultivated land. Along a circuitous rural route the house is approximately five miles from the vast Wain-scotia campus where Jamie Stiles teaches, or has taught, sculpture in the fine arts department for the past nine years, and I am a student enrolled in the liberal arts college—my twin majors are biology and art.

I am still a University Scholar. I don't any longer work part-time on campus, since I am no longer living in a university residence.

A census taker would be frustrated seeking to determine exactly who lives in the goldenrod-colored farmhouse on Heron Creek Road, Wainscotia Township. For the place is always open to Jamie's friends, acquaintances, fellow-artists and fellow pacifists/anti-nuclear protesters; frequently they are strangers passing through on their way elsewhere, who are known to Jamie, or recommended to him by mutual like-minded acquaintances. Also there are likely to be Stiles relatives on the premises, temporarily or permanently: a male cousin of Jamie's who'd dropped out of the agriculture school at WSU years before; a morose older half-brother who works in a local stone quarry, and who weighs three hundred pounds; a ravaged hard-drinking stoic uncle who'd had a twenty-year career in the U.S. Marines and who'd been severely wounded in the closing week of World War II, in Germany.

And, to my surprise, two children aged five and eight, not Jamie's children but the abandoned children of an older sister of Jamie's who'd departed several years before, leaving nothing in her wake but the children and their clothes and toys—"They're a little sad-hearted but very sweet kids, Mary Ellen. You'll love them."

It is true, I will love Chloe and Tyler—in time. I am sure of this.

The significant fact about the children, I guess you could say, is the color of their skin: a rich mocha-brown.

In all of (rural) Wainscotia Township there is probably no one else with mocha-brown skin like my little step-niece Chloe and my step-nephew Tyler.

Jamie and I will have our own children sometime soon. This is our hope.

Much of the farm property isn't tillable soil but there are a number of acres that are fertile enough to be leased by neighboring farmers, which provides a much-needed source of income for the household, and there is a half-acre behind the house where we can plant a few things—tomatoes, green beans, sweet corn, carrots, cucumbers, melons . . .

In time the care of this ambitious vegetable garden will fall to me, I think. (As the care of Chloe and Tyler will fall to me.) By the time Jamie brought me to the farmhouse in late summer everything had been planted but there were weeds choking the smaller plants, and the corn and melons had been ravaged by deer and raccoons; what flourished most was a bed of basil, catnip, and mint, which grow like weeds, and a small jungle of hollyhocks and wild rose.

I was eager to clear away weeds and thistles. But Jamie laughed at me.

"Sometimes you come too late to a garden, the way you might come too late in another's life. Best just to take things as they are. 'One breath at a time.'"

Walking through the overgrown garden, with Rufus at my heels, sniffing and bounding into the dry-rustling corn, I am suffused with happiness. I think—*All this was waiting for me. I didn't know.*

In my former life—(which I can remember only vaguely, like something glimpsed through frosted glass)—I don't believe that I lived on a farm, worked with the soil, grew things. Yet, I have confidence that I can learn.

The smells of a garden, in late-afternoon sunshine, or after a quick flashing rain—so beautiful, they leave me feeling faint.

Jamie and his friends are continually repairing the house—shingled roof, shutters, rotting porch, steps. Jamie has a plumber friend, a friend with a backhoe, a friend who digs cisterns and wells. He has (commercial) painter friends as well as (artist) painter friends. His closest sculptor-friend is a welder. Jamie himself is very handy, and strong; he has to be prevented from lifting things that might throw out his back, or break it altogether. For a reticent person he seems to thrive in a whirl of communal activities. Meetings of the local branch of SANE are usually held at Heron Creek Farm. Though sometimes Jamie drives to Madison, or farther still to Chicago. (Chicago! How very far away that seems to me. Since being struck by lightning, I tell myself that my traveling days are over.) Jamie's artist-colleagues work in their studios and eat with us, most nights. And their wives, girlfriends, children eat with us. Parents arrive, and stay for the night, or several nights. Elderly grandparents too are welcome. (But please don't die on the premises! Jamie jokes about such things, which don't seem funny to the rest of us.) Of course, there are poetry evenings—many (of us) are poets. (H. R. Brody is a friend of Jamie's.) There are musical evenings—(Jamie plays drums). Even the young niece and nephew have school friends, who are invited to the house often, brought by their parents who stay for dinner as well. Because WSU has seemed to be exploiting some instructors and staff workers Jamie has been trying to organize a union without having realized how much time this would consume, and how quarrelsome people can be when you are trying to help them. One night at dinner, which had sprawled out of the house, onto the porch and onto the grass, I counted twenty-six adults and children before I gave up.

Thinking—*There is no time here for sorrow. I am too busy!*

Jamie identifies himself as a "multi-media" sculptor. His great model is Rodin. He has fashioned strange and striking works of art out of scrap metal, including wrecked cars and tractors; he utilizes iron (which he allows to rust, in a "natural progression"), stainless steel, aluminum, brass, wood, clay, fiberglass and other materials, even papier-mâché; yet he's a traditional sculptor too, whose most successful commission has been a Korean War memorial for Wainscotia Township.

At the university Jamie Stiles is highly regarded as an original and important artist; at the same time, his political involvement with SANE, and his general pacifist/anti-war statements, have made it difficult for his departmental chairman to promote him, still less to give him a permanent appointment with tenure at WSU.

Jamie is kept on, however—"kept on." Semester after semester, year after year.

"The department likes me well enough—I mean, most of the guys on the faculty are my friends. I've known them for years. I've helped them with their work. But the dean of the college, and the president— they're afraid of my 'notoriety.' They've been hearing that there's a 'rabid Commie' in the art department. One of the trustees thought that I'd been arrested in 'some sort of protest riot.' So part-time employment is the best I can hope for."

Wistfully Jamie spoke, and yet boastfully. I had to rush to him then, to kiss him.

Soon after I was discharged from the rehabilitation clinic and had come to live at Heron Creek Farm, Jamie took me to see the Korean War memorial in front of the county courthouse in Wainscotia Falls. Though made of stainless steel the figures of the eleven soldiers, ground troops on parole, were unnervingly lifelike; you could almost imagine that they were breathing, and that their stony skin was actual skin. They loomed above the viewer slightly larger than life-size, at about seven feet in height. Their faces were both youthful and ageless. Their hands—their fingers—were particularly lifelike. Names of the Wainscotia Township dead had been carved in stone on a parapet surrounding the sculpture, and with this too Jamie had taken a good deal of care, rejecting several fonts before he chose the one he finally used.

There was a good deal of positive publicity in local newspapers regarding *Ground Patrol: Korea 1950–1955*. Relatives of soldiers who'd died in the war were deeply moved by Jamie Stiles's memorial and wrote letters to him, each of which he answered. (Jamie had not yet become involved in anti-war protests, fortunately!) His model for the memorial hadn't been Rodin but a revered midwestern sculptor of the early twentieth century named Harry Hansen, at one time promoted as the midwestern Rodin, who'd executed more than two hundred memorial sculptures during his fifty-year career. Jamie seemed embarrassed by the sculpture though I praised it as moving, tragic, beautiful; he said, humbly, "It wasn't my idea to do a 'realistic' memorial, but that's what they wanted. I tried to explain to the township board that what they wanted was an old-fashioned kind of sculpture that had been valued in the past, before photography; the rendering of human faces and figures so close to human that they appear human. Sculpture today is more likely to be abstract than realistic. I tried to explain, but . . ." In the end if he'd wanted to accept the commission he'd had to create the kind of memorial the citizens of Wainscotia Township wanted, which he did.

"But it's very powerful, Jamie. It is."

Seeing the figures of the eleven soldiers transformed by Death was deeply moving. I could not speak for some time as Jamie circled the memorial, staring at it. An artist is one who never believes what others say about his work—perhaps that was it. Jamie could not see what I saw and could not believe what I believed about his sculpture.

On the soldiers' heads and shoulders were chalky-white bird droppings. This, we tried not to notice.

Though finally I wetted tissues in a nearby puddle and tried to wipe the droppings away, with limited success.

When we returned home Jamie showed me his framed award from the Wisconsin Council of the Arts for Sculpture, 1957. He seemed both embarrassed by the reward, and proud of it.

"Jamie! Congratulations."

Only three years before but Jamie had looked younger then. He'd been thinner, his face leaner, and his jaws clean-shaven.

Jamie Stiles without a beard! The young man in this picture wouldn't have approached me on the university campus, possibly.

Seeing his young face I felt tears gather in my eyes. For when this photograph had been taken I hadn't known Jamie Stiles. He hadn't known me. And it was quite likely that we would never meet.

Indeed, how was it possible that we'd ever met? Ever glimpsed each other? It was not possible. Yet it had happened.

Tears ran down my cheeks. I was overcome with joy indistinguishable from grief. At such times Jamie comes to me, and silently gathers me in his arms.

Jamie's strong arms. Jamie's heavy body like a fortress. His comfort is immediate and unquestioning.

I have you, I will protect you. I love you.

In Jamie's studio, in the old red barn. We've fashioned a small studio for me in the hayloft, to which I climb by a ladder. It's a private space that looks out over pasture-land and down into Jamie Stiles's workspace. I can watch him below but he isn't likely to watch me.

My artwork, so-called, is of a much smaller scale than Jamie's. I have no interest in heroic or monumental works. I'm content to wander outside sketching for hours with pencil, charcoal, pastel chalks, then return here and work on my sketches. I've experimented with portraits—my little step-niece and my little step-nephew, residents and visitors, Jamie's ex-Marine uncle who calls himself, with some measure of irony I am not able to gauge, "Captain Shalom."

In the loft I have a workbench of about six feet in length, that Jamie made for me. Jamie has stretched canvases for me and encouraged me to experiment with paints.

Often, I gaze over the edge of the loft floor, at Jamie Stiles below. He's a restless figure, burly, muscular, yet like an athlete he is agile on his feet, alert and curious. The sliding barn door to his studio is usually kept open except on cold days. He works with fire, sometimes. He works with spray paint. He has fashioned sculptures out of old broken floor lamps, discarded baby carriages, bullet-ridden STOP signs; scrap metal, fiberglass, window glass, aluminum and brass rods. I think that his work is not only strangely beautiful in its own way but "profound"— "important." I don't think that it's naïve of Jamie Stiles to be thinking in terms of Rodin, not Harry Hansen of Whitefish Bay.

Jamie has the ability to totally lose himself in his work. No matter how much he's worried about, for instance, the financial upkeep of Heron Creek Farm, or the insanity of U.S. nuclear testing in the Southwest, or whether he will have an instructorship at WSU in the fall, his concentration on his work is complete as that of a lone child who has lost himself in play. He's pitiless on himself when his work isn't going well, which is fairly often; he's stubborn, easily discouraged; it makes me sad that he sighs often, runs his fingers through his hair in a gesture of exasperation, or despondency; that he pulls at his beard, that seems to me a beautiful bristling beard, of the hue of mahogany, curlier than the hair on his head.

Yet, so much of James Stiles seems beautiful to me! I could stare and stare at the man, even in his soiled bib-overalls worn without a shirt beneath, and his weather-worn sandals.

When Jamie makes love to me he is awkward, tender, hesitant—he fears hurting me, or crushing me. And it is true that Jamie's considerable weight takes the breath from me, and makes me worry that my ribs might crack. The fierce thrusts of his body cause me to shudder in pain, which Jamie interprets in another way. I never betray the slightest discomfort for I think only of Jamie. I think of my need to love, and to be loved.

Never in my life before this have I loved any man—(I am sure)—yet by instinct I've known that I must not hurt Jamie's feelings. The slightest tone of reproach or criticism of his work—never. I would never undermine Jamie Stiles's sense of himself as a man, an artist or a sexual being.

The truths I reveal to Jamie Stiles are those "truths" that will nurture Jamie's love for me. For only Jamie Stiles's love for me can validate the love I feel for him, so powerful it leaves me faint and breathless.

It must be—*I came so close to dying. Now, nothing matters except this life.*

Some evenings, we watch TV.

On a sofa we sit holding hands. We are open about our affection for each other—(this is Jamie's way, in the expression of affection generally)—and not at all embarrassed about seeming sentimental, even when "Captain Shalom" grunts wryly in our direction, passing with heavy steps through the living room on the way to his quarters at the rear of the house.

We're rarely alone watching TV. The prime hours are 8:00 P.M. and 9:00 P.M. Jamie laughs as loudly as the children laugh at the foolish pranks of Milton Berle, Lucille Ball and Desi Arnaz; Ozzie and Harriet are household favorites, as well as Arthur Godfrey, Lawrence Welk, and Phil Silvers. Jack Benny, Sid Caesar and Imogene Coca require more thought, like Jack Paar, *Truth or Consequences*, and *What's My Line?* Sometimes, Jamie falls asleep while watching TV, exhausted from a full day of work, and I don't wake him, but continue to grip his hand tight. TV images wash over us. Our most torturous thoughts are obliterated in the bluish-flickering TV light.

In our lumpy brass bed in Jamie's longtime bedroom on the second floor of the house we lie entwined in each other's arms. Here we talk, and kiss; we kiss, and make love; sometimes a sensation comes over me, that I am in the arms of someone else and not Jamie Stiles—someone whose name I have forgotten. I shudder with dread, but don't cry out, and manage not to weep.

For life is *now.* Life is not thinking, not reflective or backward-glancing; life is forward-plunging; life is the present moment as, on TV, it is always *now.*

And I think—*I am in the right place, at the right time.*

To celebrate our wedding in late October, Jamie's poet-friend Hiram Brody gave a large, festive party for us in his Victorian house in the Faculty Hills neighborhood of Wainscotia Falls, and wrote a "sprung love sonnet" for the occasion. At the party, in addition to Jamie's many friends, was a dazzling mix of writers, artists, sculptors, musicians, university professors, and their wives; here were such Wainscotia luminaries as Amos Stein, Myron Coughland, my former employer Morris Harrick, Carson Lockett III, and A. J. Axel—all of whom were friends of H. R. Brody's and, I wanted to think, admirers of Jamie Stiles's sculpture. (The most distinguished of these professors, judging by the deference paid to him, was Professor Axel of psychology, who made only a brief visit at the gathering, and left after the first champagne toast. Mr. Brody said proudly of his friend that A. J. Axel had just received the "largest federal government grant ever given to any research scientist in the State of Wisconsin" to help establish the Wainscotia Center for Social Engineering, of which Professor Axel is the founding director; the Center is to pioneer in the behavioral conditioning of anti-social, psychopathic, and subversive personalities.) To this gathering, white-haired Mr. Brody read his "sprung sonnet" in a richly dramatic voice; it was a poem containing an echo, he said, of a sonnet of Shakespeare's—*Let us not bar the twining of true love but celebrate Love's fixed star . . .* Everyone applauded loudly; Jamie wiped tears from his eyes. He didn't understand most poetry, Jamie said, but he often cried just the same when he heard it.

I thought Mr. Brody's poem was strange, and beautiful. I did not quite understand it, either, but it brought tears to my eyes.

Jamie and I had been married that morning by a justice of the peace at the Wainscotia Falls courthouse, with just a few witnesses from Heron Creek Farm. The fatherly justice had expressed surprise and a little concern that the bride seemed to have no family, or at any rate no family members who'd come to the wedding, but I smiled and assured him that Jamie Stiles was all the family I needed.

(One of many kindnesses Ardis Steadman had done

for me, in addition to boxing those possessions of mine which I'd left behind in Acrady Cottage, was to provide me with a birth certificate out of my university file, which I needed in order to be married. This birth certificate, with an ornate gilt seal from the State of New Jersey, was not a document I could remember having seen before; it stated that *Mary Ellen Enright* had been born in *Pennsboro General Hospital, Pennsboro, New Jersey,* on *September 11, 1942,* and that her parents were *Constance Ann Enright* and *Harvey Sterns Enright.* Were these my birth-parents? Or were these simply fictitious names someone had provided, for a birth certificate? The names meant nothing to me—not a stir of emotion. But I remembered Dr. Cosgrove speaking of *New Jersey.*)

In black ink, with a fountain pen, H. R. Brody copied "Wisconsin Epithalamium" inscribed to *Mary Ellen* and *Jamie,* signed and dated in the poet's flowing signature, on a stiff sheet of parchment paper, which Jamie has framed to hang in our bedroom. "It's like having a handwritten poem by Robert Frost, or T. S. Eliot," Jamie has said. He is deeply moved by the poem, as I am. Sometimes one of us reads it aloud to the other, as we prepare for bed.

I thought—*I have always loved this person. I have always known this person. Before I was born, I loved him.*

Shortly after this, a strange and disturbing thing happens.

I am not sure how to speak of it. So much in my life has floated beyond language, like a high scudding cloud so distant it can't be identified, I have lost confidence in my ability to comprehend many things, let alone explain them.

I have not tried to avoid "Captain Shalom" for I have not wanted to hurt the man's feelings, nor do I want to hurt Jamie's feelings; but there is something unnerving about Jamie's ex-Marine uncle, that hasn't only to do with the poor man's ravaged face, his hairless battered head, and unblinking rheumy eyes; or his breath that smells of something metallic, like coins held hotly in the palm of a sweaty hand. In our household, in which there are so many individuals coming and going, in the kitchen, on the stairs, in the living room and hallways, not to mention in and out of bathrooms—(there are just two bathrooms for all of us, one on each floor; but there is an outhouse between the house and the hay barn, that Jamie says had been in use when he'd been a boy, not so long ago)—you are constantly encountering the same people yet you're usually on your way elsewhere, hurrying past them with a murmured *Excuse me!*—or no words at all. The intimacy born of sheer proximity is a curious phenomenon—there is something mocking in it.

Jamie's middle-aged ex-Marine uncle uses crutches sometimes, though not always; often he can make his way upstairs by hauling himself hand over hand along the banister, and his method of descending stairs is a kind of free-falling plunge. The one thing you must not ever do is offer to assist him: this error, I made shortly after coming to live at Heron Creek Farm.

The man had stared coldly at me. His eyes were fierce and glaring. Along the left side of his face was a zipper-like scar, and a portion of his upper lip was missing. His teeth were grayish, like the teeth of a malnourished child. His breath was coppery-hot. The ex-Marine who called himself Captain Shalom knew how to render me helpless, by not speaking as I stammered an apology.

Finally he said in an ironic, gravelly voice, "When I need your help, 'Mary Ellen,' I will request it. Thanking you beforehand."

The way in which Captain Shalom pronounced *Mary Ellen* allowed me to know that he did not think much of the name, or the subterfuge which such a name can validate.

Jamie has been concerned about his uncle's "mental health" but—what can he do? Captain Shalom refuses to see any doctor, even local doctors; he flies into a fury at the suggestion that someone might drive him to Milwaukee, to see a VA doctor (that is, a psychiatrist). Jamie says that unless he overpowers his uncle and ties him up, and bundles him out to the pickup, it isn't likely that anything can be done for the veteran.

"Does he have a gun? Guns?"—this was my innocent query.

"No firearms are allowed on this property. That is understood."

How was this a satisfactory answer? Jamie was incensed, that I should even suggest this.

I think it's likely that Captain Shalom keeps a gun, or guns, in his room. (This room, awkward for the disabled man to access, was his choice when he'd moved in, Jamie has explained.) But I think it's likely that, if Captain Shalom feels the impulse to fire one of his guns, he would not kill any of us—(out of contempt, or indifference)—but only himself.

For Captain Shalom is heroic, in his tortured way.

I have tried to "sketch" him—though only by memory. I would like to take photographs of his face when he isn't aware of me—but that isn't likely.

Captain Shalom is both jocular and despondent, by turns; his moods are not so very different from Jamie's but more frequent, and unpredictable. By mid-afternoon he's likely to be moderately drunk, which gives to his manner a playful, bitter-ironic air; as he is a wreck of a man, an object of pathos, he isn't given to hypocrisy, if for instance someone tells him, as visitors to our house invariably do, meaning to be kind, that he is *looking good* he will say dryly, "Really? In whose eyes?—yours, or mine?"

Or he will say nothing but grunt in a way to convey disgust, amusement, contempt; and lurch his way past, with the gleeful rudeness of the disabled for whom condescending kindnesses from the *abled* are particularly insulting.

Between "Captain Shalom" and "Mary Ellen Enright" there is an uneasy sort of truce, I think. As I am Jamie Stiles's wife, Jamie's uncle believes that he should respect me; he's dependent upon Jamie for a place to live and a household, for his own marriage ended shortly after he'd been discharged from the VA hospital in Milwaukee, and had returned to his wife and children in Racine with both physical and psychiatric problems. Yet, as I'm a young woman of only nineteen, an undergraduate at WSU, and, since coming to live at Heron Creek Farm, as Jamie Stiles's dear companion, a fairly attractive young woman with a quick bright friendly smile, it is quite possible that Captain Shalom resents me, as men often resent women who are unattainable to them, as women. It is the case that when Captain

414 · JOYCE CAROL OATES

Shalom and I are alone together in a room or in a hall-
way, we move past each other with averted eyes, and
indrawn breaths. Captain Shalom is exceedingly polite
with me at mealtimes, and often volunteers to help with
kitchen cleanup, a chore Jamie mostly avoids with the
excuse that he must return to his sculpting studio for
an hour's work or so before quitting for the day; at such
times, I'm grateful if others in the household help out
in the kitchen, for being alone with the ravaged and
embittered ex-Marine is painful, and makes me very
self-conscious.

*Here is a man who sees through you. Your happiness,
your relentless smile, even your "love."*

Yet, Captain Shalom is an obsessive reader, and has
accumulated a library of secondhand books in his room;
unlike the rest of us, he rarely watches TV, and never
without snorting in derision and distaste. (Anything on
TV that has to do with soldiers, armed forces, veter-
ans, "war" he particularly scorns; but also pacifists,
anti-war protesters, and SANE—to Jamie's disappointment.) Often I see Captain Shalom limping outside with
a book from his library, in good weather; he has found a
place to read overlooking the pond, and has strung up
a hammock there, for his own, private use. (Yet Captain
Shalom has invited me to lie in the hammock any time
I wish, an offer I would never take up for it seems to

hold a veiled threat.) One warm afternoon when Captain Shalom went out to read in his hammock by the pond, I hurried upstairs to his room, to examine his books; though I knew that they were mostly historical books about war, as Jamie had told me. (I thought of searching for his guns, but could not so violate Jamie's uncle's privacy. I could not bring myself to look, for instance, through the man's bureau drawers, or between the mattress and box springs of his bed.)

Captain Shalom's room was sparely furnished, with no carpet on the floorboards; there was a table, a single chair, a floor lamp that looked as if it had been salvaged from a junkyard. Surprisingly, the room was relatively neat, for Captain Shalom had made his bed as if he were in a barracks—tight-drawn, corners tucked in, the single pillow perfectly positioned. (I smiled to think how Jamie would never think of making any bed in which he'd slept. He kicks his covers off, leaves the bedclothes rumpled and churned-looking.) There was only one actual bookcase in the room, that stood about five feet high; but everywhere were books, some of them oversized picture or photography books, on the floor and table, on a windowsill. Hesitantly I pulled out a book from the bookcase, noting its place so that I could return it, and Captain Shalom would never know, but when I opened the heavy hardcover book I saw to my surprise that there were *no words on the page*—no printed words.

I turned pages, and all were the same: blank.

On the book's spine there was nothing as well. On the book's cover.

Shaken, I replaced this book and opened another at random. And this book did have printed pages, but the print was blurred and incomprehensible as if it had melted; and a third book I opened, now quite frightened, and this too had pages that were incomprehensible to me, not like words in a foreign language but hieroglyphic-like words that did not use familiar letters. And the thought came to me, chilling yet somehow calm—*That's because you are dreaming. In a dream, you can never read print.*

Quickly I replaced the books, and quickly retreated downstairs to the first floor of the farmhouse. I have never returned to Captain Shalom's room since.

My injuries will never disappear entirely, I've been told—they are "neurological deficits." Always I will be susceptible to migraine headaches. I can't "play catch" as most others can in the household—playing with my little step-niece and my step-nephew, for instance, is embarrassing, since I so often fumble the ball. In chill, damp weather, both my knees ache. My eyesight begins to fade at sundown. My eyes are weak, and water easily. A mild agitation will precipitate heart palpitations even when I am otherwise serene.

And I still cry, for no evident reason.

And Jamie comforts me at such times, without asking me what is wrong. And Rufus too, if he hears me.

This afternoon, visitors are arriving. I think they are friends of Jamie's from Madison—anti-nuclear activists, who are also artists. I have no idea how many people will be eating meals here for the next several days but I will have help in preparing these meals, and cleaning up in the kitchen afterward. Strangely, there is a kind of calm amid so many people, and commotion—and then, I can retreat to my loft in the hay barn anytime I wish, or nearly.

Always room for one more at Heron Creek Farm—this is Jamie Stiles's dictum.

Anytime you are in the neighborhood of Heron Creek Farm, or anywhere in the vicinity of Wainscotia Falls, Wisconsin, you too are welcome to drop by here with all the others—of course.

Please come! I would so like to meet you. Stay with us as long as you like.

Acknowledgments

S pecial thanks to Greg Johnson for reading this manuscript with his usual care, thoughtfulness, and sympathy; and for my husband Charlie Gross for his continued support.

THE NEW LUXURY IN READING

We hope you enjoyed reading
our new, comfortable print size and found it
an experience you would like to repeat.

Well – you're in luck!

HarperLuxe offers the finest in fiction and
nonfiction books in this same larger print size and
paperback format. Light and easy to read, HarperLuxe
paperbacks are for book lovers who want to see
what they are reading without the strain.

For a full listing of titles and
new releases to come, please visit our website:
www.HarperLuxe.com